A SUBMARINE—— CORAL TRENCH LIKE A LOCOMOTIVE THUNDERING DOWN THE TRACKS

At first, Gray assumed that it was the Oscar they'd come to these waters to find and kill, but one glance at the shadowy form told him that he was wrong. He requested data from the warbook, and got it:

ALFA CLASS ATTACK SUBMARINE

WEIGHT 3,680 TONS (SUBMRGD) SPEED 50 KTS+

Behind the first Alfa came a second, and behind the second, a third . . .

"My God," Koch said, his voice sounding shaken over the laser circuit. "I'm reading three Alfas. It's the god-damn cavalry."

"Yeah," Gray said. "*Their* cavalry."

SHARUQ

BILL KEITH

HarperPaperbacks
A Division of HarperCollinsPublishers

This is a work of fiction. The characters, incidents, and dialogues are products of the author's imagination and are not to be construed as real. Any resemblance to actual events or persons, living or dead, is entirely coincidental.

HarperPaperbacks   *A Division of* HarperCollins*Publishers*
10 East 53rd Street, New York, N.Y. 10022

Cover illustration by John Berkey

First printing: July 1993

Printed in the United States of America

HarperPaperbacks and colophon are trademarks of HarperCollins*Publishers*

❖ 10 9 8 7 6 5 4 3 2 1

PROLOGUE

Assassin and victim, hunter and hunted, the one stalked the other with deadly, high-tech prowess across two hundred miles of open water. A gale brewing well to the east of Jamaica had already stirred wind and waves as far west as the Yucatán coast. Rain-laden cumulus clouds piled mountain upon white mountain in the late-afternoon sky, with promise of an evening storm.

The quarry, unsuspecting and nakedly vulnerable, plowed ahead through roughening seas with ponderous, black-hulled grace. Three days out of Maracaibo, steaming northwest toward the Yucatán Channel, the *American Castle* was a VLCC—the bland and understated acronym stood for very large crude-oil carrier— a supertanker longer than three end-to-end football fields and broad enough abeam to shrug off the rolling seas with contemptuous ease. Her twenty-four storage tanks, arrayed in three rows of eight beneath that long, long deck stretching from bow to far-aft superstructure, were filled to capacity with Venezuelan

1

crude—two million barrels of industrial lifeblood bound for the petrocomplex terminals off Texas City.

Two hundred miles to the east, the hunter tracked its prey. Like the supertanker, she, too, was a giant among her own kind, 470 feet long and as massive as a modern guided-missile cruiser. Rather than overcoming the turbulent swell on the surface, however, she avoided it, sliding silently through twilight waters at periscope depth. Nets of green-filtered sunlight rippled across the flanks of the submerged giant. Only the slender, spearhead-tipped finger of a satellite communications mast broke the surface, tasting the steady stream of targeting data relayed from a reconnaissance satellite four hundred miles overhead. Those transmissions were the huge submarine's only link with her prey, invisible now well beyond the western horizon.

Once a Soviet SSGN—a design code-named Oscar by NATO—she now served different masters. Her new name was *Sharuq,* an Arabic word meaning "east" but referring specifically to the sirocco, the hot, easterly wind of the Mediterranean that foretells changes in heaven and the death of kings.

Twin-screwed, with a tubby eighteen-meter beam and a long, rather squat sail—the conning tower of earlier generations of submarines—the Oscar was swift, silent, and deadly. She carried a typical warload of twenty-four antiship and antisubmarine torpedoes; her main armament, however, consisted of twenty-four SS-N-19 antiship cruise missiles fired from tubes set vertically between the SSGN's inner and outer hulls, an arrangement that explained her broad girth. Hatches, six on each side, extended along *Sharuq*'s hull to either side of her sail. One hatch, on the port side forward, was already open, exposing the rounded tips of two missiles.

A sudden explosion of compressed air propelled the first missile upward into the sea. A moment later it exploded from the depths in a cloud of spray, bursting from watery darkness into sunlight. The second ship-killer followed close behind the first, wings unfolding, booster rocket igniting in white flame for the seconds necessary until the ramjet sustainer motor could cut in.

At a speed of better than fourteen hundred knots, the twin killers required seven minutes to race from their launch point southeast of Cuba's Isla de la Juventud to the *American Castle*'s position entering the Yucatán Channel. They were sea-skimmers, hurtling westward scant meters above the water's surface to avoid their target's nonexistent defenses. Well before they'd completed their journey, their onboard targeting radars had switched on, and the missiles' idiot-level computer brains identified the strongest return as their target.

Six minutes after launch, both missiles were picked up by the *American Castle*'s radar, but an excited watch officer misidentified them as low-flying MiGs out of Cuba. It was an honest mistake; since Castro's death several years before, that unhappy island had been ruled by a military junta. Though its government no longer even pretended to be Communist, Washington still regarded Cuba with wary neutrality, and the situation was unstable enough to worry the captains and owners of all merchant shipping transiting the strategic choke points east and west of the island.

American Castle's radioman was still trying to raise the presumed MiGs when the first cruise missile, traveling at Mach 2-plus, slammed into her deck just forward of her superstructure, penetrating the thin hull like a bullet cutting through sheet tin and detonating inside Storage Tank 16.

In the so-called tanker war of the 1980s, supertankers had proven more or less invulnerable to air- and shore-launched cruise missiles, taking hits and sustaining damage, but never enough to cripple the ship or cause more than minor losses to the cargo. The weapons in most of those attacks had been Exocets, however, French-designed antiship missiles loaded with 165 kilograms of high explosive. By comparison, each SS-N-19 carried 1,000 kilos of HE, a warhead as massive as—and more powerful than— that of the Germans' dreaded V-2 of World War II.

The explosion ruptured a dozen storage tanks and snapped the supertanker's keel, sheered off the flat, white superstructure and left a tangled ruin of charred debris trailing aft across the stricken vessel's stern. Bow and stern rose, heaving skyward out of flame-shot sea. The second cruise missile struck the forward hull a few heartbeats later, slashing open the remaining intact storage tanks. Orange flame engulfed the tanker from end to end as stored petroleum detonated like a bomb. There were no survivors, there *could* be no survivors in that inferno.

Long minutes later that blast rumbled like distant thunder in both Cozumel and Havana and rattled the bridge windscreen of another tanker thirty miles to the south.

Hours later, as darkness fell across the western Caribbean, the mingled oil and wreckage of the *American Castle* continued to burn beneath a black, inverted pyramid of smoke. The tropical sunset was overshadowed by the angry glare of firelight reflected from that volcanic canopy, and tourists in Cancún watched the false dawn hover above the Yucatán Channel to the east.

And in Washington, D.C., the President's National Security Council was already convening what promised to be a long, late-night meeting.

CHAPTER
1

C-22 Osprey Transport
One hundred miles east of Cape Hatteras
March 28, 0910 hours

Commander Thomas Morgan Gray twisted in the hard folding seat, straining against the encumbrance of his harness for a clear look through the aircraft window. There was little to see yet; a solid deck of clouds had masked the ocean's surface ever since they'd left New London almost two hours earlier.

They were pulling 350 knots, he guessed, at an altitude of about 7,000 feet. His window was in the shadow of the Osprey transport's wings, and the morning light shining off glacier-white clouds spread beneath that deep cerulean sky was dazzling. Turning again, facing the row of folding seats along the opposite bulkhead, he leaned back in his seat and felt the throbbing hum of the tilt rotor's engines transmitted through the aircraft's fuselage, alert to any change in pitch or vibration.

Like all pilots everywhere—and Navy aviators in particular—Gray disliked being a passenger in an aircraft. Having another hand at the stick carried with it a curiously helpless feeling, a sense of being out of control.

That unpleasant realization only reinforced the sour attitude that had been building for the past several months, ever since he'd been told that his squadron was being deactivated, in fact. It was still only just beginning to sink in that he would not be flying again . . . at least, not for the Navy. No more cat shots hurtling off a carrier's bow. No more heart-stopping rush dropping into the box after he'd called the ball, deck sweeping up to greet him, hitting the deck and throttle full forward in case he missed his trap and boltered, followed by the savage yank and adrenaline high as his tailhook caught the three-wire.

Any hours he logged from here on out would be at the controls of his father-in-law's Beechcraft.

Not for the first time he found himself chin deep in doubts about just where his naval career was headed now. Damn it, he was an *aviator*—Navy flyers never called themselves "pilots"—a man who'd invested ten years of his life in carrier aviation. Aviators, as any Navy man knew, were a notch or ten better than pilots, if only because their airfield was a postage-stamp-sized piece of steel deck, pitching and rolling in three dimensions as they guided ten tons-plus of high-tech aircraft in for a trap—often in spray, rain, snow, or the black shroud of a moonless night.

What the hell did Project Orca want with *him*?

Incuriously, he let his eyes stray to the other faces up and down the tilt rotor's cabin. Four other men had been herded aboard the Osprey that foggy, New London dawn. Two lieutenants and a j.g., all three looking painfully young and fresh-scrubbed and with the gold wings of naval aviators just like his, peeking out from beneath their open flight jackets above the rows of colored ribbons pinned to their khakis. The fourth man was a chief, a stocky, heavy-set black man who'd settled far back in his seat with his arms folded across his chest, his legs stretched across the aisle, and the bill of his cap tugged down over his eyes. Gray counted the gold service stripes running up the left arm of his dress blue uniform and whistled to himself. Seven hash marks, at least twenty-eight years in; that guy had been Navy damned near since Gray had started elementary school . . . and probably longer. Above the bright-colored rank upon rank of ribbons on his left breast was pinned, not an aviator's wings, but the twin silver dolphins of an enlisted submariner.

The Osprey's cargo master, another Navy chief in khakis and a battered blue cranial—Navy slang for a padded safety helmet—made his way aft toward Morgan's seat. "God, the stews on this flight're ugly," the first chief said, not stirring as the man stepped across his legs.

"Well now, Ah tell ya," the cargo master replied, stopping for a moment and grinning wickedly at the other chief. "Where you guys's goin', damn near anything'll look real good after the first few weeks. Me, I'm an old married man with all the trimmin's, so I don't have to *dream* about gettin' any for the next four months like you poor pud-pullers do!"

"Hey, Spam in a can needs lovin', too," the passenger said, unfolding his arms and pushing back his hat. "Even if his best friend is a strong left hand!"

Both chiefs cackled at that, and Gray had the feeling that the exchange had been for the benefit of the white-faced trio of junior officers. Few words had been exchanged among the passengers since they'd boarded the C-22 Osprey at New London. It was as though each had been involved with his own personal gloom.

By contrast, the submarine chief didn't seem unhappy, only indifferent. The others, though, must have made the same career decision Gray had been forced to make, and all three looked like they were regretting it. He'd tried starting up a conversation with them when they'd first boarded the VTOL transport, but the difference in rank had kept their responses to his questions to "yes, sir" and "no, sir" and little more.

Well, the four of them shared the same problem, a problem that existed throughout the Navy. While no one was willing to admit that aircraft carriers had just become as obsolete as World War II battlewagons, the Pentagon's decision to slash the Navy's CV force from eleven carriers to four had left dozens of highly skilled and expensively trained fliers for every one available aircraft; there simply weren't enough empty cockpits to go around, and a hell of a lot of good naval aviators were winding up on the beach, taking early outs, or like the four of them aboard the Osprey transport, taking a real leap into the dark and signing on for new programs like Orca.

The two chiefs exchanged a few more good-natured comments with each other, their voices too low to be heard above the drone of the Osprey's engines. Then the cargo chief moved the rest of the way aft until he was balanced over Morgan's seat. "'Scuse me, Commander," he said. "But the Skipper thought you might like a look at your new home."

"Thanks, Chief," Gray replied. He started unbuckling his harness. "I'd like that."

"Watch your step, sir." The chief turned and led the way forward, past the other passengers.

"How much longer?" he called, following. He was surprised to find that he was hungry for conversation.

"'Bout five minutes," the chief called back. "Timing's kind of tight on this one, y'know. We got a twenty-minute window when we can transfer you guys." He jerked his thumb toward the aircraft cabin's overhead. "May-san."

Gray grunted understanding. *Me-san,* from the Japanese *me,* for "eye," was the generic name for Tokyo's current line of radar spy satellites. Rather than parking them out in geosynch where they could monitor one part of the world all the time, the Japanese followed the old Soviet practice of putting their spy sats into highly elliptical orbits, with the slow-moving apogee positioned above the area they were interested in. Orbital mechanics gave them a high loiter time above their target but also created a hole in their observation window while they whipped around the far side of Earth at perigee. At any given moment there were three Me-san spy sats up, in staggered orbits designed to increase their coverage, but by carefully observing their orbits it was possible to time activities between the setting of one satellite and the rising of another when activities the U.S. military preferred to keep secret could be carried out.

Gray wondered where the current round of East–West tensions would end. The Japanese had not filled the power vacuum left by the disintegration of the Soviet Union fifteen years before . . . not quite. So far they preferred to remain in the background, concentrating on building up their worldwide lead in trade and technology and, more and more of late, in advancing themselves as the world's peacekeepers. Their *Chowa*-series satellites promised to fulfill the old

American dream of an effective shield against ballistic missiles, even while they rendered aging giants like the *Nimitz* and the *Theodore Roosevelt* obsolete. Certainly there was no immediate threat of war with Japan, despite the latest spate of anti-Tokyo riots and demonstrations in the States.

The real danger lay in Japan's military help to the new Islamic union, which was not an immediate threat to the U.S. only because it was not a maritime power. Japan, as she had since the 1930s, desperately needed oil, while the Mahdi's government in Cairo needed advanced weapons systems and the know-how to use them. The trade alliance between the two had been inevitable from the start, but it was worrisome, nonetheless. No one knew just how much intelligence the Japanese were passing on to their Islamic allies. It was entirely possible that data acquired by the Me-sans on American ship and plane movements was ending up in Cairo hours later.

"Won't they get suspicious if they see you just turn around in midocean and head back the way you came?"

"Nah." The chief grinned. "The Japs're used to us scurryin' back and forth by now. Besides, we're not goin' back to New London this time. Soon as we make the rendezvous, we'll be heading on down to Kings Bay. If they're watching us at all, they'll never know we stopped to let you guys off."

Kings Bay. Technically, that was Gray's new duty station, though according to the orders he carried in a manila folder tucked away with his personal belongings in his duffel bag, he wouldn't be seeing the place for quite a while yet. Kings Bay, tucked away on the Georgia coast just north of the Florida border, had been designed as a port for American boomers back in the eighties, an Atlantic counterpart to the big Pacific SSBN base at Bremerton.

Now, though, it was the headquarters for Project Orca, and his new home when he wasn't at sea. Wendy, Gray's wife, would be moving down there from Connecticut sometime next week, getting herself and the kids settled into base housing.

He wondered how long it would be before he would see them again.

The Osprey's cockpit was just large enough for two men seated side by side. Lieutenant Commander Pauli, the pilot, twisted in his left-hand seat to shake Gray's hand. "Howdy, Commander," he said, pushing his helmet's pencil mike back out of the way. "Thought you might like a look-see."

"Thanks." Gray hunched back against an instrument console as the copilot, a lieutenant with WHITTIER stenciled across his helmet, unbuckled himself from the right-hand seat, then squeezed aft past Gray.

"All yours," Whittier said. "Uh, don't touch anything, sir."

"I'll try to remember that."

As he sat down, the Osprey was already bumping a little as it descended into the cloud deck. Gray wished he'd been able to come forward earlier; the Osprey's rather bulbous cockpit gave an excellent view forward and to either side, and he would have liked to have enjoyed that clear, deep sun-blasted blue sky for a little bit longer.

Then the light turned dingy gray and visibility dropped from miles to feet as they dropped into the cloud deck. Water misted against the windshield. Moments later, at 2,000 feet, they broke through into the clear.

It was raining below the clouds, a slow, steady drizzle heavy enough to make Pauli switch on the windscreen wipers. The water below was steel-gray, wave-crinkled, and thickly spotted with whitecaps.

There was a change in the sound of the engines as the Osprey dropped lower. Pauli had pulled back on a prominent lever by his right leg, swinging the big engines mounted at the end of the wings from horizontal to vertical. The transition from forward flight to hover took about twelve seconds, and at the end of that time the Osprey was hanging on its rotors like a helicopter, almost motionless relative to the sea.

"Where are they?" he asked. The sea was empty, the nearest land one hundred miles to the west. For a moment Gray hoped rather wildly that they'd missed the rendezvous, that the Osprey would have to take them on to Kings Bay. Wouldn't *that* be a surprise for Wendy and the kids?

"We're a couple minutes early." Pauli leaned forward in his seat, staring off to starboard. "There," he said, pointing suddenly. Gray sighted along the outstretched finger.

The masts broke the water first, periscopes, radar, a satellite communications antenna, rising in line-ahead above a feather of white wake. The massive sail followed, water streaming down the sides, the upper section long and squat and centered on the teardrop shape of the lower half. The hull followed, emerging from a cascade of water, bluntly rounded at the bow, squared off astern beneath the towering rudder.

"Big sucker," Pauli said. Gray, transfixed by the sight, could say nothing.

She was huge . . . a true giant of the depths. Words failed him completely as he glimpsed minute figures appearing on the weather bridge at the leading edge of the sail that gave him an indication of the vessel's true size. One hundred seventy meters long, twenty-three meters wide, over 30,000 tons displacement . . . the raw numbers failed to make her size real. The sight of her bridge crew, perched three stories above her deck, gave meaning to those numbers and brought a hard lump of apprehension to Gray's throat.

Whittier stood behind Gray's seat, peering over his shoulder at the apparition cleaving majestically through the chop. "Super-PLARB," he said. PLARB was a Russian acronym for *Podvodnaya Lodka Atomnaya Raketnaya Ballisticheskaya,* or nuclear-powered ballistic missile submarine, what the British called a "bomber" and the Americans a "boomer."

"What a monster," Pauli added. "The Russkis damn sure built 'em big."

"She's American now," Gray said, finding his voice at last. As the Osprey dropped to within fifty feet of the surface, he could make out the small American flag painted on the sail, just below the bridge cockpit. The wake, a vast arrowhead of white froth reaching aft from the rudder, was beginning to disperse as the sub slowed in the water. He was unable to tear his eyes away from her great, dark bulk.

"*Leviathan, Leviathan,*" Pauli called into his helmet mike. "This is Echo Tango Three-five with passengers aboard. Ready for approach."

Leviathan.

The name fitted the gray-black sea monster perfectly. She was as long as an Ohio-class Trident submarine, longer by three feet than the Washington Monument was tall, but her beam was nearly twice the American boomer's girth. From the air she looked impossibly broad as her flattened hull plowed forward through the choppy sea. Having her sail riding far aft on the hull instead of forward, as with Ohios and other American subs, gave her an ungainly appearance.

She was a Typhoon-class submarine, the largest undersea vessel in the world, and she was T. Morgan Gray's new ship, his home—at least while she was at sea—for the next two years.

Slavnyy Revolutsiya, the *Glorious Revolution,* was *Leviathan*'s original name, and she'd once been numbered among America's deadliest adversaries. One of eight Typhoons built at Severodvinsk in the 1980s, she'd been an important part of the U.S.S.R.'s strategic nuclear deterrence force until the August Coup and the breakup of the Soviet Union. In the mid-nineties, however, her SS-N-20 ICBMs had been removed and she'd been put up for auction; Russia was less interested in nuclear deterrence by that time than she was in feeding an unhappy population. The United States government, with reasons of its own for keeping the struggling Russian democracy afloat, had purchased *Leviathan* and a sister Typhoon for $1.5 billion apiece.

The Osprey descended toward *Leviathan*'s bows as the huge sub slowed. The entire surface appeared to be covered with dark gray tiles, each shaped to fit the curve of the hull. Gray could clearly see the double row of missile hatches, etched into the deck forward of the sail, ten to each side. That missiles-forward configuration was unique to the Soviet Typhoons. All other ballistic missile submarines in the world had their missiles mounted aft, behind the sail. It gave the monster a racy look, despite its ponderous bulk.

Gray could see several life-jacketed and helmeted men standing on the deck forward of the missile hatches. One wigwagged at the Osprey with a pair of bright yellow chemical light cones.

"You'd best get aft, sir," Pauli said. "Watch that first step gettin' off!"

"Thanks for the ride, Commander."

Back on the Osprey's cargo deck, the cargo master was passing out life jackets and making sure each passenger had his properly fitted and cinched. "We can't actually touch down," he told them as he handed a jacket to Gray. "The Skipper'll hover while you go out the stern ramp. Mind your step, and watch the rotor wash. They won't like it if they have to stop and fish you guys out of the drink."

Gray had been told he could bring only a single small bag—a canvas satchel the size and shape of a high-school gym bag. He retrieved it, checked to see that his orders were still tucked away safely inside, then lined up with the others, facing aft. He could feel the Osprey slipping sideways in the air; the motion was similar to what he'd experienced more than once in a helicopter, but it felt steadier, more stable. The cargo master pressed a large red button on one bulkhead and the back of the compartment opened, part of the deck dropping away as a ramp yawned, and he felt a blast of cool, wet air from outside.

"Right!" the cargo master called. "Go! Go! And good luck!"

Gray followed one of the lieutenants down the angled ramp. A crewman in dungarees was waiting for him on the sub's deck, reaching up to take his arm and steady him as he jumped off the ramp.

It was a two-foot drop to a surprisingly steady deck. With a swell running about three feet and a lot of chop and whitecaps, he'd expected the vessel to be rolling heavily, but the waves scarcely affected the Typhoon at all. Like an iceberg, the sub kept far more of her bulk hidden beneath the surface than was visible above.

He ducked to clear the twin-stabilizer tail of the Osprey and allowed the crewman to lead him forward. He clung to his bag with one hand and the bill of his hat with the other; the rotor wash was fierce, lashing at his body like a living thing and blasting the sea alongside the sub flat in two enormous circles. His khakis were instantly soaked by the mix of rain and wash-blown salt spray. As the last man came off, the Osprey dipped its nose behind them and began picking up speed. In seconds it had vanished into the leaden clouds, leaving the submarine alone in a wide, empty ocean.

A lieutenant in helmet and life jacket waited forward by an open hatch. Gray wasn't certain of the protocol required; in the traditional Navy, he'd be expected to step aboard, salute the ensign aft, salute the Officer of the Deck, and intone the age-old formula "Request permission to come aboard." But *Leviathan* was not in port, there was no ensign flying aft, and the lieutenant by the hatch was motioning with urgent "hurry up" motions of his hand.

"Request per—"

The lieutenant cut him off. "Move your ass! Sir!" He was propelled into the narrow opening of the hatch in the deck. A ladder squeezed down through a steel-walled, three-foot pipe that seemed to last forever.

He felt like he was being swallowed alive.

CHAPTER
2

SSCVN-1 *Leviathan*
One hundred miles east of Cape Hatteras
March 28, 0920 hours

The steel pipe ended but the ladder kept going down, emerging in a brightly lit room smelling of oil, steel, paint, and men. Gray stepped off the lower rung and onto a linoleum tile deck in a large compartment made cramped by piping, conduits, heavy equipment, folding bunks, and as an oddly homey touch, string bags of potatoes and carrots hanging from the piping. The compartment was square—somehow, he'd been expecting the interior bulkheads to conform to the rounded shape of the sub's outer hull—and brightly lit by fluorescent panels nestled within the maze of wires, steam pipes, and ventilation ducts that snaked across the low overhead.

The room was dominated by massive racks cradling blunt-snouted missile shapes, each a good six yards long and almost two feet thick, filling the center of the compartment and lining the port and starboard bulkheads. From those, Gray surmised that he must be in *Leviathan*'s torpedo room. An array of eight round, gleaming doors like pressure-cooker

19

lids, four above, four beneath, took up much of the forward bulkhead; dangling on chains from two of the hatches were signs reading WARNING! WARSHOT LOADED.

A dozen men in dungarees watched from bunks or casual attitudes about the compartment. No one shouted "Attention on deck," the usual formality in the Navy when an officer entered a room. He'd not really expected it aboard a sub; special circumstances always superseded protocol aboard ship. Still, the silence that greeted him reinforced the strangeness of the situation, making him feel like an intruder in an alien world. No one said a word until the crewman who'd led him to the hatch nearly dropped on his shoulders from above with a sharp "Gangway! Make a hole!"

Moving aside, he watched as the rest of the passengers and deck party crowded down the ladder one after another. Someone called, "This way, gentlemen," and he and the others allowed themselves to be led aft.

At least he assumed it was aft, away from the bulkhead with the eight torpedo-tube doors. His descent through the narrow hatchway and the strangeness of his surroundings had left him completely disoriented. There were two watertight doors going aft from the torpedo room, set side by side but leading through short corridors that angled down and sharply right and left.

Stepping through the one on the right, Gray felt as though he'd been dropped into one of those fool-the-senses houses at an amusement park, the kind that deliberately disoriented people in oddly angled passageways before letting them enter queerly tilted rooms where objects appeared to roll uphill, and the laws of gravity and perspective seemed temporarily suspended.

Aft of *Leviathan*'s torpedo room was the missile room, a fraction of it, at any rate. The Typhoon's twenty missile tubes were divided between two side-by-side pressure hulls, ten to each, and they extended vertically through three decks as well. The compartment they were in now was huge, half the length of a football field, though it was less than thirty feet wide and much of that space was taken up by the single line of gleaming white tubes lined up along the inboard bulkhead.

The overhead was so high the compartment felt like a cathedral after the low overhead of the torpedo room, but the visible portion of those huge, deck-to-overhead cylinders visible along one bulkhead still comprised less than a third of the tubes' total length. Though *Leviathan* was no longer a ballistic missile submarine, those tubes had been designed to accommodate the largest sub-launched ballistic missile, or SLBM, ever produced, the three-stage, fifty-foot-long SS-N-20 Sturgeon.

Now, of course, they held completely new weapons, the reason Gray had been offered the chance to volunteer for Project Orca.

Volunteer, right. As though he'd had a choice.

Two men were waiting for the newcomers as they entered the missile compartment. One, a chief, wore spotless khakis. The other, a small, lean, wiry man, wore blue coveralls with colorful patches on arm and chest that gave him the look of a space-shuttle crewman. He sported a captain's silver eagle pinned to his collar, the only indication of rank the man wore.

"I'm Captain Ramsay, gentlemen," the captain said

as the dripping wet newcomers came to an uncertain halt. "Welcome aboard *Leviathan*. Sorry we had to rush you aboard, but our orders require us to stay out of sight of the Japanese spy sats." He singled out the chief, standing to Gray's right. "You're Chief Huxley, right?"

"Yes, sir," the man said.

"You look a little uncomfortable in those blues."

"They caught me in transit, sir. From Norway. Didn't have a chance to change."

"I'm sure the Chief of the Boat can get you squared away." The eyes shifted to Gray, diamond hard and very bright. "You must be Commander Gray."

"Yes, sir."

"Welcome aboard, son. I understand your dad was a submariner."

"Uh . . . yes, sir."

"I'm sure you'll fit in just fine." He turned to the chief standing beside him, hands on hips. "Chief, these men are wet and they're dripping on my deck. Get them squared away and deliver them to the wardroom in, make it thirty minutes."

"Thirty minutes, aye, aye, Captain." The chief looked the five of them up and down as though he weren't quite sure where he was going to fit them in an already crowded boat. Gray became aware of a number of discrete noises that seemed to echo from the bulkheads around him, creaks and groans mingled with a distant rumble.

"Well . . . gentlemen," the chief said after the captain had left. "I'm Chief Delano and I'm the COB, the Chief of the Boat. Bring your gear and follow me." There was another ominous creak from somewhere overhead.

"Uh . . . Chief?" the j.g. said. His face looked, if anything, whiter than it had aboard the Osprey. Gray hoped it was an effect of the compartment's fluorescent lighting.

"Yes, sir?"

"How long, uh, before we submerge?"

A faint smile creased the COB's face. "Feel the deck, sir?"

"Beg pardon?"

"The deck." He moved his hands, pointing forward. "It's slanting, bow down. We went decks awash about the moment you stepped into the torpedo room. Right now we're at five degrees down bubble and, oh, maybe fifty feet. Still periscope depth." The smile deepened, creasing into an unpleasant grin. "But we're *going* to devils five."

"What the hell's 'devils five'?" Gray wanted to know.

"You aviators have your own buzzwords, right? You talk about a target at 'angels five'—"

"And we mean five thousand feet, right," one of the lieutenants said. "What are you saying, Chief, that we're going down five thousand feet? That's impossible!"

"Five hundred feet, actually," Delano said with a grin. "A mere nothing. Take us maybe another two minutes."

Now that the COB mentioned it, Gray could feel the cant in the deck, slight but definite. He tried to picture the huge sub dropping into the depths, surrounded by dark water, and failed.

"Space is at a premium, I'm afraid," Chief Delano explained as he led them aft. "Even on a Typhoon. Commander, I'm afraid we're going to have to park you in the MEJO locker until we can work out better accommodations."

"That's okay, Chief," Gray replied. "Just so it's not inside a torpedo tube."

Delano laughed. "You might have more room in a tube, sir."

"How many men on a Typhoon, Chief?" the other lieutenant wanted to know.

"She was designed for a Russian crew of one hundred thirty. Maybe sixty of those were officers, but the Russkis never trusted their enlisted men the way we do, and they weren't as careful with their training. With the new automated systems, and with the boat's missile crew no longer needed aboard, we were able to pare that back to a complement of one hundred twelve, including twenty officers. But you Orca guys have added thirty more to our muster list, counting the enlisted technicians, so we're a bit cramped for space. Don't worry, though. We're not hot-bunking yet."

Navy protocol still demanded a rank-dependent hierarchy in the quality of accommodations, but space for anything was a luxury aboard a submarine. Even on a Typhoon, it was usually only the Captain who had a cabin to himself. Senior officers normally bunked two or four to a room, but aboard *Leviathan*, Gray would have to rack out with the MEJOs. He knew the acronym from his rotations aboard carriers. It stood for "marginally effective junior officers" and usually referred to ensigns and j.g.s. For now, though, the eighteen officers assigned to Project Orca would be sharing quarters, while Chief Huxley quartered in the goats' locker with the boat's other chiefs. Gray actually welcomed the arrangement. It would give him a chance to get to know his men better.

The MEJO quarters, located off to the side of the main deck starboard missile compartment, were walled off by thin, pressed-wood privacy dividers. Once they'd been occupied by Soviet Naval Strategic Rocket Force officers assigned to the *Slavnyy Revolutsiya*'s SS-N-20 systems. Eight narrow bunks or "racks" folded out from the bulkhead in a long space just wide enough for two men to squeeze past one another. An identical compartment was located on the port side, opposite "Sherwood Forest," the ominous rows of side-by-side, ten-foot-thick missile tubes.

Five officers were in the quarters when they walked in, three lieutenants and two j.g.s lying on their racks. "Fresh meat!" one of the lieutenants exclaimed. Then he noticed Gray's collar insignia. "Oh, 'scuse me, sir," he said, and rolled off the bunk.

"Don't get up," Gray said. He extended a hand. "Commander Gray."

"Lieutenant Koch, sir," the other said, shaking hands. "This here's Lieutenant Hernandez, Lieutenant Franklin, and Lieutenant j.g. Dominico."

Gray noticed that Koch had not introduced the other j.g., who remained in his rack with an arm across his eyes, taking no interest in the newcomers. *Trouble there,* Gray thought.

"Mike Seegar," one of the lieutenants from the Osprey put in. He was tall, sandy-haired, and had the cocky directness that Gray associated with most of the aviators he knew. "Call sign 'Cigar.'" He pronounced it like his last name, with the accent on the first syllable.

"Joseph R. Young," the other lieutenant off the

Osprey added. He was shorter than Seegar, with wiry black hair and a mustache. "The mighty Joe Young. Call me 'Monk.'"

"And I'm Oz." The third lieutenant in the MEJO quarters was a young black man with an easy grin. "Oz Franklin."

"Oz?"

"'Cause I don't think we're in Kansas anymore."

"And you?" Gray asked the j.g. from the Osprey.

"F-Frank Wilder, sir," he said.

"Well, it's damned nice to see someone else from the bird-farm Navy," Koch said. "Bird farm" was Navy slang for an aircraft carrier. "It gets kind of cold and dark and lonely down here."

"So," Hernandez said. He was a short, dark-skinned Latino with a neatly trimmed mustache. "Where're you guys coming from? Before they ran you through the gauntlet at New London, I mean."

"Me'n Monk were at NAS Oceana," Cigar replied. "VFA-157."

"*Roosevelt*," Gray added. "They brought her back to Norfolk, and the next thing I knew they were telling me I could fly a desk or come down here."

Koch shook his head. "Hope you made the right choice, sir."

"Hey, sir," Lieutenant Young said. "We heard you drove F-22s."

The F-22 was the newest combat fighter in the Navy's inventory, derived from the long-delayed Advanced Tactical Fighter program. "Yeah, but mostly I drove Hornets. VFA-171. How about you?"

"We're all Hornet drivers here," Franklin said. "I think that's what qualified us for Orca. What's your call sign?"

"It was 'Cold Steel,' back in the days of my youth," Gray said, smiling. "Lately, though, it's been 'Assistant CAG.'"

"Well, I guess you're CAG now," Seegar observed. "You're skipper of our new squadron, right?"

Gray laughed. "CAG," standing for "Commander Air Group," was a leftover term from World War II, back when carriers had air groups instead of air wings.

"Well, actually I guess that makes me a C-S-G instead of a C-A-G," he said, spelling the acronyms. "But I'm not sure how to pronounce that." He cocked his head, curious. He'd just placed their squadron number. "VFA-157. The *Abraham Lincoln*?"

"That's right," Young said.

"Were you on her in '02?"

"Damn right," Seegar said. "We were on CAP when things went down."

He shook his head. "Man. You guys are lucky to be here." He read their faces and thought it best to change the subject. "So, how does it feel to be in submarines now?"

"You mean, how do we feel about losing our wings?" Young shrugged. "When they passed the word that Fighting 157 was being canned, I was mad as hell. Fucking budget cuts . . . and what had happened to the *Abe*, of course. But they'd already kept us at Oceana for three years, flying training missions, so it wasn't like we were still going off bird farms, right? Just like you, sir, we had a choice between flying desks at Norfolk or . . . this." His expression as he glanced around at the MEJO compartment suggested that he wasn't entirely sure he'd made the right decision.

Gray knew exactly what Young was feeling, or

thought he did. He was beginning to think that he'd made a mistake by assuming that he could substitute *this* for the career he'd trained for all his adult life.

He couldn't help but remember that his father had been a sub driver . . . and that the elder Gray still considered volunteering for submarine duty the biggest mistake he'd ever made in a career that had extended from 1969 to its abrupt termination in 1984.

"Well, we're sub drivers now," Gray said. He glanced at his watch. "Hey, we'd better get squared away for our welcome-aboard speech. Which bunk's mine?"

Personal gear, he learned, was stowed in a flat compartment revealed by unlatching and lifting his mattress, and there was also a narrow locker for his uniforms.

Not that he had that much to stow. His orders had specified the single carry-on bag, so besides an electric shaver and a few toiletries, all he'd brought aboard was a single extra uniform, tightly rolled, and some spare socks and underwear. He spent several minutes trying to decide which uniform was the more suitable for an interview with the captain—the one creased by a two-hour flight and still damp from his soaking topside, or the one creased from its stowage in a gym bag. He opted for dry clothes over wet—the wrinkles weren't *too* bad in the permanent-press material—and he took some time to wipe the salt from his shoes. First impressions counted for a lot in the Navy.

How the hell, he wondered, did men like Delano keep themselves looking like a Navy recruiting poster, living this way for months at a time? Compared with his quarters aboard the *Theodore Roosevelt*, where he'd had his own room, desk, and even a wall safe for valuables, these were spartan quarters indeed.

As he dressed he glanced again at the j.g. still lying alone in his rack in the corner. "How about you, son?" he asked. "What's your name?"

"You don't need to pretend you're interested in me, sir," the man said. He did not move, and he kept his arm thrown across his eyes. "Soon as they can pull it off, I'm out of here."

"His name's Phillips," Koch said. Gray heard an edge in his voice, almost a sneer, or an accusation. "He VD'd."

Phillips sat up suddenly. Gray judged that he might be twenty-four, maybe twenty-five, but his eyes looked *old*. "I'm not a coward, goddamn it! It's just this whole fuckin' idea sucks!"

"Easy, man," Oz said.

"They don't have a fuckin' clue how to use us, so they're gonna fuckin' throw us away!"

"Whoa, there, son," Gray said. "Who's 'they'?"

"Them. Admiral Delacroix and the REMFs back in D.C." He rolled over in his bunk and refused to say another word.

Before he'd left New London, Gray had learned that three of his fellow passengers aboard the Osprey were replacements. Young, Seegar, and Wilder were all being flown out to *Leviathan* to bring Orca up to strength. According to the roster he'd been given, Orca called for a squadron complement of sixteen officers, including himself as squadron CO. *Leviathan* had set sail from Kings Bay one week earlier, with ten of those slots filled.

Three days earlier, two of those men had elected to "VD," or opt for a voluntary dropout from the program.

Now Gray and the three replacements had brought the squadron strength back up to twelve, still four short but enough to get the program off to a decent start.

Phillips, he realized, was an early casualty.

Among naval aviators, the opportunity to "turn in your wings" offered an escape for men who feared they'd lost the edge. It happened. Not often, but it happened. Gray had seen aviators shaken into near catatonia by a hairy night trap or the raw shock of punching out after a critical systems failure in flight.

Making that decision, however, was a kind of voluntary self-exile. It was an admission that they no longer had the "right stuff," the drive and the guts and the inflated self-esteem that drove combat pilots, and that made them outcasts. Other aviators no longer associated with them, and such men were yanked off the carrier and out of the squadron as quickly as the transfer could be arranged. Generally, they wound up in less demanding arms of the fleet, driving COD transports or tankers. Their fellow aviators talked about them in the past tense, as though they'd crashed and burned.

Something of the sort had happened to Phillips, Gray realized. Unable to hack the special demands of life aboard a submarine, he'd quit. That was his privilege, of course, but Gray wondered what had made him do it.

So far as the others were concerned, it seemed, he was already gone.

CHAPTER
3

Wardroom, SSCVN-1 *Leviathan*
March 28, 1005 hours

*L*eviathan's wardroom was a carpeted, wood-paneled compartment on the main deck opposite the officers' mess. Though there was room in one corner for a coffeepot and hot plate, most of the deck space was taken up by a table with an imitation wood-grain top and green, plastic seats, arranged like a large corner booth in a restaurant. Commissioning plaques, unit emblems, and awards hung on the bulkheads, most of them displaying the alien symbols of the Cyrillic alphabet, and there were several framed paintings and photographs. One painting was of the U.S.S. *Pittsburgh* surging ahead beneath the surface, while a photograph showed the conning tower of a sub, its diving planes rotated vertically, protruding above the ice as crewmen in parkas stood beneath a pale blue sky.

Captain Ramsay had joined the five newcomers in the wardroom and sat at one end of the table with a steaming mug in his hand.

"Go ahead and grab yourselves coffee," he'd told the others when he came in. "You'll find things a little less formal down here than you might have been used to aboard a flattop."

Gray decided that he liked the Captain, an easygoing man whose eyes and words occasionally revealed a flash of steel beneath the mild exterior. He was clearly a professional, with the unspoken self-assurance that said he knew his business.

"Well, gentlemen," Ramsay said when they were all seated. "This is your official welcome-aboard talk. I've got things to do and so do you, so I'll keep it short.

"People, Commander Gray here has been brought in as skipper for the Orca Project. You will answer to him and through him to me." He nodded toward the tall, black chief, who was still wearing his dress blues. "Chief Huxley here happens to be one of the moving forces behind Project Orca. With the initial design group, am I right, Chief?"

"Yes, sir. Design and testing."

"In other words, he knows the SFV-4B Barracuda, he knows the Barracuda's systems, and he knows ULTRA-C and SUBVIEW. I'm sure his presence aboard will go a long way toward making Project Orca a complete success.

"Gentlemen, you've heard the line already but I'll spout it again, just so we understand each other. Submariners have the toughest damned job in the Navy. The food's good, but the rest of it—the crowding, the isolation, being out of touch with your family ashore—it all sucks. That's why they're volunteers, every one of them. They only make it into the boats after rigorous screening to make certain that they can adapt psychologically to the routine." He smiled, a wintery twitch at the corner of his mouth. "We don't allow any claustrophobes down here.

"Normally, submariners come aboard after months of training at the submarine school in New London, and even then they're on probation. It takes a year for a submariner to win his dolphins.

"Now, because of the rush with Project Orca, most of your training focused on Orca technology and you've had to skimp on the training and familiarization with conventional submarine systems. I'm not even sure how much you've had, but I imagine this all probably feels pretty weird to you, and maybe a little scary.

"I want you all to understand that I'm available if you need to talk to someone . . . and that includes if you decide that you can't hack it and you want to cash it in. Just say you want a VD and we'll pull you off Barracuda duty and see to it that you get taken off and sent ashore at the first available opportunity. My Executive Officer is Commander Parker. You can talk to him as you would to me. Also, you've already met Chief Delano, my Chief of the Boat. Definitely a father figure if ever there was one. You can take your problems to him if you need to, too. Everybody else does, and that includes me.

"I'm a nice guy but I expect my orders to be obeyed instantly and with snap and absogoddamn-lutely by the book because if someone screws up, it can result in the loss of a very expensive submarine, not to mention killing every man on board. However, since we're practically living in each other's laps day in and day out, you'll find we're not as fanatical about the shined shoes and the pressed uniforms as they are aboard the skimmers. Talk to the other officers and men aboard. They'll help you get shipshape.

"And that's enough gab on my part. Any questions?"

"Yes, sir," Young said. "They packed us off in such a rush, they didn't even tell us what the flap was about. Why are we in such an all-fired hurry?"

Ramsay smiled. "That's the Navy for you. Well, you were scheduled to come aboard at Kings Bay in another four weeks, right?" There were nods and several murmured assents from around the table. "First off, we came up with a couple of VDs and we needed to fill the hole. Orca still isn't up to strength, yet, but it's better now that you guys are aboard.

"The hurry-up was caused by recent developments in the Caribbean. Last Monday, a supertanker in the Yucatán Passage was struck by at least one cruise missile and sunk. The attacker remains unidentified, but it's a good guess that it was a former Soviet cruise-missile submarine, and that means an Oscar. Since I doubt that the Japanese are patrolling the Caribbean, I think we can assume that the attack was carried out by the Islamics.

"Yesterday, this squadron received orders to proceed at full speed to the area off southwestern Cuba. We're to be on the lookout for this pirate, though Washington hasn't made up its mind yet whether we're going to sink him or call him dirty names. Our orders read, quote, protect American shipping in the area by all means at your disposal, unquote. And that, to the best of my ability, is what I intend to do."

A tall, khaki-clad shape stepped into the doorway. "Well said, Captain."

"Attention on deck!" Seegar called, but the figure waved them down before they could get to their feet.

"You jump up every time I walk in on you aboard this boat and you'll never get anything done. Captain? Do you mind if I join you?"

"Of course not, sir," Ramsay said. "Gentlemen, allow me to present the commanding officer of this squadron, Rear Admiral Vincent Harriman Delacroix."

He was tall, powerful, silver-haired, and crag-faced, probably in his late fifties, Gray judged.

"Good morning," the admiral said. "As I'm sure you know, admirals don't generally travel aboard submarines." He cocked an eye at Ramsay. "But then, most submarines are skippered by commanders, not captains. *Leviathan* is in a class by herself.

"This vessel is the flagship of something new, an undersea squadron designated Submarine Flotilla One. Normally, when a sub skipper makes captain he ends up squadron commander, and that means he gets posted to a nice, safe desk ashore or aboard a nice, fat sub tender. Ramsay and I have been able to break the rules because *Leviathan* is the Navy's testbed for ULTRA-C."

Gray knew what ULTRA-C was, of course. Underwater Laser, TRAcking and Communications, had been on the drawing boards for years, but only recently had the bugs in power supply and control been finally licked.

The concept of a submarine battle group was not new. The Germans had pioneered the use of wolf-pack tactics in the Second World War, tactics that the United States had used with great success, on a much smaller scale, in the Pacific. But for submarines to coordinate their movements and attacks they had to communicate with one another, and until recently, the only way that had been possible was for them to surface and use the radio.

For most of the time since World War II, however, throughout the long years of the Cold War, submarine warfare had been a solitary struggle. A submarine's stealth, its invisibility in the wide, deep waters of the ocean, was its greatest strength, and every time a sub approached the surface to communicate with other subs or with its base, it threw that advantage away. Submarines had become lone-wolf hunters, occasionally rising to periscope depth to receive orders, but never transmitting unless breaking radio silence was absolutely necessary.

ULTRA-C was changing that. *Leviathan* and her two escorts, both old Los Angeles–class attack subs, were able to communicate with one another underwater, using blue-green laser beams that could penetrate the sea for miles with only slight loss of signal.

"Commander Gray," the admiral said sharply, flinty eyes meeting his. "You've already turned in your orders?"

"We gave them to a yeoman a few minutes ago, sir."

"Good. Have you read them?"

"Yes, sir."

"How do you interpret them?"

Gray pursed his lips. "As commander of the new SFV-4 squadron, I'm to evaluate its performance in an actual deployment, and the performance of Orca personnel. I'm also to use my experience as an aviator to evolve combat tactics for the SFV-4B. Uh . . . COMSUBLANT kind of gave me carte blanche on that one, Admiral."

"What do you mean?"

"Well, no one really knows what the SFV-4B Barracuda can do. Oh, they know the specs, how fast it is, how it phases with ULTRA-C, and all that, but I don't think Washington knows yet whether they've developed a new kind of minisub . . . or a hot, undersea fighter plane."

"You know the answer to that one already, don't you, son?" There was something about Delacroix's voice that set off a warning flag in the back of Gray's mind. The man was digging at something.

"I'm not sure I know what you mean, sir. I've had simulator training with the Barracuda, of course, but—"

"The SFV-4B Barracuda is a minisub, Commander. Sophisticated, fast, and maneuverable, but it is *not* a jet fighter and it is not a toy. I know, I know, I've heard the jokes about the 'SF' in 'SFV' standing for 'Science Fiction,' but the Submersible Fighting Vehicle was intended as a support craft for more conventional submarines. I should tell you now, right up front, that I feel the Pentagon's decision to post aviators to this project was a grave mistake. Aviators, in my estimation, are too prone to . . . call it flights of fancy. They're too likely to read things into the technology that simply are not there."

Gray blinked his surprise, then exchanged glances with Young and Seegar. They looked as puzzled as he felt. Wilder was glancing from face to face as though searching for clues as to how to react. Huxley kept his face impassive.

In fact, Gray wasn't sure yet what he thought of the Barracuda, and he damn sure didn't know how to employ it tactically. But his orders had been to find out and make suggestions, not to accept the preconceived pronouncements of another naval officer, no matter what his rank.

"I will keep the Admiral's opinions in mind as I carry out my evaluation," Gray said slowly. "Naturally."

This time Delacroix blinked. "Indeed." He didn't sound pleased with Gray's evasive answer. Ramsay looked uncomfortable. "That's all I have to say, Captain," the admiral said abruptly. "Thank you for letting me address them."

He all but stormed from the wardroom.

"Was it something we said?" Monk asked.

"Admiral Delacroix is a longtime submariner," Ramsay said. He didn't sound as though he approved or disapproved of the admiral's behavior. He was simply stating a fact. He nodded toward the painting of the *Pittsburgh*, and the photo of the sub surfaced in the Arctic ice. "He skippered both the *Billfish* and the *Pittsburgh* back in the eighties. After that he drove trucks."

"Trucks, sir?" Seegar asked.

Ramsay grinned. "Attack-sub slang for boomers. The big missile boats. Anyway, he's had a hell of a lot of experience in submarines, people. Don't sell him short."

But Ramsay's tone of voice almost seemed to be saying something else, something about Delacroix's inability to handle the new and rapidly changing technologies that were everywhere making today's high-tech obsolete.

Gray wondered whether there was going to be trouble organizing a Barracuda squadron under a man who didn't really believe in them.

Flag Cabin, SSCVN-1 *Leviathan*
March 28, 1015 hours

It wasn't that he didn't believe in the Barracuda. It was just that his concept of tactics had not yet made the leap the new technology demanded. Admiral Delacroix knew well that *Leviathan* was like no other submarine in history, and he knew that she incorporated technology that was likely to completely change the character of submarine warfare. Delacroix knew all of this, and accepted it.

But he still didn't like it.

Delacroix had been a submariner for twenty years, and he was a master of both sonar and attack-sub tactics. ULTRA-C seemed to him more like science fiction than anything else, and he was damned if he'd let the landlocked double domes back at RAND and DARPA compromise sound tactics with their wild and impractical schemes.

So much had changed since he'd commanded subs of his own, back in the eighties, before the collapse of the U.S.S.R. and the end of the Cold War. The only reason he'd left the boats was his promotion to captain. Four-stripers simply did not command submarines then, so he'd been bumped first to squadron command aboard a tender, and later to a staff job with COMSUBLANT at the Pentagon.

He'd made rear admiral just before the *Abraham Lincoln* disaster in the Persian Gulf, and when the Navy Department started scrambling to redirect America's naval strategy, Delacroix had been the logical choice for COMSUBFLOT-1.

At least, that's how his boss back in COMSUBLANT had explained it. Commander, Submarine Flotilla One. His mouth twisted, etching sour lines down his long face. Delacroix was not known for his tact, or for his ingratiating manner. He'd long since decided that somehow, sometime, he must have stomped on some pretty high-ranking toes back in the COMSUBLANT hierarchy. Nothing else would explain his exile from a quiet desk in the Pentagon's E-ring to . . . here, riding herd on a project that sounded like it ought to reside among the pages of some pulp sci-fi mag.

A personnel file was lying on his desk and he opened it, leafing through the first few pages.

Commander Thomas Morgan Gray. Thirty-five. Naval aviator . . . *former* aviator, rather. CO of VFA-171 aboard the *Roosevelt*, then Assistant CAG, same ship. Son of a career naval officer . . . a sub driver, ironically enough. Delacroix remembered hearing about *that* imbroglio, back in the early eighties, a damned, ugly mess. From everything he'd heard, Commander Gray—the father—had been a decent officer.

So far, the son had been a model of Navy efficiency, straight four-ohs. Married . . . two kids . . . stable . . . intelligent. He'd volunteered for Orca and managed top-third marks at the Groton sub school. Not too shabby for a latecomer.

At least he wasn't trying to prove something, like most of the other ex-aviators in Orca.

Or was he? The fact that his father had been a nuke skipper could have a lot to do with his deciding to volunteer for subs. Delacroix had noticed that he was still wearing his wings, and that smart-assed weaseling over the interpretation of his orders hadn't escaped the admiral's notice either. Clever bastard. He would have to keep a close eye on Gray. No matter what the guy's psych profile said, a duty change like this would be pretty rough.

And Admiral Delacroix tolerated no weakness in his command.

Damn *all* Navy aviators, anyway! Delacroix decided that he was going to have to keep a close eye on all of them. Fortunately, this bunch probably wouldn't last long. With this new crisis brewing in the Caribbean, it was entirely possible that *Leviathan* and her battle group would be in combat within the next few days, and that was bound to shake out the men from the boys. It always did.

Delacroix very much doubted that this bunch had what it took to be submariners.

Quarters, SSCVN-1 *Leviathan*
March 28, 1340 hours

Later, in the MEJO quarters, T. Morgan Gray was also wondering if he had what it took to be a submariner. By his own admission his dad hadn't. Who did he think he was trying to fool, making the big leap from flyboy to . . . to . . . fishboy?

Commander Chester A. Gray had joined the Navy in 1969, at the very height of the Vietnam War and two years before his son had been born. He'd volunteered for subs right out of OCS, been accepted for nuclear training, and worked his way all the way to the top, serving in a dozen different boats. He'd trained for every department, though since he was on the track to commanding his own boat someday, the vast majority of his experience had been in reactor engineering. He'd gone aboard his first command, the Sturgeon-class attack boat *William C. Russell* in 1984, three days before Morgan's thirteenth birthday.

On her very first patrol, the *Russell* had encountered a Soviet sub. It was part of the old Cold War game, of opponents stalking one another in the depths, unheard and unseen. It was a game pursued

in deadly earnest; should war break out, it was vital
that the enemy's submarine force be neutralized fast,
especially his missile boats. At that time, the Cold War
had entered a new and more dangerous period;
Reagan was in the White House and the United States
was shipping Stinger SAMs to the rebels in
Afghanistan. Chernenko was in power in the Kremlin,
while few outside the Soviet Union had even heard of
Mikhail Gorbachev.

Russell's target had been an old Echo II–class boat,
an old and noisy sub that fired Shaddock antiship
cruise missiles from elevating launchers stowed flush
with her afterdeck. *Russell* had encountered her at
800 feet in the waters over the Newfoundland Basin,
halfway between St. John and the Azores. Maneuvering
by passive sonar alone, "Chesty" Gray had brought
the *Russell* in on the Echo II's six, dead astern of the
Soviet sub in that blind spot known to submariners as
her baffles. The Echo's own propeller noise and wake
wash kept her from hearing the American boat.

Suddenly, the Russian sub's sonar aspect had
changed. She was swinging around, coming to port,
then hard to starboard in a full one-eighty designed
to bring her back on a reciprocal course. It was a
maneuver Soviet skippers often pulled to clear their
baffles; American submariners called it "Crazy
Ivan."

There'd been nothing like SUBVIEW in those
days, only the steady sonar track from dead ahead
that suggested that the other submarine was now
heading directly toward the *Russell*. Gray had hesitated,
uncertain. Should he swing port or starboard, dive or
blow ballast? Warning the Russian sub with an active
sonar ping could make the situation worse; like a

game of chicken on the highway, there was no way to know which way the other guy might jump.

At the last possible instant, Gray had ordered *Russell*'s Diving Officer to take her down. Every man aboard could hear the other boat's approach by that time, a whooshing noise mingled with the rising *throb-throb-throb* of the Echo II's twin screws. It sounded like he might be passing overhead . . . he was going to miss. . . .

The shock had thrown men to the deck and caused a dozen injuries. *Russell* had heeled far over to port, then righted. There was no obvious damage, but Gray had ordered *Russell* to the surface.

As they rose through the water sonar had heard the other sub die.

In the inquiry that followed, it was determined that the Echo had almost missed the *Russell* completely, passing just above her deck as she dropped away beneath. At the last moment, though, the Echo's starboard screw had slammed into *Russell*'s sail. The impact caused little damage to the American sub, but it badly sprung the Soviet vessel's starboard propeller shaft. Water had poured in through a torn gasket, flooding the Echo's after-engine compartment, slamming through to the forward compartment, knocking out critical power, drowning batteries. . . .

Chester Gray had been listening through a set of sonar headphones. He'd heard the shriek of metal groaning, then caving in, the rumble of heavy machinery slamming against the pressure hull and icy water flooding compartments, even, he imagined, the terrified shrieks and death screams of a hundred Russian sailors.

The water over the Newfoundland Basin is deep,

16,000 feet in places. He heard the hull collapse as it passed 2,000.

On his bunk in the MEJO quarters aboard *Leviathan,* Morgan Gray stirred, shoving aside the unwanted memories. His father had retired after that cruise. The inquiry had cleared him of improper conduct, but somehow he'd never been able to clear himself. His decision, though he could not possibly have known it ahead of time, had doomed one hundred men. The fact that they were the enemy, at least in the political sense, made no difference. In fact, after that watch the elder Gray had always wondered if he would have been able to order a torpedo launch if a real war broke out.

It was not a question a sub skipper could ask. He'd lost the edge. He'd quit. And Thomas Morgan Gray had always been just a little leery of the submarine service. He'd not even considered subs when he went through OCS but put in instead for flight training at Pensacola. His father, retired now, had been delighted when he learned his son was pushing jets.

Gray hadn't figured out yet how to tell him that he'd volunteered for submarine duty. So much about Orca was still classified anyway, it had been a lot easier simply not to write.

Rising from his bunk, Gray dismissed increasingly dark thoughts and started removing his uniform. He would take a quick shower, wash the salt out of his hair, then hit the paperwork. Here he'd just arrived aboard his new duty station, and already he had a backlog of work, going over the personnel records of the men in his squadron, checking their evaluations and test scores, planning how to organize the squadron.

The Navy, he thought, didn't run on diesel fuel, nuclear power, or even coffee. It ran on paperwork.

Maybe, he thought, *it wouldn't be so bad, sitting behind a stack of paper at a desk job in Norfolk.*

Maybe that's where I belong.

CHAPTER
4

U.S. Navy P-3C Orion
Forty-eight miles south of Isla de la Juventud
March 28, 1746 hours

"**MAD! MAD! MAD!**" the voice of ET2 Rodriguez called over the intercom system. "Popping smoke!"

Lieutenant Commander James Nixon glanced out the left-hand cockpit window, scanning the waves five hundred feet below for . . . something, *anything* breaking the crinkled gray of the surface, but of course he saw nothing. If there was a submarine down there, it was submerged.

The P-3C Orion was an old aircraft, dating from the early eighties, but Nixon still preferred it to the newer P-7s that were replacing them. Even in the twenty-first century, there was a place for big, four-engine turboprops like this one, able to patrol for ten hours at a stretch, hunting submarines with a sophisticated EW suite that could ferret them out both acoustically and electronically; the big aircraft's tail was drawn out into a long, narrow "stinger" that housed its Magnetic Anomaly Detection gear, or MAD. Rodriguez, one of the Orion's ten crewmen, had

46

just registered a MAD trace as they flew through the magnetic distortion induced by the passage of a large, metal body beneath the ocean's surface.

A submarine, in other words. The Orion's prey.

Nixon put the Orion into a hard bank to the left, bringing it back onto a reciprocal course. Excitement sang in his blood. For the past three months, he and his crew had been operating out of "Gitmo"—the U.S. Naval Air Station at Guantanamo Bay, Cuba—flying daily patrols aimed at tracking the continuing flow of drugs heading north out of Venezuela, Colombia, and Panama, a chore that Nixon liked to compare to using F-29 interceptors for tracking down speeders on the turnpike. The day before, however, there'd been a sudden change in orders. The Gitmo P-3 squadron was now on antisubmarine patrol, relentlessly searching corridors south of the Cuban bight all the way west to Mexico. Scuttlebutt had it that an oil tanker had been sunk, probably by a sub. It was possible that they'd just picked the bastard up.

White smoke spilled from a patch on the sea ahead, marking the point at which Rodriguez had got his nibble. "Okay, back there," he said over the intercom. "We'll drop a standard pattern. Phil, patch a PROBSUB alert through to the *Roberts*. They're closest."

"Coming up on the first mark," his Tactical Officer called. "Three . . . two . . . one . . . *mark!*"

A silvery canister *chuffed* from the Orion's belly, emerging from one in a pattern of round, aft-facing slots. A parachute blossomed, steadying it as it fell toward the water. Moments later, a second canister followed . . . then a third.

Sonar remained the key to finding submarines.

Sonobuoys could be either passive or active—that is, they could float silently, listening for the noise of a passing submarine, or they could send out sharp, high-frequency pings of sound that reflected back from whatever happened to be in the water. Since they already suspected that a submarine lay beneath that patch of the Caribbean, the P-3 crew was laying a pattern of active sonobuoys. In his cubbyhole on the Orion's port side halfway back, sonar technician 1st class Harry Anderson pressed headphones to his ears, listening for the radioed transmissions from the first buoy.

UIR Oscar-class SSGN _Sharuq_
Forty-eight miles south of Isla de la Juventud
March 28, 1747 hours

As so often happened in submarine warfare, the hunter had become the hunted. Two days after the destruction of the _American Castle,_ reaction to the attack had been sharp and purposeful, though the United Islamic Republic's SSGN _Sharuq_ still held the advantage.

Five times in the last thirty hours, _Sharuq_'s sonar operators had reported sounds from the surface that were almost certainly American antisubmarine warfare aircraft. This time, those sounds had been followed by the telltale splashes of sonobuoys.

Within _Sharuq_'s control room, a crowded compartment surprisingly narrow for so broad a vessel, men stood at their stations with an urgent, expectant air. A muffled ping echoed through the hull, and the men tensed, many glancing upward, past the clutter of pipes and wiring and fluorescent lights in the overhead and toward the unseen surface of the sea.

Captain Siraj al-Badr glanced forward at his Diving Officer, who was standing just behind two men seated side by side. *Sharuq*'s planesman and helmsman silently gripped the large joysticks set into the consoles in front of them as *Sharuq* continued her dive. A second ping sounded from overhead, more muffled now, and distorted. "Depth," he snapped.

"Passing one hundred twelve meters, Captain," the Diving Officer replied. "Holding at fifteen degrees down bubble."

"Conn, sonar," a voice crackled over the intercom. "We're passing through the thermocline now. Signal strength falling off. I don't think they got a solid fix."

A third ping sounded . . . this one so faint and garbled it could not possibly have transmitted useful information back to the surface. Al-Badr turned, looking aft at the small figure in nondescript coveralls who stood beside *Sharuq*'s chart table.

The man adjusted his glasses, his Oriental features expressionless. "You see, Captain?" he said, his Arabic fluent but thickly accented and almost comically stilted. "In these waters there is frequently a temporary temperature discontinuity at this time of day well above the normal thermocline."

"So you said," al-Badr replied gruffly. He still did not like the idea of this, this foreigner—and an infidel, at that—aboard his ship. Christians, even Jews, were *ahl al-kitab*, the People of the Book, men who at least believed in God, however imperfectly. The Japanese, however, with their strange mix of Shinto, Buddhism, and technocapitalist materialism, were truly alien people who worshiped nothing that al-Badr could recognize; they were not to be trusted.

Still, Cairo had saddled him with this Japanese advisor, a naval officer who was supposed to have an extensive technical background with Oscar-class submarines. Al-Badr had to admit that the man's advice had been useful so far. "Are they likely to pick us up magnetically?"

"Not at this depth, Captain," the advisor said. "The danger now is that the aircraft will call in helicopters or surface ships. These could employ dipping sonars that can be lowered to three hundred meters or more."

"We will not be here by the time they arrive," al-Badr replied. "Helm! Come left twenty degrees! Engineering! I want revolutions for thirty knots!"

"We will not be able to listen for enemy ships at that speed," the Japanese advisor pointed out.

"Of course not. However, we already know where our next target is, and where it will be tonight. I intend to be waiting for it, and I want no American ships or aircraft watching over my shoulder when I give the command to fire."

Leveling off at 400 meters, the great submarine slipped silently toward the southwest.

U.S. Navy P-3C Orion
March 28, 1752 hours

"Sorry, Skipper," Anderson said. His sonar plot on the big, circular board in front of him showed one possible contact, bearing at two-three-five from the first sonobuoy, then nothing. "I'm sure we had something down there, but it was gone before I could get a second look at it. I think he pulled the plug and slipped beneath the afternoon effect."

"Okay, Anderson. Pass what you got to comm. Maybe the *Roberts* can pick up the trail."

"Right, Skipper."

The Orion had already been on the homeward leg of its patrol. Nixon and the other men aboard were stiff and tired after more than eight hours aloft, and they were eager to touch down again at Gitmo. Sub hunting was exciting, but they were more than happy to pass the responsibility on to someone else now.

One hundred miles to the south, the guided-missile frigate *Samuel B. Roberts* acknowledged the Orion's radioed message and swung onto a new heading. At twenty-nine knots she would be in the sighting area in less than four hours.

UIR Oscar-class SSGN *Sharuq*
March 28, 2135 hours

The Captain had ordered her speed cut back to a silent, five-knot crawl. Now *Sharuq* rose slowly through ink-black water, climbing back to periscope depth.

She'd looped far to the west and south before swinging back to her new hunting grounds, stopping every so often to listen carefully with passive sonar. Once, her sonar operator had thought he'd detected another vessel, a surface ship running on a single screw, but the contact had been faint and distant, and quickly lost. The sonobuoy-dropping aircraft had not returned.

It was time now for a final fix on the target . . . and then the kill.

Chusa Yoshio Katatura stood in *Sharuq*'s attack center next to the torpedo status board, a place, he judged, where he would be out of the way. Hours before, the submarine had been rigged for red in order to save the officers' night vision in case they needed to use the periscope. Officers and men stood or sat side by side in that crowded compartment, going about their duties with a silent efficiency that barely concealed their excitement.

Closing his eyes, Katatura imagined he could sense all of the 130 men of the submarine's crew sealed away within the long, steel cylinder of *Sharuq*'s pressure hull, men keyed to fever pitch by the certain knowledge that this was not an exercise. They'd been on alert for almost four hours, ever since the last American subhunter had overflown them. He could smell their excitement, and their fear, sharp odors blending with the sour-mingled stenches of paint, urine, cooked meat, and too many people crowded into too small a space.

Opening his eyes again, he was assaulted by the flicker of lights and display monitors cramming the attack center's bulkheads, the displays bright in the blood-lit compartment. *Sharuq*'s combat crew waited at their stations, hands poised at their consoles, the expressions on their faces ranging from fanatic excitement to confusion, from near worship of their Captain to outright fear.

All of them looked out of place, confined here in this high-tech cylinder. Many were little more than children, many of them, fresh-faced youngsters who should have been in school instead of prowling the depths of a sea so far from their homes and families. The rest were rough, bearded men who looked like they would have been more at home on camelback than aboard a modern nuclear submarine, despite their swaggering bravado and blue naval berets and the UIR naval insignia on their khaki uniforms.

Yaban-jin, Katatura thought. *Barbarians, all of them . . .*

Sharuq, too, was out of place. Her career . . . no, *his* career, Katatura corrected himself—unlike the West, Russians thought of their ships as male—his career had begun twenty years before, at Severodvinsk on the White Sea, where the huge submarine had joined the Soviet Union's Red Banner Northern Fleet as the *Komsomolets Ukrainyy,* an SSGN, known to the West only by the NATO code name Oscar. Larger than all but the big ballistic-missile submarines, *Komsomolets Ukrainyy* and his brother Oscars were weapons designed to counter America's supercarrier battle-groups in a war that ultimately had never come.

Instead came the events of 1991, and suddenly there was no longer a Ukrainian Young Communists' League . . . or a Soviet Union, for that matter. For a time, there'd been rumors that the *Ukrainyy* might be scrapped, but then, in the late nineties, he had been one of four Oscar SSGNs purchased by Japan; five years later, as the rekindled firestorm of Islamic fundamentalism swept across the Arab world, toppling and burning and remolding governments, he'd been refitted and sold again, this time to the fleet of the newly born United Islamic Republic.

And *Chusa* Katatura—his rank was equivalent to that of a full commander in the Western navies—was part of the sale, his services sold to the UIR as a military advisor, someone who could explain to the Arabs the complexities of their new toys . . . and the best way to use them. At last, after twenty years, the *Ukrainyy*—now the *Sharuq*—was being used as his designers in far-off Severodvinsk had planned, to stalk and kill, not aircraft carriers, but the larger and even more vulnerable supertankers upon which the United States depended for its very economic life.

"Sooner or later we will face the Americans again across the broad arena of the Pacific," Admiral Tetsuya Hagiwara had told him, just hours before Katatura had departed Tokyo for Cairo, then Havana. "Perhaps the enthusiasm of our Islamic friends will prepare the way for that day, *neh?* We cannot hope to challenge the Americans directly in a conventional war, not yet . . . and they would never dare challenge us with nuclear weapons. But after they have fought the marshaled forces of a united Islam . . ."

Perhaps. And perhaps the war, the *final* war that everyone had expected for so many years, and that in the end had never materialized, was about to begin after all. The sinking of the *American Castle* might well have been the first shot fired in that war.

His clients seemed singularly eager to continue this bloodletting. Could they truly be ignorant of the firestorm they were igniting in the world beyond their vessel's pressure hull? Or did they simply not care?

That thought carried with it a small stab of shame, carefully concealed. His own government had made this moment possible, Katatura realized; worse, they'd made it inevitable by selling advanced weapons systems to Cairo. Tokyo, too, was playing with fire and had been ever since they'd adopted the new constitution eight years earlier.

Proponents of the new Japanese policy were always quick to point out that Tokyo was simply introducing order into a system that would have proceeded in any case, chaotic and unchecked. The mountain of weapons—conventional and nuclear submarines, aircraft, missiles, vehicles—available on the international arms markets since the collapse of the Soviet Union was bound to reach the Third World anyway, one way or another. By supporting Great Islam, by becoming the arms brokers for the UIR, Japan was only helping guarantee the stability of an increasingly fragmented and self-destructive world.

Katatura did not agree, though propriety and duty had kept him from speaking out. He was beginning to realize, however, that he was as out of place here as desert barbarians aboard a submarine . . . or a high-tech Russian vessel sailing under Islamic colors.

He wondered again if he could fulfill his mission here with these people. For two years he had lived in the United States, completing graduate work at UCLA. Later, after he'd served as executive officer aboard Japan's first nuclear submarine, he'd returned for two years more, assigned to the staff of the Japanese naval attaché in Washington. He knew the Americans, spoke their language far better than he did this crude and barbaric Arabic, and for the most part, at least, he did not—*could* not—share in the fashionable wave of anti-American sentiments now sweeping his home country.

Gimu alone kept him going. Duty …

Captain al-Badr, too, was thinking of duty as he brushed past the Japanese military advisor and stepped onto the low platform surrounding the periscope well. His orders were at once explicit and vague: *Sharuq* was to sink as many American oil tankers in the Caribbean as possible and to record the American military response, but at all costs he was to preserve his new command intact and undamaged, even if that meant fleeing to the safe haven of Cienfuegos.

He was also to show to his Japanese "guest" how easily the Yankees could be embarrassed and how efficiently *Sharuq* could be handled and fought. Al-Badr realized that Cairo was interested in impressing their Japanese patrons, but he suspected that playing such cozy politics with infidels was a mistake.

That, however, was not his decision to make. It was time for another demonstration, and to that end he had brought *Sharuq* back to periscope depth. He touched an intercom switch. "Sonar, Captain. Do you have any contacts?"

"Negative, Captain," the sonar operator's voice came back. "All clear."

"Up periscope."

Al-Badr caught the handles of the scope as they rose from the deck, pressing his face against the padded ocular and riding the tube as it slid into the extended position. Far above his head, the one-eyed tube broke the surface with a phosphorescent wake that flashed pale white in the darkness. The eyepiece presented al-Badr with a ghostly, green-limned view of waves moving beneath a black sky; he had engaged a thermal imager that would make the heat plume of a ship or aircraft stand out like a beacon. Swiftly, he walked the scope in a full circle, checking the entire horizon, then flipped the upper mirror into the sky-watch position and walked it around once more. No ships . . . no aircraft. *Sharuq* was alone in the wide, dark ocean.

"All clear," he said, confirming the sonar operator's report. "Raise satellite antenna and ESM."

Aft of the periscope, two more masts slid vertically from the Oscar's sail. One of them, called "Rim Hat" by the West, sniffed the air for electronic traces of their quarry or of nearby hunters. The other, slender, sharp-tipped like a conical spear point, was code-named "Pert Spring." In seconds, it had locked onto the transmissions of a reconnaissance satellite passing far overhead.

"*Me*-One-four-nine acquired," the Communications Officer announced, naming one of the current flock of Japanese spy sats. "Target select . . . scanning . . . We have the target."

"Down scope." Al-Badr stepped off the low stage in the center of the compartment and joined the Communications Officer and his Executive Officer, who were leaning over a large television monitor at the satcom console.

"Well, Ali?" He nodded toward the screen, which displayed a black-and-white image. The contrast had been lowered, but the picture was still brilliant in the red light. "What have we found this time?"

Commander Ali Ibrahim, *Sharuq*'s Executive Officer, had pulled out a heavy, green-covered book filled with page after page of photographs and statistics. Carefully, he leafed through the book, pausing occasionally to study again the ship visible on the display.

The freeze-frame image had been captured in radar waves rather than light, so incidentals such as lettering on the hull or a flag flying at the truck were invisible, but details of hull, deck, and superstructure stood out with astonishing clarity, viewed from overhead as though photographed by a passing aircraft. The fact that it was night with a heavily overcast sky meant nothing. Even the wave patterns were perfectly recorded in sharp focus, and the supertanker's wake through heavy seas stood out like a dazzlingly white arrowhead laid across the dark, metallic ripples of the water.

The image changed, replacing itself from top to bottom with another view of the same ship, one recorded seconds later. Unable to process the satellite data in real time, *Sharuq*'s computer displayed a new scene every few seconds, updating the view from space in slow-motion, frame-by-frame segments.

"*Amatex Rainbow*," Ibrahim said after a moment, looking up from the book with one finger marking his place. "Oil tanker, Liberian registry."

"Liberian!" Al-Badr snorted. "A flag of convenience. She is American!"

"Yes, sir. The cargo owner is listed as Amatex Petroleum, Houston. Length one hundred ninety meters, capacity twenty-eight thousand tonnes." Ibrahim snapped the book shut and looked up with a crooked grin. "Not so fat a target as the last one, Captain."

Al-Badr smiled. "Fat enough, Ali. Fat enough for us to present the Americans with a second funeral pyre as a gift. Weapons Officer!"

"Sir!"

"Ready Falcons three and four. Our birds have acquired a taste for South American oil!" Turning, surveying the red-lit attack center, he saw again the Japanese advisor, watching him with black and expressionless eyes. "Unless you have something to add, Advisor?"

"You have handled your ship exceptionally, Captain," the Japanese officer said in that curiously backhanded fashion of his. "I might suggest only that you lower your other masts. Now that you have your target fix, you no longer require the satellite feed."

Al-Badr considered this. He'd lowered the attack periscope but had left the ESM and satcom masts above water. A nearby enemy warship or aircraft could easily pick them up.

There'd been nothing on the ESM, however. "We will leave them up," he decided. "We will record the destruction of the American tanker."

The Japanese merely nodded, the slightest of bows, and al-Badr turned away with a scowl. It bothered him that he could never be sure what the advisor was thinking.

He must be writing a report on me and on the crew, he thought to himself. Such a report could determine whether *Islam'azim,* Great Islam, received any more advanced weapons systems from Tokyo, and it would certainly determine whether or not al-Badr got to keep his new command. *What is in the infidel's heart?*

"Range to target," al-Badr snapped.

"Two hundred eighty-five kilometers," the Weapons Officer replied. His long fingers flicked across switches set in long rows on the bulkhead missile firing panel, *snap-snap-snap,* each touch calling an amber light to life. "Inertial navigation set. Self-arming initialized. The missiles are on internal power. All readouts show green."

Al-Badr listened to the litany of prelaunch status reports, and all thoughts of the unwanted naval advisor and his reports faded away. "Flood missile tubes three and four."

Snap-snap. "Tubes flooded, Captain."

"Open outer hatch."

Snap. "Outer hatch number two open. We are ready to fire."

"Allah akbar!" Al-Badr's face gleamed with savage joy. "Fire three!"

The Weapons Officer's hand came down on the

third of a series of buttons mounted on the missile firing panel. Al-Badr heard the deep-throated *whoosh* of compressed air flinging the missile clear of the submarine, like muted thunder beyond the control room's starboard bulkhead. The deck canted slightly to port, then righted again as water was automatically pumped from port to starboard ballast tanks, compensating for the sudden loss of trim.

"Three fired, Captain."

He waited, counting the seconds. Loosing the second bird too soon after the first could have unfortunate consequences. "Fire four!"

The thunder repeated itself, and the attack center crew exploded in a roar of *"Allah akbar!"*

God is great!

From across the compartment, the Japanese naval advisor watched the cheering and the clenched, thrusting fists with a disquieting aloofness.

The SS-N-19 Falcons
Tuesday, March 28, 2141 hours

The first missile streaked toward the surface on expanding clouds of compressed air, nestled within a buoyant capsule that was jettisoned as it broached. Two solid-fuel rocket boosters nestled beneath the swept-back wings fired, and the Falcon emerged from the waves in an explosion of spray and fire-lit smoke. Wings unfolded, biting the night air. The flame from the engine flared like burning magnesium, illuminating sea and smoke and sky.

Seconds later, the boosters burned out and dropped away and the Falcon's turbojet sustainer kicked in.

Guidance systems engaged, steering the ship-killer in the general direction of the target, still invisible far over the western horizon.

Behind it, the second missile emerged from the black water in a flare of dazzling light.

CHAPTER
5

U.S. Navy SH-60F Oceanhawk
March 28, 2141 hours

"My God!" Lieutenant Lawrence Willis shouted, pointing out the starboard side of the helicopter's cockpit window. "Did you see it?"

"What? What?" Lieutenant Commander Francis R. Barnett, called Barney by his friends, had not seen anything, but it was clear that his pilot had. "What've you got?"

"I don't know . . . a flash, like. Two of them, one right after the other."

"Lightning—"

"I don't think so, Lieutenant. Looked like a goddamn missile. It's gone now. . . ."

Barnett checked his instruments, eerily green-lit in the darkened cockpit. Willis, occupying the helicopter's right-hand seat, was pilot and aircraft commander. Barnett, in the left-hand seat, was ATO—the Airborne Tactical Officer. That made him the mission's tactical commander as well as backup pilot and gave him the responsibility of monitoring the helo's ESM, or Electronic Surveillance Measures, and radar. A third man, STG 2nd class Milhouse, was manning the sonar gear aft.

There was nothing on radar, though there was enough chop in the sea that he didn't necessarily trust that. A target flying close to the waves could be lost in the sea scatter.

"Take us up higher," he told Willis. It occurred to him that the helo's low altitude must have masked them from the sub. Otherwise, they wouldn't have risked a launch. "Let's get the big picture."

The Oceanhawk's powerful Rolls-Royce/Turboméca engine thundered to a higher pitch, and the ASW helo climbed rapidly into the night. It had been traveling low and slow, pausing occasionally to take samplings of the sea with its AQS-13F dipping sonar, but now it needed altitude to extend its radar horizon.

A blip appeared on Barnett's radar screen, small and fast moving. As he stared at it, double checking its speed, it split into two.

"Damn!" He switched his helmet mike to the tactical frequency. "Snakepit, Snakepit, this is Cobra One."

"Cobra One, Snakepit. We copy."

"Snakepit, we have two bogies, repeat, two bogies at three-two-five, relative bearing two-seven-three, range two-five miles, speed one-four-three-oh knots. Looks like someone just popped a coupla cruise missiles."

His first thought had been that the missiles were heading for the *Samuel B. Roberts*, the Perry-class frigate the Oceanhawk was operating from, but the course was all wrong for that. The *Roberts* was twenty miles to the southeast, while those birds were headed west, and in one hell of a hurry to get there.

As he fed the tracking data back to the *Roberts,* he wondered who was shooting . . . and just what their target was.

UIR Oscar-class SSGN *Sharuq*
March 28, 2141 hours

Chusa Katatura watched the exultation around him, the frenzied shouting, the clenched fists jerking in the air, and imagined that the red-lit scene was the very image of the Christians' Hell.

He disapproved strongly of the display. It put him in mind of scenes he'd watched on CNN during the Islamic revolts, of crowds of filthy, bearded men shouting and chanting as they mindlessly fired their automatic weapons into the air. Dozens of casualties were reported after each of those wild victory celebrations, the victims of stray rounds falling from the sky; the half-savage warriors never seemed to learn that their celebrations killed people . . . or care.

The crew's celebration now could kill them all. Sound traveled marvelously well under water, and the Americans were as good or better than the Japanese in the sensitivity of their passive sonar equipment. If an American warship happened to be close by . . .

"Uskut!" the *Sharuq*'s Executive Officer barked. "Silence! Silence in the boat!"

At last! Katatura made a mental note; the command had been too long in coming—and it should not have been necessary in the first place.

Slowly, far too slowly, order returned aboard the submarine. Chests heaving, eyes bright with emotion, the officers and crewmen in the attack center watched their Captain with excited anticipation. Katatura glanced at his watch, noting that it would be another five minutes and some seconds before the Falcons reached their target.

The conventional warheads of the SS-N-19s each carried one ton of high explosive, but they could just as easily pack 100 kilotons of nuclear devastation, five times the destructive power that had once been unleashed on Katatura's home city of Nagasaki. There had been a great deal of discussion back in Tokyo, Katatura knew, over whether or not to supply the UIR with nuclear warheads, as they had repeatedly requested. So far, the decision had been made to neither help nor hinder the Third World's global race for nuclear weaponry; the UIR almost certainly had mastered the design of fission weapons already, and they were rumored to be working now on the next logical step—the hydrogen bomb.

Katatura tried to imagine thermonuclear warheads in the hands of these savages, and shuddered.

"Conn, Radar," a voice called over the intercom.

Al-Badr picked up a microphone. "This is the Captain. What do you have?"

"ESM has detected radar emissions, bearing one-eight-zero." The voice sounded as though the speaker was out of breath, his excitement raw and hard. "Contact identified as probable APS-124."

"An American helicopter, Captain," Katatura said. "The APS-124 radar means it is either an SH-60B Seahawk or an SH-60F Oceanhawk."

Al-Badr's eyes bored into Katatura's from across the attack center, harsh and angry. As though blaming him for this unexpected turn. "Have they picked us out yet?"

"I would say yes," the sonar officer replied. "The signal strength is strong."

"Lower the satellite and ESM masts," the Captain ordered. "Diving Officer, take us down. Make depth eighty meters."

"*Ya sidi!* Eighty meters!"

Most likely, it was just plain bad luck that an ASW helicopter had been close by when the Oscar had launched its missiles. If they'd been listening with their sonar at the time, they might well have heard the cheering of *Sharuq*'s crew. Unfortunately, the passive ESM trace could not tell them the helicopter's range. It might be fifty kilometers away . . . or hovering directly overhead.

No, if it was that close, *Sharuq* would already be dead. Katatura had tremendous respect for the Americans. In the past decade of revolutions, depression, and splintered nationalism throughout a disintegrating world, they'd lost much of the superpower status they'd enjoyed for half a century after World War II, but their technological and military prowess was still formidable.

The deck tilted sharply beneath Katatura's feet as *Sharuq* plunged into darkness.

U.S. Navy SH-60F Oceanhawk
March 28, 2144 hours

"Okay, he's heard us and pulled the plug," Barnett said. "But we nailed a solid track on him. Silly bastard."

The sub skipper, whoever he was, should have pulled all his periscope masts down as soon as he'd launched, but for some reason he'd left them up, probably because he was tied into a recon satellite feed and wanted to watch the show. It suggested that he was inexperienced . . . or careless. Either way, he'd just given away the store.

The Oceanhawk raced north at its maximum speed of 126 knots.

"Cobra One, Cobra One," crackled in his helmet headset. "This is Snakepit. Your submarine contact designated Alfa One. Be advised we are launching Cobra Two to assist. Over."

"Copy, Snakepit. Do we have weapons free, over?"

"Stand by, Cobra One. National Command Authority is assessing, over."

Barnett pursed his lips. The "National Command Authority" meant the President or the Secretary of Defense. God, this was higher stakes than he'd thought.

"Roger, Snakepit. Cobra One, standing by."

UIR Oscar-class SSGN *Sharuq*
March 28, 2145 hours

"Leveling off, Captain. Eighty meters."

"Helm, come left thirty degrees. Engineering, make revolutions for twenty-five knots."

"*Ya sidi!* Coming left thirty to two-four-zero."

"Speed twenty-five knots."

Katatura listened to the litany of orders and ritual response as the hull creaked and groaned under the intense pressure outside. Pain bit at his palms, and he realized his fists were tight-clenched, the nails pressing into the flesh. He forced himself to relax. Nearby, the Exec hissed something in Arabic which Katatura didn't quite catch, but he picked up the word "Guantanamo."

"Advisor!" al-Badr rasped. "Is that possible? Is this aircraft out of Guantanamo?"

"We are too far from their base at Guantanamo Bay, Captain," Katatura replied quietly. The SH-60s had a patrol radius of less than two hundred kilometers, and the U.S. naval base was four times that distance to the east. "It must be an ASW helicopter from one of their ships."

"What kind of ship?"

"Most likely would be one of their Perry-class guided-missile frigates. They carry SH-60s for antisubmarine patrol."

It was possible that the Americans were escorting their oil tankers now. It was also possible that they had a task force in the area, one actively searching for the *Sharuq*. Which? Katatura wondered. It was important that he know, if he was to effectively shape al-Badr's strategy.

"A frigate!" Al-Badr fixed Katatura with diamond-hard, unfriendly eyes. "How could your expensive radar satellites miss such a threat?"

"Perhaps it would have been better had you directed it first to scan the entire area, Captain." Katatura's voice was cold and level. He disliked this kind of confrontation, but he sometimes despaired of teaching these people anything. "It is unfortunate, but our reconnaissance satellites provide data only on those areas for which you request it."

"And we cannot waste time examining every potential target within a thousand kilometers. Never mind. We should have expected an American response sooner or later. Helm! Bring us left fifty-five degrees to one-eight-five. Increase revolutions to thirty-five knots."

One-eight-five. Almost directly toward the contact. What did al-Badr have in mind? Katatura wanted to ask, but it was important that he maintain his distance, especially when the Captain was being deliberately rude and confrontational. To be drawn into the argument would be a kind of surrender.

Most important, his duty required him not to challenge the Captain's authority in front of his crew. Katatura could advise and suggest, but to openly question a Captain's orders, especially during combat, would be deadly.

Minutes passed. Al-Badr gave the order to cut *Sharuq*'s speed to three knots, barely enough to maintain way. In silence, then, they crept forward, straining to hear the unseen opponent at the same time the opponent must be trying to listen to them.

"Captain!" the Weapons Officer said quietly. "Our first Falcon should be at the target in five . . . four . . . three . . . two . . . one . . . mark."

It was eerie, listening to the silence that followed. The countdown was not necessarily accurate, of course, since it represented the straight-line flight time to the target and did not take into account the possibility that the missile had had to circle while its radar acquired the target. Still, the initial target fix had been accurate enough that both missiles had probably flown straight in. One hundred seventy miles to the west, the skies must be ablaze.

Here, though, there was only silence and tense anticipation. Katatura had almost expected the crew to break into another round of unrestrained cheering and was glad to see that they had discipline enough not to. The Yankee might be listening for them at that very moment, with sonobuoys or dipping sonar.

"The second missile should have struck."

"Very well," al-Badr said with a grim smile. "We shall hear the full story over Radio Havana in the morning. Diving Officer! Take us to periscope depth!"

"*Ya sidi!* Periscope depth. Planes, ten degrees up bubble."

"Engineering, increase revolutions to fifteen knots. Weapons Officer. Prepare Sea Snake."

Katatura's eyes widened at that. Sea Snake! Was al-Badr actually contemplating an attack on the American helicopter? He wanted to say something, to suggest that *Sharuq* take refuge instead in the depths. Al-Badr's hard eyes stopped him, however, before he could open his mouth.

Macho pigheadedness. The English phrase came unbidden to Katatura's mind. Al-Badr was acting as though Katatura had somehow challenged his manhood.

Ping!

The chirp of the sonar rang loud and clear in the attack center, the sender obviously close by. "Conn, sonar! AQS-13F contact, very close, bearing two-five-three."

The AQS-13F was a dipping sonar, one lowered from a hovering helicopter into the sea above the suspected location of the target submarine. It confirmed for Katatura that the unseen hunter was an SH-60F Oceanhawk. The older Seahawks did not carry dipping sonars.

Ping!

"Periscope depth, Captain."

"Raise ESM and radar array. Stand ready with Sea Snake!"

"Breaking surface, Captain."

"Up periscope!"

The sonar pulses were coming more quickly now. *Ping! Ping!*

U.S. Navy SH-60F Oceanhawk
March 28, 2153 hours

"Contact!" the enlisted sonar tech called over the Oceanhawk's intercom. "Bearing zero-seven-three, range five thousand yards!"

"Hot damn!" Barnett told Willis. "We dropped almost right on top of 'em!" He opened the intercom. "Okay, Milhouse. Reel it in!"

"Think Washington's made up their mind yet?" Willis asked.

"We'll damn well find out." He opened the tactical channel. "Snakepit! Snakepit! This is Cobra One. We have submarine contact. Request weapons free, over."

"Cobra One, Snakepit. Copy. Wait one." Static crackled. "Cobra One, Snakepit. Standard ROEs are in force."

"Copy, that's standard ROEs." Barnett exchanged wry glances with Willis. The standard rules of engagement allowed them to fire if they were fired upon. "Listen," he told the pilot, who as aircraft commander also rode the helo's weapons triggers. "If that guy even thinks about launching, you take him down."

"You got that right, sir."

"Hey, Skipper?" Milhouse called. "Fishin' line's coming up. Listen, I was getting some funny noises on the contact when I shut down. Might be surfacing noises."

"Thanks, kid." Willis was already taking the helicopter higher. Stars gleamed through rents in the overcast. "Snakepit, Snakepit. This is Cobra One—"

UIR Oscar-class SSGN *Sharuq*
March 28, 2155 hours

Sharuq's radar and ESM masts dragged up out of the water, clawing a long, furrowed wake. At a range of more than two miles, they were invisible from the Oceanhawk, but masts and wake together made a splendid radar target.

"Captain! Radar! Strong ESM contact at two-five-three! Helicopter search radar!"

The periscope was still sliding up from its well. Al-Badr rode the gleaming cylinder, already swinging to face the proper bearing. The scope's thermal optics picked up the enemy helicopter the instant they broke the surface; against a jet-black sky, the Oceanhawk's fish shape glowed green, with brilliant flares of white light marking engine exhausts and rotor heads.

Twenty years before, the British had experimented with a submarine-launched antiair missile, or SLAM, then dropped the idea. Submariners had not liked the system, not when their best defense against air attack had always been a deep and silent dive. There'd been rumors, though, that the Soviets had installed a similar system on their diesel-driven SSKs.

But the Japanese had improved on both the SLAM and the Soviet air defense systems with Sea Snake, a cluster of six-foot tubes bundled to *Sharuq*'s snorkel. At the Weapons Officer's command, *Sharuq*'s snorkel rumbled in its sail housing, spearing up through the dark water and emerging above the surface.

With great deliberation, al-Badr closed his finger on a red button on the periscope grip, triggering a laser directed through the periscope optics. A brilliant point of light appeared on the target, visible only through the thermal optics and to the Sea Snake's guidance systems.

"Target acquired," al-Badr announced. "Fire!"

One of the tubes abaft *Sharuq*'s snorkel popped open in a burst of smoke, and a sender lance rocketed into the night, trailing white flame. Al-Badr stayed hunched against his periscope eyepiece, keeping a pinpoint of laser light steady on the approaching helicopter.

"Missile has locked on," the Weapons Officer announced from his console. "Missile is homing. . . ."

U.S. Navy SH-60F Oceanhawk
March 28, 2155 hours

"SAM! SAM!" Barnett cried. He could see the surface-to-air missile's white-hot exhaust. "Snakepit, we have been fired on—"

"Torpedo away!" Willis called. The Oceanhawk lurched skyward as the 800-pound Mk 50 torpedo dropped from the starboard weapons pylon. A parachute streamed behind it, steadying it, keeping it from going into a tumble and guaranteeing that its nose would hit the water at the proper angle. Willis recovered smoothly from the load displacement pitch, dropped the helo's nose, and accelerated. Speed, as naval aviators said, was life.

The torpedo struck the water with a splash, its sonar homer going active almost at once.

The Mk 50 lightweight torpedo was a relatively new replacement for the older Mk 46 air-dropped ASW torpedo. Like the SFV-4B, it was nicknamed the Barracuda, a minor bit of terminology confusion that was not entirely coincidental. Like the revolutionary fighter sub, the Mk 50 had been the first of a new breed, driven not by a propeller, but by a high-speed seawater pump jet. The design made it faster and deeper diving than conventional torpedoes, as well as making it extremely quiet. Its AYK-14 onboard computer allowed it to compute minimum-energy interceptions and gave it the capability to make multiple attacks. In other words, if the Mk 50 missed on the first pass, it would swing around and try again.

In the sky, meanwhile, Willis spotted a brilliant star dipping and weaving as it erratically followed the Oceanhawk's course. Assuming that the SAM was heat-guided, he turned the helicopter hard toward the oncoming missile, a maneuver that would both let him maneuver inside its turning radius and effectively hide the aircraft's hottest engine parts.

Laser-guided, the missile slammed into the Oceanhawk's canopy directly between Willis's and Barnett's seats, penetrating the aft flight deck bulkhead before exploding. Flame erupted from the side window panels, and then the fuel tanks detonated in a pair of savage, secondary explosions. Burning furiously, the wreckage arced toward the sea.

*　　*　　*

UIR Oscar-class SSGN *Sharuq*
March 28, 2155 hours

"Got him!" al-Badr sang. In the night sky above the sea, flame and shattered wreckage spilled from the darkness. *Sharuq*'s sonarmen heard the debris hit the water with a roar a mile to the west.

"Captain, Sonar! There is something. . . ."

"What is it?"

"Sir, I can't tell. Something in the water, not wreckage. It is coming toward us."

Katatura broke the spell that had held him, unmoving, beside the torpedo fire-control panel and strode aft toward *Sharuq*'s sonar room. It was a narrow compartment aft of the attack center, made crowded by three seats, with a fourth man, the Sonar Officer, standing behind three enlisted men, all wearing bulky headsets. A deadly suspicion possessed him. . . .

Sonar displays on the bulkhead gave visual read-outs of what the technicians were listening to, projecting narrow, vertical tracks that looked like waterfalls arrayed side by side on glowing, green-tinted screens. Each track registered a different sound frequency, drawn from the background noise, enhanced, and graphically displayed by *Sharuq*'s sonar computer. Two showed the characteristic trail of V stacked upon V of a contact, one at the frequency of a high-speed pump, the other registering the hiss of something moving at high speed through the water.

"Captain!" he snapped, using the intercom but calling loud enough to be easily heard out in the attack center. "This is Katatura! Contact is high-speed torpedo, bearing one-seven-three, range two thousand meters—"

"Dive! Dive!" al-Badr yelled. "Helm, come hard left.

Countermeasures! Stand by *hadaf qati,* starboard side!"

The problem with the American Mark 50, Katatura thought, was that it didn't *sound* like a torpedo. It lacked the whine of propellers, and relatively untrained sonarmen could be confused the first time they heard it.

Fortunately, Katatura's submarine training had included extensive courses on American ASW technology. He'd spent long hours listening to the sounds of an approaching Mk 50 and watching the cascade of Vs they generated on a sonar screen. How long did they have? Mark 50s traveled at forty-five knots . . . make it a minute and a half to cover two kilometers.

Sharuq's deck canted ominously to port, and Katatura had to put out a hand to brace himself. The huge sub was describing a tight turn toward the approaching torpedo, and diving at the same time. The seconds dragged past. The Oscar was cumbersome in close combat, slow to answer the helm, slow to build up speed. The Mark 50 had a range of at least twelve kilometers, so outrunning the thing was not an option.

"Range!" al-Badr demanded.

"Twelve hundred meters!" Eight times *Sharuq*'s length.

"Now!" al-Badr yelled. "Fire countermeasure! Cut engines!"

With a pneumatic hiss-*thunk* of air, a blunt-ended canister ejected from *Sharuq*'s hull and sped into the watery night, broadcasting the sound—very loud—of an Oscar-class submarine. At the same time, *Sharuq* went quiet; though her reactor coolant pumps continued to throb, the diminutive brain of the approaching Mk 50 was suddenly presented with a choice between a quiet target and a loud one.

Unerringly, it chose the loud target, canting its rudder to bring it to port.

Hadaf qati was Arabic, roughly, for "deadly target," and it was the product of a joint Japanese-Islamic research program carried out for the past three years. The problem with normal countermeasures was that once a torpedo had been distracted by them, it tended to hunt around until it reacquired its target.

Hadaf qati was something new. Possessing active sonar of its own, it tracked the approaching torpedo. Just before the Barracuda reached it, the cylinder exploded.

It was a tiny explosion—not much high explosive could be packed into the miniature torpedo's small warhead—but it was enough to create a pressure wave racing out from the blast. An instant later, the nose of the Mk 50 impacted that moving wall of water, a very *hard* wall that detonated the torpedo's warhead.

Aboard *Sharuq*, the sonarmen whipped off their headsets, and Katatura sympathized with them. He'd heard the ringing shock through the sub's double hull himself, and he'd not been wearing earphones. Even with electronic cutouts to safeguard their hearing, the sonarmen must have been jolted by those two closely spaced blasts of raw sound.

Turning, he saw Captain al-Badr standing in the doorway to the attack center.

"Perhaps," al-Badr said slowly, "we can learn to work together after all."

For the first time, Katatura allowed emotion to show on his face. He smiled. "Our survival demands that we do just that, Captain."

Al-Badr reached out and clapped him hard on the shoulder, a distinctly un-Japanese gesture that Katatura normally disliked.

This time, though, it felt strangely reassuring.

CHAPTER
6

Situation Room Support Facility
Washington, D.C.
Wednesday, March 29, 0953 hours

There are several presidential situation rooms. Best known is the one located one floor beneath the Oval Office, which consists of a single small and rather austere conference room with adjoining equipment areas and communications center. Contrary to the high-tech image portrayed in fiction, the conference room is so cramped that it doesn't even have the space for large-screen projection equipment.

It is so small, in fact, that in the 1980s President Reagan's staff ordered the construction of a supplementary complex in the Executive Office Building next door to the White House. This Crisis Management Center, later renamed the Situation Room Support Facility, occupies Room 208, a large room one floor up from the Vice-President's office with a vaulted ceiling and gilded, nineteenth-century decor. It is rich with history, the same room from which Secretary of State Cordell Hull unceremoniously evicted Ambassador Nomura and peace envoy Kurusu on a certain Sunday afternoon late in 1941.

The President was thinking of the room's more recent history as he entered it, his heels clicking on the gleaming parquet floor in unison with the steps of his Chief of Staff and two military aides. The Support Facility was generally reserved for the senior White House and departmental staffs, while the President continued to use the older, smaller Sit Room in the White House West Wing basement. The pace of modern technology, however, of global communications and satellite-relayed newscasts, of real-time reconnaissance satellite imagery and direct C^3 links with individual unit commanders in the field, had begun to make the original Sit Room superfluous. Even though it was a longer trip along the subterranean corridors between the White House basement and the Executive Office Building, the President found it more useful to attend the crisis management sessions in Room 208 than to wait for the same information to be further compressed, evaluated, and digested for a presidential briefing in the Sit Room.

Forty or more men and women were already seated around the huge, diamond-shaped table in the middle of the room, all coming noisily to their feet as he entered. The restored, nineteenth-century decor surrounding them was strictly superficial; ornate, wooden cabinet doors were open to reveal television monitors tuned to CNN and the major networks, and most of the east wall was taken up by an enormous display screen. Behind that wall were four rooms filled with projecting equipment, three powerful VAX computers, and communications links to the Pentagon and all of the national security agencies.

"Sit down, everybody, sit down," the President said, taking his place at the head of the table. He nodded to several of the faces around him, the Joint Chiefs and the Secretary of Defense. The DCI. The President's National Security Advisor. Many of the faces present were familiar but nameless, soldiers of the vast, bureaucratic army of staff members, aides, and assistants that linked the presidency with the rest of the government.

An agenda had been laid out at his place on the table, but he already knew what was on it. The Caribbean situation had held the number-one priority on the PDB for the past three days.

The President's Daily Brief, the fifteen-page memorandum with which he began each working day, had been heavily weighted for some time with news of developments in Africa and the Middle East; the United Islamic Republic—with technical assistance from Japan—was rapidly emerging as the new world superpower, one bent on filling the power vacuum left by the Soviet Union's demise fifteen years before.

Now, though, the emphasis had shifted to the Caribbean, and in particular to the slender threads of the shipping lanes connecting the South American coast with the United States. The destruction of the *American Castle* two days before could well have been the opening shot in an undeclared war by the UIR. The loss of a second tanker and an American helicopter early that morning seemed to confirm it.

"Very well, gentlemen," the President said. "Let's get started. Neil?"

Neil McIntyre was the President's National Security Advisor, a lean and wizened man with long, white hair and sideburns beneath a nearly bald scalp. He looked drawn this morning, as though he'd not gotten much sleep.

"Thank you, Mr. President," McIntyre said, rising. "To keep things short and sharp, that flash bulletin this morning has been confirmed. Just before dawn this morning, another tanker, the *Amatex Rainbow,* was sunk in the Yucatán Channel by cruise missiles fired from a submerged submarine. The launch was actually observed by one of our ASW helicopters. Unfortunately, when the helo moved in for a closer look, it was shot down by a surface-to-air missile, presumably launched from the same submarine. If we could see the graphics on this, please?"

The room darkened, and the large screen on the east wall illuminated, showing a map of the northern Caribbean, from the Yucatán to Haiti, from Cuba halfway to Venezuela and Colombia. Twin red circles glowed side by side southwest of Cuba's Peninsula de Guanahacabibes. Another showed the helicopter crash site fifty miles south of Cuba's Isla de la Juventud, and a green zigzag ticked off with time lines marked the movements of the *Samuel B. Roberts* through the region over the past ten hours.

McIntyre walked around the table, pulling a telescoping pointer from his jacket pocket and unfolding it as he talked.

"Our assumption is that at least one UIR cruise-missile submarine is operating in these waters," he continued, moving the pointer against the screen and indicating the general area around where the helicopter had gone down. "And that their orders are to interdict the sea-lanes between South America and our Gulf and Atlantic coasts. All such traffic now is constricted at two choke points . . . here in the Yucatán Channel west of Cuba, and over here, in the Windward Passage between Cuba and Haiti."

"How do we know it's the UIR?" the President asked. "What about Cuba?"

"I can answer that, Mr. President," a distinguished-looking man in an expensive gray suit said from the left side of the table. Richard G. Cabot was the current Director of Central Intelligence, head not only of the CIA, but of all America's intelligence agencies. His usual aristocratic Bostonian reserve was creased and rumpled this morning. He, too, had not been getting much sleep lately.

"The Cuban Navy possesses only three submarines," he said, "Kilos, conventional, diesel-powered SSKs purchased from Russia ten years ago as replacements for the much older Foxtrots transferred to Cuba by Moscow in the late seventies and early eighties. They are strictly attack subs, carrying torpedoes or mines. They don't carry cruise missiles . . . specifically they don't carry cruise missiles with a two-hundred-mile range, like the ones that sank the *Castle* and the *Rainbow*."

"We have some interesting photographs here, Mr. President," McIntyre added. He raised his voice slightly. "Let's see series one."

The map of the Caribbean was replaced by an enormous, black-and-white photo of a submarine cruising on the surface, taken from the air off the port bow. The detail was exquisite, so sharp that the President could make out the faces of several men standing on the weather bridge atop the long, low, characteristically Russian sail.

Before running for the White House, the President had been a Senator, serving two terms on the Senate Arms Committee. He knew the distinguishing marks of Russian submarines quite well. This one he recognized immediately as an Oscar, broad and flattened, with over three quarters the immense beam of a Typhoon, and eight tenths the length. The vessel's huge, flattened girth was apparent in the near bow-on photo; the upper deck was broad and flat and so wide that the sail seemed small and isolated. He could easily see the row of six rectangular hatches to either side of the sail, each hiding two SS-N-19 cruise missiles, and the ragged patchwork effect left by missing anechoic tiles.

"Taken last week outside Alexandria Harbor," McIntyre said. "We've identified her as either the *Sharuq* or the *Rih Sadid,* two of four Oscars purchased by the UIR two years ago from Japan. Both have been stationed at Alexandria since their transfer, apparently as part of a submarine training program. Ten days ago this one set sail without warning. We tracked her as far as Gibraltar, then lost her in the Atlantic.

"She's designed to operate against surface shipping . . . especially big surface vessels like our carriers. For that purpose, she carries twenty-four cruise missiles, with either nuclear or conventional warheads."

"Neil," the head of the Joint Chiefs, General Paul Drummond, interrupted. "Is there reason to believe she could be carrying nukes?"

"No, sir. We've still not been able to confirm that either the Russians or the Japanese have transferred nuclear weaponry to the Islamics. The conventional warhead on an SS-N-19 is bad enough, though. One ton of high explosives."

"So the Arabs have started sniping at our oil tankers," the President said slowly. He leaned back in his seat, letting his eyes close. He was beginning to think that he should have taken his wife's advice and

not run for a second term. The world was coming
apart around him, the disintegration getting worse
every day, and there wasn't a damn thing he could do
to stop it. "In God's name, why?"

"Yeah, just what do they expect to prove, anyway?"
Vincent Sarlucci, the Secretary of Defense, said from
his seat at the table. "They haven't declared war. They
haven't made a single damned move toward war. If
they're sinking tankers, it's piracy, pure and simple."

"Harassment, Mr. Secretary," Cabot replied. "And
economic leverage. When the UIR organized and cut
off our oil from the Persian Gulf, we were able to shift
the bulk of our pipeline network to South America . . .
barely. You remember that brouhaha, I'm sure."

There were nods and grunts of agreement from
around the table. The Panic of '02 had been worse,
far worse than the Arab embargo of '73.

"In any case," the DCI continued, "eighty percent
of our oil today comes from Mexico, Venezuela, and
Suriname. This one submarine is in a position to cut
our oil imports by half, maybe more. It doesn't even
have to *sink* the ships . . . just scare the owners and
the insurance companies into stopping the sailings.
That large a cutback could lead to another depression."

Oil. The problem hadn't gone away in the seventies,
not by seven million miles. There was only so much of
the stuff to go around and it was still absolutely vital
for a modern industrial nation, not just for gasoline
and heating oil, but for petrochemicals, medicines,
and especially plastics. The world's largest reserves
were still in the Middle East, but the UIR controlled
them all now, and the UIR was not exactly a friendly
government. "Murdering, blaspheming Satans reek-
ing with the blood of martyred innocents" was how

one Cairo newspaper had described Americans only the week before, and that had been an editorial by one of their moderate religious leaders.

His pledge to safeguard the environment, especially his promise to eliminate America's dependence on nuclear power, had helped get him elected, the first president of the twenty-first century. Perhaps, he thought wearily, that was a campaign pledge he should have broken.

"One submarine?" Admiral Christopher Shapley, Chief of Naval Operations, hammered the polished surface of the table with one fist. "One damned submarine is not going to hold America up for ransom. We've already got ships in the area. And we have the *Leviathan* battle group heading south now. We'll hunt the bastards down and ram their missiles down their throats."

Henry Strauss, the Secretary of State, gently cleared his throat. "With, ah, all due respect to my distinguished naval colleague, Mr. President, things will not be as easy as that. The Japanese, as always, pose an unfortunate threat, a threat that we cannot ignore the way we did in '02. The *Lincoln*, you know. We can't risk another military disaster like that."

"Neil?" the President asked. "Do you think the Japanese would get involved again?"

"Unlikely, Mr. President. They don't want to be perceived as the bad guys by the world press. They'd prefer to play this out behind the scenes. But I have to agree with Mr. Strauss. Just the possibility that they might uncork Sky Shield is going to force us to sit back and think this over. If they did decide to come in with the Islamics again, well, they could pick off our surface ships pretty much at their leisure."

The President considered this. Who would have imagined ten years before that the Japanese would succeed so spectacularly where the United States had failed? The Strategic Defense Initiative—Star Wars—was an American idea, but the Japanese had taken the idea and run with it after the U.S. decided that the notion would be too costly, orbiting a series of satellites capable of destroying ICBMs within seconds of launch. They'd managed it without any of the high-cost, high-tech lasers or particle beams that had slowed SDI research in the U.S., too, patterning their design after the Air Force's low-cost Brilliant Pebbles concept. Their Sky Shield satellites used magnetic railguns to launch two-kilo lengths of iron-sheathed depleted uranium—"crowbars" in popular military usage—along extremely precise paths and at extremely high speed. Only partially vaporized by the brief reentry, the dense projectile cores struck their targets with deadly accuracy at speeds exceeding 25,000 miles per hour. Ballistic missiles in flight vaporized under that kind of impact, and even underground silos and bunkers were not entirely safe. What was even worse from the American point of view, though, was the fact that Sky Shield was also effective against conventional weapons, even against vehicles as small as individual tanks or personnel carriers.

And during the Gulf crisis four years earlier, Tokyo had sided openly with the UIR when the United States threatened to intervene in the Gulf, launching a salvo of projectiles against the U.S.S. *Abraham Lincoln* as she approached the Straits of Hormuz.

Officially, that salvo was supposed to have been a warning, a pattern of four crowbars bracketing the *Lincoln* at a range of less than a mile. That, certainly, was the story presented to the public by Washington, and Tokyo had issued a formal apology within hours of the disaster, even offering to pay for the ship and recompense the families of the 4,000 sailors who'd died when the supercarrier exploded.

But the President and every man and woman in Room 208 knew that that final crowbar, hurtling out of space at seven miles a second and tearing through *Lincoln*'s crowded flight deck, had been dead on target. There was no way the Japanese could have permitted an *accident* of that magnitude, not with the whole world watching and her new alliance with oil-rich Cairo on the line. The sinking of the American carrier had been a warning, all right, a very sharply worded and direct one giving notice that now Japan held the military high ground of space.

"Surface ships," the President said, repeating his Security Advisor's words. "Okay, so surface ships are out. What about submarines? What about *Leviathan*?"

The CNO glanced at his wristwatch. "*Leviathan*'s battle group is off Miami now, Mr. President. She'll be in the area within another twelve hours. Say, twenty-two hundred hours."

"Yes, but can she find the bastard? The Orca concept is still untested."

Admiral Shapley shrugged. "She's got two nuclear attack subs with her, Mr. President. *New Haven* and *Charlotte*. Charlie Logan and Bruce Katkowski are two of the best sub drivers we've got. And Admiral Delacroix knows his stuff. They'll nail him."

"Are they all we've got?" the Defense Secretary wanted to know.

"I've passed the word to CINCLANT. They're scrambling every attack boat on the Atlantic. But the

Leviathan group'll definitely be on the scene first."

"One thing still bothers me, Mr. President," the DCI said.

"And that is?"

"This guy's sitting out here in the middle of our lake. The Caribbean. He's got to know that we're going to land on him with everything we've got. And that worries me."

The President allowed the slightest of smiles. "I thought we wanted to get the bastard."

"We do, sir. But Mama raised all her boys to be suspicious when the other fella says, 'Here I am! Come get me.'"

"You sound like you suspect a trap," Admiral Shapley said.

"Maybe not a trap, Admiral. I do wonder if that Oscar has friends in the area. Maybe a warm dock in Cuba."

"Cuba is definitely the wild card in this, Mr. President," McIntyre said. He cocked an eye at Cabot. "It might be a good idea to retask some of our spy sats to take a peek at our friends down there."

"We've been monitoring Cuba pretty closely," the DCI said. "But we can increase our surveillance, if you think that would be a good idea, Mr. President."

"Do it," the President said. "And keep me posted, Dick. I don't want any surprises down there. There's too damn much riding on this."

"Yes, sir."

"And Admiral?"

"Yes, Mr. President?"

"I *want* that Oscar. Dead, on a platter. He's killed two of our ships, one of our aircraft, and God knows how many people. I don't known whether he's trying to start a war or not, but by God, if he wants one, let's give it to him!"

"Aye, aye, Mr. President. *Leviathan* and her SSN group'll take him down."

"I hope so, Admiral. Because if they don't, we could find ourselves in the middle of the nastiest little war this side of World War II. And between you and me, I don't think this country is ready for it."

The President rose and left Room 208. Behind him, the NSC began their contingency planning.

Because, if there *was* a trap, if the Oscar had escorts or allies in Cuba, then *Leviathan* and the two attack subs with her might well find themselves out-matched.

CHAPTER
7

Gray stood in the narrow shower cubicle, naked except for his plastic thong sandals, turning to let the stream of water blast the soapsuds from his chest, face, and arms.

Fresh water for personal use was not a problem aboard *Leviathan*. His father had told him often enough about the sharply rationed water aboard older boats, about how submariners in World War II had been lucky if they even had one shower during a sixty-day patrol. For one thing, the stalls made excellent storage lockers for canned food and vegetables. The men literally had to eat the space empty before they could use it; once they did, there were still only two showers aboard, one for the officers, the other for eighty men, and the batteries and the galley always had first rights to fresh water.

Leviathan's distillation plant produced plenty of water every day, and the big submarine was roomy enough that even the head abaft the missile-deck MEJO quarters had its own stall. Gray luxuriated in the warm blast for a moment, then reached for his bottle of dandruff shampoo.

So far, life aboard a nuclear sub wasn't as bad as he'd been afraid. After one day, though, his body hadn't yet snapped into the shortened daily schedule. Six hours on followed by twelve off made for an easily managed duty schedule, but it was guaranteed to confuse a person's biological clock, especially when there was no way short of looking at his watch to tell whether it was night or day in the first place. Still, he'd stood watch and watch more than once in his naval career so far, and he knew it would only be a matter of a few days before his body caught up and adjusted to his schedule. He'd been up until almost 0500 the night before checking stores for the Barracudas and had finally racked out about 0540. He'd slept soundly in his narrow bunk until past noon, despite the steady, scuffling movement of men through the compartment and along the passageway outside.

Probably the worst part of the arrangement was the simple fact that, as CO of the new Barracuda squadron, there was no reason for him to fit into *Leviathan*'s watch schedule in the first place. There was plenty to do, of course, checking out the Barracudas' electronic systems, sensors, and computers; reviewing the records and training scores of each of his men and interviewing those men personally to get a feel for the squadron; working up training plans, maintenance schedules, and requisition forms. But the SFV-4 squadron rarely had to interact with *Leviathan*'s other officers and men.

The boat's crew remained a quiet, almost introspective group, as though the submariners' old nickname, the Silent Service, had taken on an added and very personal meaning for them. Gray knew from his training at New London that submariners were expected to be quiet, steady, easygoing, and unexcitable men. Those who weren't were weeded from the program long before they ever got near a submarine.

Still, the reserve shown by the officers and men he'd met so far aboard *Leviathan* seemed to have more to do with the fact that he was an outsider than anything else.

Eyes shut against the lather from the shampoo, he vigorously massaged his scalp beneath the flow of water.

It took a year for a new man to win his dolphins, the silver pin of a submariner. There was bound to be some distance from the crew until he and the other former aviators had demonstrated that they had the submariner's version of the right stuff.

He finished rinsing, then turned off the shower.

That was odd. The water wasn't draining from the stall. It sloshed about his ankles now, almost reaching to the bottom of the stall's frosted door. Stooping, a minor feat of contortion in the narrow cubicle, he used his fingers to clear the mesh cover above the drain. When he stood up, a large mass of dark brown hair adhered wetly to his hand.

Stepping out of the shower, he retrieved his towel and briskly dried off. Using a corner to wipe the steam from the room's mirror, he peered at his scalp. It took only a moment to confirm that the lost hair was definitely his. Gray normally wore his hair quite short on the back and sides, and longer on top. The hair on top of his scalp was thinner now, and as he teased at it with a plastic comb, more hair came away in the teeth.

"I'm not getting that old," he told himself, more curious than alarmed. Wrapping the towel around himself, he retrieved his soap and shampoo, then flip-flopped back to his quarters. After dressing, he combed his hair and retrieved another handful from the comb.

Seegar walked in a moment later. "Hey, Skipper?" He sounded worried.

"Yeah?"

"What do you know about radiation sickness?"

"You were stationed aboard a nuke carrier how long? What's the matter?"

"I dunno. Probably nothing." He reached up a hand and rubbed lightly at his scalp. "Just I've been losing a lot of hair since we came aboard this tub, and I've heard that happens if you get too many rads. Monk and Flasher are shedding, too, and so are some of the other guys in the squadron. What you think, sir? Is it something we should see the boat's Doc about?"

Gray smiled and shook his head. "Don't worry. I'll talk to the Doc. But I don't think it's anything to fret about."

Fifteen minutes later, Gray was in *Leviathan*'s mess hall, waiting for one of the boat's "galley slaves" to bring him his food. While there was a separate ward-room for officers forward of the galley, the main mess deck aft served anyone, officer or enlisted, at any time of the theoretical day or night. Traditionally, food had always been of supreme importance aboard a submarine, one of the few exciting points in a day of unvarying, gray-walled routine. On surface ships and ashore, men stood in lines to be served cafeteria style; aboard subs, however, with space, as ever, at a premium, mess hands brought the trays to the tables and took orders for coffee or drinks. Dinner today was a Navy-wide favorite, "sliders"—hamburgers—served with fries, corn, and canned pears.

About a dozen other men were in the mess hall at the moment. The big midday meal was already over, but the compartment performed double duty as rec hall and lounge for off-duty personnel. Four enlisted men were playing cards at a table in one corner, while two more played chess in another. Three men were seated at the table next to his, talking with Wilder, Dominico, and Monk Young. The aviators were eating, or trying to, while the others nursed coffee mugs or sodas.

Gray was mildly surprised . . . and pleased. He'd been wondering if his squadron was going to complete their entire first cruise aboard *Leviathan* as pariahs.

"Oh, it's grim, Ah tell ya," one lanky, sandy-haired man with a dolefully long face was saying. He shook his head sadly. "Most folks just don't realize what the pressure down here can do to a man. Why, the pressure on our hull goes up fourteen-point-seven pounds per square inch for every thirty-three feet we go down. See, sir, what that means, is at thirty-three feet your pressure's twenty-nine-point-eight psi-absolute. That's the weight of all that water plus the weight of the air above it, what you call your one atmosphere. At one hundred feet, your pressure's just a bit shy of sixty pounds per square inch, but that ain't shit. One hundred feet, why, that's practically right up on the roof.

"Now, *Leviathan* here's designed for cruising at a

depth of, oh, say a thousand feet. That's how deep we are right now, s'matter of fact. Down here, your pressure's squeezing against every square inch of your vessel with a pressure of over thirty-three tons per fuckin' square foot!"

Wilder licked his lips. He didn't seem particularly interested in his hamburger. "H-how deep can we go, anyway?"

"What you think?" the doleful-looking man asked one of the others. "Fifteen hundred?"

"'Bout that, Deep Six."

"Okay, fifteen hundred feet. That's supposed to be our safe operatin' depth."

"'Course, that's not really an absolute, y'know," one of the others chimed in. He was a solemn-looking man with red-blond hair and a bushy mustache. "'Specially in these Russian boats that, well, just between you and me, they're really shit, y'know? If y'got micro-cracks in the struts or a bad weld in the pressure hull, well …"

"That's right, Murph," the one called Deep Six said agreeably. "But, y'see, sir, the depth you got to be concerned about is usually set at one point seven times the safe operatin' depth. One-point-seven, that's the safety factor, see? So for *Leviathan,* that would be, lessee, about twenty-five hundred feet. Down there, it's hairy, man, let me tell you. Eighty-one tons plus on every goddamn square foot of hull. And, y'know what that's called, don't you?" As Dominico shook his head nervously Deep Six leaned forward dramatically, his fingers gripping the edge of the table. "Why, that's our *crush* depth!"

Wilder made a small, strangled noise in the back of his throat. Dominico laughed nervously. "I don't know about the depth outside, but I think it's getting kind of deep in here already, guys."

"God's truth, sir," Murph said, shaking his head. "Shit, do you know what happens to a guy what gets hit with that kind of pressure all at once? I saw one, once, that came up from just a thousand feet. A hard-suit diver, one of them new research jobs." He shook his head, lips pursed in sympathy. "Suit failure, y'know? A boot seal gave way, down where the pressure was almost a quarter ton on every square inch of that poor bastard's body. Christ, they had to scrape him out of his helmet with a sponge and a spatula! Everything was kind of . . . squished, y'know?"

"Hell," Deep Six said. "They shoulda saved the trouble 'n just buried him at sea in the helmet. Say the words an' drop it right over the side, kerplunk!"

"Tell me something," Gray said, raising his voice enough to be heard at the next table. "We learned all about pressure back in New London. But what about radiation? Is that a problem on these boats?"

Deep Six swiveled on his bench, a broad grin on his face. "'Scuse me, sir. Didn't see you come in. Yeah, Ah tell ya, radiation can be a real problem on these boats. 'Specially ex-Russian boats like this one."

"He's right," a man with remarkably large, sad brown eyes said. "You know, don't you, how many nuke subs the Russkis lost 'cause of fires or rad leaks or meltdown casualties?"

"Casualty," in submariner terminology, meant an accident or problem of some kind and had nothing to do with whether or not there were injuries. "Nope. Can't say that I do."

"Oh, hell, must be twenty, maybe twenty-five now," Deep Six said. "Russian boats, now, they got a bad,

bad safety record. Since World War II, the U.S. Navy has lost exactly two submarines in accidents, the *Thresher* and the *Scorpion*. But the *Russians . . .*"

"Bad construction," the sad-eyed man said. "Like Chernobyl. It's a fact!"

That struck a chord with Gray. He thought about his father, and the accident that had beached him.

"They always used to say that Russian nuke submariners could see in the dark," Murph put in. "That's because they *glowed* in the dark!"

"The thing about radiation, see," Deep Six continued, warming toward this new subject, "is it's so fuckin' sneaky. You can't see it, can't taste it, can't smell it. It could be in the air. In your food . . ."

Gray took a big bite of his hamburger. "Yeah?"

"That's right, sir. Sometimes the detectors don't catch the little leaks. Or, up where they have you aviators sleepin', could be some residue from when those missile tubes had MIRV warheads. You never know! Radiation sickness? Usually starts with your hair startin' to fall out. In clumps. Then the headaches, the puking. Your gums start to bleed, and you start loosin' your teeth. . . ."

"Hey, these guys're tryin' to eat their dinner," Murph said.

"I don't think I'm all that hungry," Dominico said.

"Oh, I tell you, rad sickness is a nasty way to go. It's the way they build these Russian boats. Like shit. Right, Dee-Dee?"

"Fuckin-A, Murph," the sad-eyed man said. "Hey, did you hear about the Mike they lost? When was that, Deep?"

"Must've been '89, thereabouts."

"Yeah. Anyway, that boat was a prototype, first of

her kind, and man, she was sweet. Fast. Deep diver. And qui-et. On her second cruise, she had a major casualty, an electrical fire in an after compartment. Now, there were these gaskets, see, that're normally made of copper. But the Russians, they'd yanked out all the copper gaskets and replaced 'em with plastic to save money."

"Probably sold the copper on the black market," Deep Six suggested.

"Could be." Dee-Dee took a swig of coffee. "Anyhow, when the fire hit it, the plastic melted right through. Let a blast of compressed air into that compartment fire and turned it into a blast furnace. The skipper managed to get her to the surface and got some of the crew off. Then . . ." He pantomimed a dive with his hand. "Down she went. They say her internal bulkheads started blowin' at two thousand feet."

"Yeah, how do you know all that if she sank?" Young demanded.

"Oh, there was a survivor," Dee-Dee said. "An eyewitness. Seems the CO and several men managed to get into an escape capsule. Only trouble was, the damned thing got hung up. Shitty Russian construction, right? They got dragged all the way to the bottom, forty-nine hundred feet straight down. When the Mike hit bottom, the capsule got jarred loose and pop! Up she came! One crewman lived to tell the tale. Toxic gas got the rest."

"That's the problem with these damned Russian boats," Deep Six said, looking about the mess hall as if carefully inspecting the bulkheads. "You just never know where some fuckin' *apparatchik* was tryin' to save a ruble or two . . . or maybe had a scam going so he could afford a dacha for his mistress."

"Goddamn it, Patterson, don't you have anything better to do?"

Gray turned and saw an officer standing behind him, a lean, balding man with glasses. His collar tabs showed he was a commander.

"Sure, Commander Parker," Deep Six said. "We was just, you know, shootin' the bull."

"Shoot it somewhere else. I want to have a chance to talk to these guys before you scare them to death."

"God, I think we were getting the royal treatment," Young said as the three sailors, Murph, Dee-Dee, and Deep Six, carried their cups forward to the galley, then left the mess hall. "I thought submariners were supposed to be stable characters!"

"They're good men," Parker said. He extended a hand. "I'm Bill Parker, the boat's Executive Officer."

"Glad to meet you," Gray said.

"Likewise. Don't let those clowns get to you, guys. They like to give newbies the business. Ron Murphy's a sonar tech second, a damned good one, too. St. Clair—"

"Who?"

"The one they call Dee-Dee. Stands for Death and Despair, by the way. A real character who likes to recite endless tales of submarine disasters. He's a first class torpedoman. Patterson's an electronics tech second, but he's been standing helm and planes watches lately. We try to rotate everybody around the boat, give 'em a feel for the whole operation."

"I hope you'll give us that chance."

"Could be. What's the matter, your high-tech pets forward not keeping you busy?"

"Busy enough," Gray admitted. "But I've been concerned about the Orca squadron mixing with the crew. We have our own work, sure, but things are too cramped down here for us to go our separate ways. There's going to be friction. Maybe trouble. I'd like to see my bunch and yours working together."

"You just stole the thunder from my welcome-aboard speech," Parker said. "Couldn't have put it better myself. Mostly, though, you guys're going to have to learn that we do things differently in the boats. On watch it's all formal, snap and polish—it *has* to be—with each order repeated back three or four times. Sounds like a bunch of kay-dets on parade, but the repetition is a guarantee against mistakes in an environment where *every* mistake is potentially deadly."

"I can understand that," Gray said. He'd heard the same sort of thing from his father. "Aboard a carrier, if the helmsman gets confused and goes starboard when the captain says port, it's embarrassing. And unhealthy for the guy at the helm. In a submarine, well—"

"You could lose the boat," Parker finished for him. "And chances are, that means losing every man aboard. Right. But otherwise, we're pretty informal down here. We have to be, living and working in each other's laps day in, day out, three months or more at a stretch. Don't sweat it. You'll get to know all of your shipmates pretty well."

"Not like a carrier," Dominico said.

"Hell, sir, there were six thousand guys on the *Lincoln*," Young said. "I was aboard her for over a year and knew maybe six hundred by sight."

Parker laughed. "Damned floating airports, complete with shopping malls. Welcome to the *real* navy!"

One of the chess players at another table looked up

from the game. "You know, don't you, sir, that there's only two kinds of ships? Submarines and targets."

"I'd heard submariners felt that way," Gray said.

"It's the truth, right, Joe?"

"Sure," his companion said. "I know you aviators think you're pretty good—"

"We're not good," Seegar put in suddenly, his voice blunt, almost belligerent. He and two other aviators had just walked into the mess hall. "We're the *best*."

"Still skimmer navy, though, sir. It's like, if you don't make it down here, all you can do is go back to the skimmers, right?"

There seemed to be no answer to that. Gray was beginning to realize that his transfer to submarines was going to force him to do some major rethinking about his perceptions of the Navy. Entering the submarine community was causing the military equivalent of culture shock.

And the chess player was right in two ways. Gray had heard the old "subs and targets" line plenty of times from his father, especially when he'd made his decision to go with naval aviation. Still, it was a valid way to look at the world if you were a submariner; surface ships were always there, in plain view, noisy and vulnerable. Submarines by their nature were secretive, appearing where you didn't expect them, striking without warning and then vanishing again into the depths.

But since the *Lincoln* incident four years earlier, skimmers were targets in another way, nakedly vulnerable to railgun attacks from space. If the Navy had any future at all, that single revolution in global military strategy might well dictate that *all* seagoing combatants in the future be submersibles. *Leviathan,* huge as she was, might be a minnow alongside the monster, undersea battleships of fifty years hence . . . or technology might, as she so often did, go the other way, scaling all warships down to the size of modern fighter planes, one- and two-man craft that could travel thousands of miles beneath the waves at speeds approaching those of aircraft.

"Anyway, Commander," Parker said, "I came down here to look you up, give you an invitation to come up to the control room when you get a chance. You might be interested in seeing what we're doing with ULTRA-C."

"I'd like that a lot, sir," Gray said. For one thing, he was going to have to learn how the sub's new ULTRA-C network was going to coordinate with the Orca laser tracking systems. "First thing, though, I want to call an all-hands meeting of the squadron. Commander, do you have any idea where we could get together? The wardroom's not going to be big enough."

"You could use the MEJO port forward," Parker said. "Used to be quarters for Russian missile technicians, like where we put you, but we just have fruits and vegetables in there now. We could clean that out, turn it into a squadron ready room. How'd that be?"

"Perfect."

"I'll order a working party to help you clean it out."

"That would be great, sir. Cigar? Pass the word. All hands at MEJO port forward, 1400. We'll pitch in with the field day, then call a meeting."

"Officers manning brooms?" the chess player said, one eyebrow askance. "This I gotta see!"

"You'll get your chance, Wojciekowski. You're on that work detail, as of now."

"So what's going down, CAG?" Seegar asked. "Another briefing?"

Gray ran a hand back over his thinning hair and grinned. "Nope. Just an idea I have to get us all into the routine down here."

CHAPTER
8

SSCVN-1 *Leviathan*
Twenty-two miles south of Key Largo, Florida
Wednesday, March 29, 1630 hours

"Welcome to *Leviathan*'s control deck."
Gray climbed up through the deck hatch
and stepped past Commander Parker,
astonished at the sheer size of the place. He'd been
aboard subs before, both as a kid when he'd been on
his father's sub on a rare visitors' day, and also at
New London. Contrary to the impression conveyed
in most movies, submarine control rooms, even
aboard the big boomers, were claustrophobic places
filled with metal cabinets and sharp corners, television monitors protruding at odd angles, circuitry
panels, consoles, and chairs.

His hurried orientation at New London had given
Gray the basic layout of America's newly acquired
Russian subs, so there should have been no surprise,
but the space was startling nonetheless. Typhoons
were as large on the outside as they were because
they actually consisted of four separate pressure hulls
inside a single enormous outer hull. The torpedo
room was one small pressure hull forward, located

above the sub's forward sonar dome. The bulk of the sub consisted of two long pressure hulls set side by side and interconnected at numerous points; Gray had heard that each had probably been derived from the inner hull of a Delta, an earlier class of Soviet missile sub.

The fourth pressure hull rode above and between the main hulls and formed the lower half of the Typhoon's huge sail. The design allowed for a control deck and attack center much roomier than any Gray had seen before. The two areas were part of the same compartment, though a block of electronics cabinets and the sonar room almost divided it in two, with the control room forward and combat aft. The control room was easily identified by the two men in dungarees and blue baseball caps seated side by side at a large console, each with his hand on a pistol-grip joystick. Screens and electronic displays were mounted on the bulkhead in front of them, including a big screen that appeared to be giving them a television view forward. In the old days, Gray knew, they'd navigated with nothing more than a bubble to show the sub's angle of ascent or descent, a fathometer to give the depth, and the repeated commands from the Officer of the Deck. Behind them, practically looking over their shoulders, sat a lieutenant in khakis.

"Helm on the right, diving planes on the left," Parker explained. "Lieutenant Driscoll there is Diving Officer of the watch. On an American sub, helm and planes are controlled by wheels." He illustrated by moving his hands in a steering motion. "The Russians seem to prefer the high-tech approach."

The deck was over twenty feet wide, even allowing for the consoles and electronics cabinets that

enclosed it. Perhaps the strangest part of the scene
was a low, raised dais ten feet behind the Diving
Officer's station, partly encircled by an aluminum
railing and surmounted by what looked like an executive's chair. The seat was occupied at the moment by
an officer in a blue jumpsuit. Gray thought it must be
Captain Ramsay, but he couldn't be sure because the
man's head was completely encased in what looked
like an aviator's helmet, except that the visor had
been replaced by black plastic and wiring that gave
him an alien, bug-eyed appearance. The letters "CO"
were stenciled across the back in white paint. Cables
trailed from the helmet, dangled over the officer's
shoulders, and vanished into a complexity of wiring
and conduits in the overhead.

The arrangement looked like a computer simulator device that Gray had used in aviation school.

"The latest thing in virtual reality," Parker said,
noting Gray's interest. "SUBVIEW. Stands for
SUBmarine Virtual Imaging Electronic Window." He
pointed to the deck below the electronics block
behind the chair. "Down there is a Cray Series IV
supercomputer, taking input from sonar, from
remote TV cameras on the outer hull, and from our
blue-green lasers. The computer—we call it 'Crayfish,'
by the way—puts it all together and feeds a picture
through those cables to the helmet. Captain Ramsay
there can wear the SUBVIEW helmet and 'see' what's
going on outside the boat. You'd like it. It's almost
like flying."

"You've got that wrong, Number One," Ramsay's
voice said, muffled by the helmet. It was a little eerie
to see the face of that helmet swing blindly toward
the sound of their voices. "It is precisely like flying.

But I imagine our guest here has already had some experience with SUBVIEW helmets. Am I right?"

"Yes, sir, you are." It was a little startling to see that blind helmet swing toward the sound of his voice. "We use SUBVIEW in our Barracudas. The only difference is we don't wear helmets. The imagery is projected onto the inside of the cockpit."

"Well, this is just the Mark I version," Parker said with a smile. "Experimental. I gather all submarines will have the Mark II someday. Even big ones like *Leviathan*."

The Captain reached up, fumbling with a clasp at the angle of his jaw. Unsnapping it, he swung the visor up, then lifted the open helmet from his shoulders and handed it to a sailor who'd come to assist him. "Thanks, son." He rose from the chair. "Actually, I'd be a little worried about driving a sub where everyone in the control room can see what I do. Call me old-fashioned, but I like it better when the crew just does what I tell them to do, when I tell them . . . and aren't being distracted by the pretty pictures. You want to give it a try?"

"Very much, Captain."

"Here." He reached into a recess in the overhead. "We'll pull down an observer's SUBVIEW for you."

He produced a second helmet, identical to the first except that the word OBSERVER had been stenciled across the back. With a little help from Parker and a seaman, Gray slid the shell down over his head, then snapped the visor down, locking it in place.

Instantly, Gray's world changed.

It seemed as though he was standing high atop *Leviathan*'s sail, looking forward. The great sub's forward deck stretched ahead into the distance, the

double row of missile hatches sharp-etched and distinct. It was like any number of underwater films
Gray had seen at one time or another, from
Cousteau documentaries to movies like *Red October,*
except that the surrounding water was wonderfully,
magically transparent, as clear as pure, green-tinted
crystal and with none of the fuzziness or murk that
usually accompanied underwater photography. It was
hard to judge distances in this alien world with no
familiar landmarks, but he guessed that he could see
ten or twelve miles before his line of sight finally
blurred into a uniform, shadowy gray-green fog. He
could see the bottom, a gray landscape of rounded
hills, gullies, cliff sides, and rolling plains, gliding
beneath *Leviathan*'s hull far below.

How far? His eyes, he knew, could easily fool him in
this watery strangeness, but *Leviathan*'s top speed was
something over thirty knots. That was a crawl compared to the Mach speeds of aerial combat, of course,
but it gave him a starting point for his perspective.
The ground was slipping away at about the same rate
as it would have had he been in an F/A-18 Hornet flying at 300 knots and an altitude of 8,000 feet. Dividing
by ten to make the speed thirty knots gave him an
"altitude" of 800 feet. He could see no real detail at
that range, he saw no individual boulders or seaweed
or whatever else might be down there. The sensation
was exactly like flying above the barren wastes of a
sandy desert, except that the "sand" was a darker
shade of the gray-green environment surrounding it.

Motion caught Gray's eye and he instinctively
swung his head to the left. The undersea world swung
dizzily to match his movement. Like an aircraft simulator helmet, the SUBVIEW system monitored his

head movements and adjusted the images being displayed before his eyes by the helmet's optics. There, perhaps a thousand feet to port and slightly astern, another submarine was pacing *Leviathan*.

She was beautiful, long and black and streamlined, with an aura of sleek deadliness about her that hinted of a killer's speed and purpose. Two-thirds *Leviathan*'s length, she was less than half as broad, her hull a perfect cylinder teardrop-rounded at the bow and tapered aft at the cruciform tail. Unlike *Leviathan*, the other sub had its sail set far forward, perhaps a quarter of the distance from bow to stern.

Curiously, the other sub appeared to have running lights, brilliant blue-green beacons mounted atop the sail and on her rounded belly amidships, as dazzling as aircraft landing lights. Those, Gray knew, were the vessel's ULTRA-C lasers. Her Captain, too, had SUBVIEW. He suppressed a sudden, illogical urge to wave.

"That's the *Charlotte*," Ramsay's voice said, startlingly close to Gray's right ear. "One of our two escorts. A Los Angeles–class attack boat, a real greyhound. I used to drive one of those, before they consigned me to driving trucks."

It was a little eerie, having Ramsay's voice speak at his side like that, but with the Captain himself invisible. Perhaps it was no different than hearing someone speaking over a flight-helmet radio, but the illusion projected by the simulator helmet was so perfect he could almost imagine he was actually standing on *Leviathan*'s weather bridge, rushing forward through the water, rather than standing on the railed dais next to Ramsay's chair on the Typhoon's control-room deck.

"This is fantastic!" Gray said. "The definition is a lot sharper than I expected."

"You're seeing a computer animation, of course, but it *is* pretty detailed. See the wakes and turbulence? That's sound you're seeing, not something that would be visible to the eye."

He could see the wakes, like fuzzy contrails streaming aft from *Leviathan*'s bowplanes, and a much larger one churning aft of the *Charlotte*'s single screw. Turning his head to look back over his shoulder, Gray could see across the back of *Leviathan*'s dorsal fin and down at her own tail. Twin vortices swirled aft of the Typhoon's two screws; the effect was like the thundering column of smoke streaming behind the space shuttle during a launch, save that the colors were all muted variations of gray, blue, and green . . . and the scene was completely silent.

"What are the numbers across the top of my display?" he asked.

He'd ignored the flickering numerals at first, since there were no identifying words or symbols with them. They appeared to be hanging in space a few inches from his forehead, above his line of sight but easily visible if he rolled his eyes up. If he raised his head rather than his eyes, the whole view shifted and he was looking toward a faint, shimmering interplay of golds and greens, sunlight, he thought, dancing on the ocean's surface twice *Leviathan*'s length overhead.

"The number on the left is range to target in meters," Ramsay said. "Measuring off whatever is in the center of your field of view. Middle number is bearing, the direction you're looking in at the moment. Right number is a voice-controlled discrete. You're showing depth below keel right now. Say

'SUBVIEW speed' out loud and it'll give you our velocity in knots. Say 'SUBVIEW ID' and it'll identify whatever you're looking at, assuming your target is in the data base or matches something in the Crayfish's sonar library. There's a list of about twenty pro-words you can use to get different data."

Gray was interested to see that he'd been fairly accurate with his earlier assessments of range. *Leviathan* currently had about 250 meters of water beneath her keel, close enough to his guess of 800 feet. The number kept flickering up and down, registering the undulations in the landscape as *Leviathan* cruised past overhead. Looking to port again, he saw that *Charlotte* was 310 meters away and at a bearing of 175, almost due south.

"My helmet has more in the way of discretes and control options," Ramsay continued. "But it's essentially the same as yours. I gather you use similar discretes in the Barracuda system."

"Yes, sir. But the imaging isn't nearly this sharp and clear. In an SFV-4 you *know* you're looking at a computer image. This looks completely realistic!"

"That's because we have the space for a bigger computer to run the imaging," Ramsay explained. "Your Barracudas don't have the room for a full-fledged Cray IV, so they make do with Cray CT Micros. Same software, but less processing power. Give the computer jockeys a few more years though, and we're going to have a damned hard time telling what's real and what's not."

"This is real enough for my blood," Gray said with feeling. "I see what you mean, though, about not wanting to distract your crew."

"We have interior SUBVIEW displays, of course.

On TV screens. The helm has a big one, and there's another in sonar."

"Do you still need sonar?" Gray asked, and immediately wished he could take it back. Stupid question.

"Oh yeah," Ramsay replied with a chuckle. "Damn right we still need sonar. You don't think I'm going to trust my boat to this newfangled science-fiction stuff, do you? Besides, there are times when we can't risk giving ourselves away."

Submarines had always presented special problems in navigation. Water was never as crystalline as the SUBVIEW system suggested, and below a depth of a very few hundred feet the sea was always so dark that human vision was for all intents and purposes useless. Other senses developed for warfare on land and in the skies above were even more limited; radio waves, for instance, were absorbed almost immediately underwater, which made radar useless and radio communications virtually impossible. The same was true of heat radiation, which was why thermal imaging didn't work.

To replace sight, then, submarine designers had relied on the one form of energy that traveled very well underwater indeed—sound. Indeed, dolphins and other toothed whales had, like bats, developed the use of sound for echolocation long before Man had arrived on the scene. Dolphins, in particular, were so extraordinarily sensitive that they could sense the differences between targets made of different types of metal, or between a hollow sphere and a solid one. Dolphins were still a lot better at getting useful information out of echoes than humans were. It was no wonder that submariners had adopted the friendly, intelligent sea mammals as their familiars in the witch world of undersea combat.

Of course, dolphins used active sonar to navigate, a technique that submariners were reluctant to employ for the simple fact that sending out loud chirps of high-frequency sound was like shouting "Here I am!" to any listening enemy. Passive sonar— simply *listening*—was safer but was useless for determining ranges or for sensing the topography of the sea bottom.

To get all of the information necessary to create its illusion of human vision, SUBVIEW had to employ both active and passive sonar, as well as the rapidly pulsed flashes from several blue-green lasers. If the Captain ordered the active sonar switched off, Gray knew, the quality of the illusion would degrade somewhat. If he had to switch off the lasers as well, the illusion would vanish completely save as vague, glowing fogs showing the direction—but not the shape, texture, or distance—of sound sources in the surrounding ocean.

And there would be times when he'd have to run blind. Any other ship or submarine equipped with the proper gear could sense laser light. In fact, for a time, back in the seventies and eighties, it had been thought that submarines were doomed because reconnaissance satellites equipped with ocean-piercing blue-green lasers would one day be able to see submerged submarines as easily as they saw aircraft carriers or tanks. That they couldn't do so yet was due more to the fact that submarines were so tiny compared to the surrounding vastness of the ocean than to any flaw in the theory. A laser-scanning satellite would have to scan enormous areas of water with a beam only a few feet thick in order to illuminate a sub, and there were countermeasure devices—laser-scattering layers of bubbles, for instance—that could serve as camouflage of a sort. So far, the advantage was still with the submarine in the ongoing global race in military technology.

But when *Leviathan* used her ULTRA-C lasers she lost some of that advantage. Scattering and attenuation made her lasers less obvious than, say, a man switching on a flashlight in a dark room, but they were still detectable from space if the satellite knew about where to look. They were even easier to see from an appropriately equipped submarine or surface vessel—again, if the hunter knew about where to look.

So there would be times, Gray knew, when they were being hunted, when Ramsay would order the ULTRA-C shut down because an enemy might be able to detect her lasers. When that happened, SUBVIEW would become useless, and *Leviathan* would be forced to revert to the technology of a decade or two before, when submarines lurked and prowled and hunted one another in a strange combination of hide-and-seek and blindman's buff.

It would be a long, long time—if ever—before submarines stopped including skilled sonar technicians in their crews.

"Ready to come back inside?"

Gray started at Ramsay's voice, so lost had he been in the computer-generated illusion. "Uh, yessir." He groped at the helmet release. "How do I get this off?"

Unseen hands guided his. There was a sharp click, and the watery universe around him was wiped away. He stood again in *Leviathan*'s control room—a compartment suddenly tight and small and claustrophobic after the vista he'd experienced "outside." Ramsay was standing beside him, a crooked grin on his face.

"I know how you feel, Commander," he said. "It's like you could stay out there forever."

"When Hollywood gets hold of this, it's going to revolutionize the movie industry."

"I gather the Japanese are already working along those lines. Movies that surround the viewer. Puts Omnimax in the same category as those cheap, three-D glasses they sometimes used to pass out at those God-awful B-movies they had when I was a kid."

Mention of the Japanese sobered Gray's mood, reminding him that this technological wonder was still basically and essentially a weapon of war. He wondered if the Japanese had this kind of system on their submarines yet . . . or if they'd sold it already to the Islamics.

"I appreciate your letting me coming up here, Captain," Gray said, reluctantly handing the observer's helmet to a seaman to be stowed back in the overhead. "Thank you."

Access to a ship's bridge was always a privilege, never a right to be taken for granted.

"Glad to have you, Commander. I gather from your schedule you're planning on taking some Barracudas out for a run at 1730 hours."

"Yes, sir, with your approval, of course. I'd like to start shaking them down before we get to where we're going."

"Fine by me. Of course, if the damn things don't work, I won't be able to stop and pick you up."

"That's another reason for doing it this afternoon, Captain, while we're still close to Florida and the Coast Guard."

"Very well, then. Keep me apprised."

The interview was clearly over. "Aye, aye, Captain. Thanks again." Accompanied by Parker, Gray made his way toward the hatch in the deck leading back down to *Leviathan*'s portside pressure hull.

CHAPTER
9

SSCVN-1 *Leviathan*
Thirty-eight miles southwest of Key Largo, Florida
Wednesday, March 29, 1745 hours

An hour later, spreading rumor had brought a number of *Leviathan*'s off-duty personnel to a passageway on the sub's second deck starboard, aft of sick bay and across from the mess hall. All twelve of the aviators of SF Squadron 1 had vanished into the small compartment sometime before, causing intense speculation among the sub's enlisted personnel, and among some of the officers as well.

At last, the door opened and T. Morgan Gray stepped into the passageway. The buzz of conversation and speculation died away instantly. Gray stood in front of them, grinning broadly, his head shaved nakedly bald. A moment later, Cigar stepped out of the compartment used by *Leviathan*'s barber, followed, one by one, by all of the rest of the aviators, every one with his skull just as naked as Gray's.

"You gotta watch out for that radiation, guys," Gray said loudly. He saw Patterson, watching him gape-mouthed from farther down the passageway, and gave him a cheerful thumbs-up. In single file, the long line of naval aviators marched in bare-headed glory past the staring seamen, heading for the missile decks forward.

Gray never did figure out exactly what they'd been mixing in the newcomers' shampoos. Someone had suggested Nair, but that stuff had to be left on for more than a few seconds for it to work, and the concoction used by the pranksters in *Leviathan*'s crew had started thinning men's hair after one or two applications. He had learned from Parker, however, that the gag was at least as old as service aboard nuclear submarines; newbies were frequently subjected to harassment ranging from the undignified to the revolting to the outright painful, and the hair-remover-in-the-shampoo trick was one of the more subtle ones. Parker had never heard of the routine being used on officers before, however.

Apparently the aviators' position aboard, not-quite-crew, not-quite-guests, was just ambiguous enough that some member of *Leviathan*'s crew had decided to extend the initiation to them. Such hazing among enlisted personnel was officially forbidden but largely tolerated; the reasoning was that men who could take a joke would fit in, while those who couldn't probably weren't adaptable enough to survive long as submariners. It also carried with it the rough justice of a rite of passage. Like the King Neptune ceremonies aboard a ship crossing the equator, the harassment served to initiate the newbie, to make him one of the gang, fully a part of an all-volunteer crew that already considered itself a cut above any other group in the Navy. Newcomers had to *earn* their dolphins.

By going along with the joke, Gray and his squadron had proven that they could take it . . . and that they didn't take themselves too seriously. Most of the squadron had taken his request—not an order—that they have their heads shaved in the spirit of good fun . . . and in scoring one up on the submarine navy.

Now, on *Leviathan*'s missile deck, second level, Gray inspected the gleaming cylinder of Tube 20. A missile inspection hatch there had been widened and stood open now on massive hinges. Inside was visible, not a ballistic missile, but a sleek shape that combined design elements of missile, aircraft, and sub. Its cockpit was open, the padded, harness-draped seat exposed to view, its back horizontal, its armrests sticking straight up and down.

At the next tube down, number eighteen, Monk Young saw Gray watching and gave him a grin and a mock salute off his gleaming scalp. In the portside pressure hull, in tubes nineteen and seventeen, Seegar and a Lieutenant Robert Hanson, one of the original Orca aviators on board, were preparing two more Barracudas for launch.

Gray was being assisted by a TM 2nd named Sprague and by Raymond Huxley, the black chief who'd flown in with Gray aboard the Osprey. "So what are you going to call your squadron, sir?" Huxley asked.

"No idea yet, Chief. Why'd you ask?"

"Oh, I don't know. Looking at you guys, the Bald Eagle Squadron comes to mind."

Sprague laughed, a little nervously. "Some of the guys are already talking about the radioactive mutants, sir. You could be the Mutant Menace."

"Sure. Or the Chrome-Dome Squadron. We could use our heads as reflectors for the ULTRA-C lasers."

"Good idea, Commander. I'll have to remember to

put that in a memo to Washington." Huxley checked off a final box on the clipboard checklist in his hands, then set it aside. "All green on the manual run-through. Ready for the squeeze?"

"Yep. Where's my helmet?"

His helmet was much like an aviator's helmet except that the visor had no outer, reflective sun-shade. Sprague handed it to him, and he slid it over his head, leaving the visor up. The interior padding felt strange against his scalp, which still burned a little from the barber's scraping.

"There. That cut the glare a bit?"

"Yes, sir. We can see just fine now."

"Okay. Give me a hand, will you?"

With Huxley's help, Gray got his feet into the open accessway, then slithered legs-first into the missile tube. His Barracuda was organized exactly like a jet fighter—its controls were laid out almost identically to those of the new F-22 fighter—but at the moment the compact little vehicle was resting in Missile Tube 20, its nose pointed straight up, which made getting into the cockpit a contortionist's feat similar to that of a Mercury astronaut wiggling into his capsule in the early days of the space program.

Once he was snuggled into the cramped cockpit, flat on his back and with his knees elevated above his head, he pulled the harness on and locked it in place, then found the communications plug and jacked it home in the receptacle in his helmet. "Barracuda One, communications check."

"Read you, sir," Huxley said. He'd slipped on a headset with microphone and was tapping the Barracuda's comm system. Once Gray was launched, he would communicate with the ship through the interlocking web of laser light transmitted from *Leviathan.* "Ready to close."

Gray flicked on the internal lights and his console power, illuminating his cramped surroundings. "Seal 'er up, Chief. See you in an hour."

The Barracuda's cockpit canopy closed over his head with a hollow clang and the hiss of a pressurized seal. A moment later, there was a second duller thump as the missile access was closed outside. He could hear the faint hum of electronics, the whine of a cooling fan buried somewhere behind the intricacies of screens and readouts in front of him.

He swept his eyes across his control panel, mentally cataloging each readout, each screen. His console mounted six Multiple Function Displays, or MFD screens. As in the F/A-18 or the F-22, most of the instruments appeared as graphics on those displays rather than as actual dials or lights. A touch of a button could completely change his console configuration. He reset his from standby mode to prelaunch, calling up a checklist on his center screen.

"Barracuda One," a new voice said over his headset. "This is Home Plate. Your mission has been designated Sierra Foxtrot. Do you copy, over?"

"Home Plate, Sierra Foxtrot One."

On an aircraft carrier, launch and recovery operations were directed from Primary Flight Control or "PriFly," which served as a control tower for the seagoing airport. Aboard *Leviathan,* the sub's missile control center had been converted to serve a similar purpose, though, so far, none of the aviators had referred to the place as PriFly. The Launch Control Officer and his staff were responsible for checking the myriad systems that powered, ran, and controlled each fighter sub, for getting the Barracudas seaborne and for recovering them after a mission without smashing them or *Leviathan*.

"Ready for prelaunch checklist," the Launch Officer said. "We have you registering at 26,400 pounds."

Gray checked an MFD readout. "Twenty-six-point-four. I concur."

"Internal power."

"Internal power on. Fuel cells reading at one hundred percent."

"Life support."

"On."

"Pressure."

"Go."

"L-CIS."

"Computer on. Program running."

There was a long pause, longer than should have been necessary to record Gray's response.

"Ah, Commander, Sierra Foxtrot Three reports a computer malfunction," the voice said after a moment. "We've scrubbed his launch."

SF-3. That was Cigar. What the hell had happened to his computer? It was an uncomfortable reminder that the SFV-4s were still experimental vehicles, untried devices subject to the teething pains of any new system. "I copy that, Home Plate. Please confirm that Sierra Foxtrot Flight will now be operating with three members, over."

"That is affirmative, One. Foxtrot One, Two, and Four."

For this initial test run, a formation of three Barracudas would do as well as four. He just hoped the breakdown didn't indicate some as yet undiscovered flaw in the system.

"Resuming preflight," the voice continued. "Laser power."

"Go."

"Sonar."

"Go."

"ULTRA-C integration."

"Go."

"Indicators."

"Go. Set for launch configuration."

"Engine."

"Power on. Pressure at nine-five and go." He flicked a switch and heard a deep, throaty hum from somewhere behind his back. The Barracuda trembled slightly at the touch of restrained power. "Mags are spooling."

"Hull."

"I read green. Integrity good. Intakes open. I'm hot and tight."

"Weapons."

"I read safed and disarmed."

"Waterfoils."

"Folded, unlocked, ready for deploy."

"Stand by to flood tube."

"Set here. Go ahead."

"Flooding Tube Two-zero." He could hear it after a moment, a dull, rumbling shudder sounding from just outside the opaque wall of his cockpit. He felt the Barracuda shudder slightly as sea water filled the missile tube.

"Clamps released," the voice in his headset warned. "Umbilicals released. Deck hatch open. Depth is eight hundred feet, speed zero-five knots, pressure three-five-six psi."

"Confirm hatch open. Sierra Foxtrot One is ready

for launch." He took a deep breath. The routine, pursued time and time again in his training during the past few months, still struck him as strangely out of place, referring to "flights" and "launch" while referring to what was still a submarine, however high-tech it might be.

"Roger. Launch in three . . . two . . . one . . . *launch!*"

There was a surge of acceleration—not nearly so strong as the zero-to-one-eighty-in-three-seconds rush of a carrier catapult launch, but hard enough to press him back against his padded seat. There was a shock and a loud clang, enough of a jolt that for an instant he wondered if *Leviathan*'s deck hatch had been left closed after all.

Then there was an unearthly silence, almost like the instant of free-fall when a catapult failure leaves an aircraft with insufficient speed to get airborne. He touched a rectangular, lighted button marked "SBVW."

The interior of his canopy, gray and featureless and close, lit suddenly with an emerald glow, as though it had magically become transparent. He was rising straight up, riding a geyser of bubbles exploding from the surge of compressed air that had fired him clear of *Leviathan*'s missile tube. To his left, he could see the Typhoon's sail like a broad, bluff, gray cliff dropping behind him.

Deployment of his waterfoils was automatic. Wings, short, stubby, and sharply anhedral, unfolded into position on either side of his hull, below and just aft of his canopy. Farther aft, the stabilizer snapped erect and locked in place. Grasping the stick on his right-hand armrest, he gently tested the controls. Words flickered across his left-hand data screen. Rudder and planes were functioning perfectly.

The SS-N-20 Sturgeon missiles originally launched by the Typhoon were forty-nine feet long, seven feet wide, and weighed 132,000 pounds apiece. The Barracuda, already under development when the Navy had acquired two Typhoons from the Russian republic, had required only the reengineering of folding wings and stabilizer to let it fit inside a Sturgeon missile tube. Measuring twenty-four feet from rounded snout to needle-slender tail, it was six tenths the length of the F/A-18 Hornet Gray had flown off the *Roosevelt*.

With his wings extended, Gray could no longer maintain his nose-high attitude. Pressing his stick forward, he brought the Barracuda's nose over, putting the minisub into a sloping dive that would carry it well clear of *Leviathan* and build up the necessary pressure for the craft's pulse-jet engine.

The SFV-4 Barracuda represented a tremendous leap forward in submarine design, one that had been anticipated for years but that had not been realized until the very dawn of the twenty-first century. Before Barracuda, every submarine from the U.S.S. *Holland* in 1900 to *Leviathan* herself operated in essentially the same way—by flooding or emptying ballast tanks to make the vessel more or less buoyant. Pump water into the tanks and the submarine goes down, achieving neutral buoyancy at a depth of around one hundred feet, with trim and dive planes controlling further maneuvers; blow the water out with compressed air and the sub goes up. Submarines, in fact, are less like undersea-capable airplanes than they are like dirigibles or hot-air balloons, dependent on positive or neutral buoyancy to change their depth.

The Barracuda represented a revolution in submarine technology, a *negative* buoyancy vehicle always heavier than the water it displaced. Drop an SFV-4 in the water and it sank. It climbed underwater precisely the same way an aircraft climbed in the air; the Barracuda's stubby wings and high speed allowed it to literally fly through the water, a jet instead of a dirigible.

The engine was a radical departure from the past as well. Rather than relying on a screw, the Barracuda operated much like a modern jet aircraft. Water entered the twin, gaping maws of the intakes forward; powerful magnetic fields induced within the water sent it astern in rippling pulses with the force of a jet engine's exhaust. The Barracuda had a top speed of an incredible eighty knots, twenty-five knots better than the old Soviet Alfas that for years had been the fastest attacks subs in the world. Theory stated that— with more power and better engines—speeds of over 120 knots were possible.

Of course, Barracudas did have their downside. An engine failure or an undeployed wing would send them into a long, long glide toward the bottom. They were rated for operations as deep as 3,000 feet and had a theoretical crush depth of almost a mile, but the pressures that far down did strange things to hull metal, even titanium and polyceramic alloys. Most operations would be conducted at friendlier depths above a thousand feet.

If the worst happened, there was an emergency ejection system that would send the entire cockpit module ballooning toward the surface—a kind of inverted parachute—but nobody was eager to test that under field conditions. Besides, electrical and mechanical systems had been known to fail, especially in combat and especially under the stress of an environment as alien as the deep sea.

Gray felt the engine take hold, felt the smooth surge of acceleration as his Barracuda banked to the left, passing the towering sail of the slow-moving Typhoon.

Now that he'd used the SUBVIEW aboard *Leviathan,* the Barracuda's optical system seemed even more limited, like animation instead of the real thing. It was very good computer animation, but the colors were just a little too bright, the surfaces a bit too slick, clean, and glossy to be mistaken for, say, a view through a transparent canopy. The major technical difference, however, was the fact that the Mark II's imagery was projected onto his canopy dome, like stars and a night sky on the inside of a planetarium, instead of through the optics of a simulation helmet. It worked exactly the same as *Leviathan*'s SUBVIEW system; sonar information, TV pictures, and the returns from small blue-green lasers mounted on the Barracuda's dorsal stabilizer and belly were fed into the small sub's Cray Micro, processed, and displayed as animation. It was the size and power of his computer that limited Gray's view.

Gray's headgear mounted tiny infrared sensors like those in attack helicopter helmets, allowing the Barracuda's computer to monitor his head and eye positions; he could engage a target—or call up more data on it—simply by looking at the image projected on his dome and giving a verbal command.

To port, now, he could see the long, lean hull of the *Charlotte.* The water appeared murkier than it had through *Leviathan*'s SUBVIEW, and he had some difficulty making out the attack sub's form. The Barracuda's ULTRA-C lasers didn't have the penetration and range of *Leviathan*'s far more powerful laser imaging system, though it was possible that the water here was less transparent than what he'd seen in the Typhoon's control room.

Passing the cliff side of *Leviathan*'s sail, he could look up and see the dazzling blue-green beacon of her dorsal ULTRA-C laser. It was not actually a steady light, but a series of millisecond flashes flicking out in all directions, firing hundreds of times within a single second. The effect was like a steady glow, however, and he felt bathed in its light. If he'd been looking at it at this range with his naked eyes, he could have been blinded. He wondered if Ramsay was watching him now from the control deck's SUBVIEW and decided he must be. Any ship's Captain got nervous when other people maneuvered small craft close aboard, and that nervousness could build toward something like paranoia when the vessels were already under eight hundred feet of water.

Gray adjusted his right-hand stick, increasing his separation from that immense, dark gray cliff. Glancing back over his left shoulder, he saw a cloud of bubbles emerging from Hatch 18. Sierra Foxtrot Two rose into view a second later, wings already unfolding. Twenty seconds later, Hatch 17 erupted in bubbles, and the third Barracuda joined the formation. Young and Hanson brought their craft under control and formed up on Gray, moving steadily aft past the ponderous vastness of the Typhoon's hull.

"Home Plate, Home Plate," he called. "This is Sierra Foxtrot One on laser channel three-niner."

"Sierra Foxtrot, Home Plate," the voice of *Leviathan*'s Launch Control Officer responded. Where radio was limited by absorption in water, the laser energy radiating from *Leviathan* and the three Barracudas could be tapped to carry modulated signals. "We read you. Captain relays the following message: 'Good launch, but if you scratch my hull I'm not going to let you back aboard.' Message ends."

Gray laughed. "Copy that, Home Plate," he told *Leviathan*'s LCO. "Tell the Captain we'll be glad to chip the barnacles off his hull if he'll pay us by the hour."

Bringing the right-hand stick back, increasing slightly the engine power by pressing the left-hand throttle forward, he pulled the Barracuda into a gentle climb that easily cleared *Leviathan*'s massive, vertical rudder, then hauled the craft around in a one-eighty turn that sent him forward up the Typhoon's starboard side. His two wingmen paced him, one on either side in close formation.

Gray had handled Barracudas many times, both in simulators and the real thing in Long Island Sound, though this was his first experience with them off an operational mother sub in midocean. The experience was exhilarating . . . almost like flying a Hornet again, except that the craft's reactions were so painfully, laboriously *slow*. He was used to a combat jet with twin afterburning turbofans, each producing 16,000 pounds of thrust. When he flicked the stick to one side and kicked in the rudder, he automatically expected the craft to snap roll into a dive. The Barracuda could roll and dive, but every movement dragged, until Gray doubted that he would ever get used to the mushy, slow-motion feel of the thing.

Leviathan was moving faster now. She'd slowed to five knots for the launch, but now she was pushing ahead once more at thirty-three knots. Gray increased his own throttle until he was drifting past the Typhoon's long, three-story sail, this time moving from stern to bow. His Barracuda shuddered a bit; he was brushing the turbulence of displaced water coming off the giant sub's hull. Glancing at his instruments, he saw he was also bucking a pretty stiff current, a virtual undersea river that flowed out of the Gulf of Mexico and through the Florida Straits, the very beginning of the great Gulf Stream. Increasing power to compensate, he studied *Leviathan*'s double row of missile hatches, all closed now. He hoped the sub's recovery system worked as well as advertised.

A gray-silver flash to starboard caught his eye. Two shapes, as streamlined as the fighter subs, matched speeds with his Barracuda, seeming to hover a few feet off his bow.

Dolphins. His computer's graphic depiction of the sea mammals was quite realistic. The sight of them filled him with a surging wonder and excitement.

"Sierra Foxtrot Leader to Flight," he called. "Everybody with me?"

"Copy, Sierra Foxtrot Leader," Hanson replied. "On your four."

"Yes, Mother," added Monk. "Tucked in tight on your eight."

"We seem to have picked up an escort."

"Roger that," Monk said. "I think they want to race."

"No contest, guys." Gray laughed. "Listen up, now. The *New Haven*'s out in front of us, about twenty miles ahead," Gray said, referring to the flotilla's second attack-sub escort. "Let's see if we can catch her . . . and find out what these hot rods'll really do."

"With you, CAG!"

"Let's punch holes in the ocean!"

He shoved his throttle full forward, accelerating rapidly. At twenty-five knots, the dolphin escort was left behind.

They flew through open water.

CHAPTER
10

A'bdin Palace, Cairo
Thursday, March 30, 1215 hours (Time Zone Zulu +2)

"*A llahu akbar!*"

Thunder broke from the minarets of mosques scattered across the seething chaos of the city, the wavering, amplified voices of the muezzins calling the people to pray.

"*God is most great.*"

"*I testify that there is no god but God.*"

"*I testify that Mohammed is the Prophet of God.*"

"*Come to prayer. Come to success. . . .*"

In his office on the third floor of Cairo's Presidential Palace, Saadeddin Matar, *al-Qayid min al-Jamahir, al-Mahdi,* President of the Republic and Speaker for one billion Muslims, was proving a point.

"No, Mr. Ambassador," he said. "Prayer is for the people. You and I are men to shape the world. We do not need to have our lives shaped by superstition."

Special Envoy Tadashi Yoshida showed no more surprise than the slightest widening of his eyes, but President Matar detected it and smiled.

"You see, Ambassador," he added, "that you can trust me. I have just put my political life into your hands."

Yoshida smiled in return. "An unworthy messenger like myself would never be believed were he to say anything against a man of your power and position. Such an admission would have to be considered as a confidence between friends, not as a weapon."

Matar nodded. "It is good to have good friends such as yourself, Tadashi." *Still,* he thought, *I would never have even whispered such a thing if my people hadn't been able to assure me, with absolute certainty, that you were carrying none of your devilish Japanese electronics hidden about your person. Friendship has little to do with global politics, especially these days.*

They were alone, of course. A servant had brought in coffee and pastries some time ago, but now the office doors were locked, and the light on Matar's desk, positioned so that others in the room could not see it, was unlit. The man with him was carrying no hidden microphones or recorders.

Yoshida bowed from his seat on the far side of the broad, cedar desk, acknowledging Matar's courtesy. "And it is as a good friend that my government has sent me to Cairo," he said.

Matar remained silent, expectant. He wanted to force Yoshida to tell him bluntly.

"Mr. Nakagawa," Yoshida continued, naming Japan's ambassador to the UIR, "has been unable to explain precisely what your ambitions are in the Caribbean. Or why you wish to provoke war with the United States."

"Does Japan oppose such a war?"

Yoshida scarcely hesitated. "Of course not. The Americans have long been our opponents . . . first in war, then in the global marketplace." He took a careful sip of coffee, barely concealing a wrinkle of distaste in his expression. Matar knew that the envoy preferred green tea . . . but this was Egypt, and Matar wanted to be certain that that fact was abundantly clear to his guest.

"They lifted Japan out of the destruction of war," he pointed out gently. "They made you a great world power."

"After maneuvering us into that war in the first place. No, Mr. President, we bear no great love for the Americans. Even if we did, it would not matter." Yoshida leaned forward, increasing the sense of intimacy between the two men. "Our economists predict that in ten years, in fifteen at the most, a major expansion by our people into the Pacific will be necessary, will be vital to our continued survival as a nation."

"Why . . . because of overpopulation?"

"That is a factor, certainly. Japan's standard of living has been rising steadily, but our small islands cannot long continue to support our numbers in comfort. But I speak more of economic factors, of our need to control a larger marketplace, as well as our own sources of raw materials."

Matar kept his expression one of polite interest. The alliance between Japan and the UIR had, from the beginning, been forged in Tokyo's need for oil. That was one raw material they would never control.

It was interesting, though, that the Japanese hunger for land, labor, and resources that had led them into World War II drove them still. The imperial generals and cabinet officers of the 1920s would have understood Yoshida's reasoning perfectly.

"Already," the envoy continued, "we have made gigantic inroads in the Philippines, filling the power vacuum left by the Americans when they abandoned those islands. Singapore. Malaysia. Independent nations all, but dependent on us for their economies.

"But these are scarcely a beginning. I am sure it is no surprise to you that we are already considering what control of such financial centers and labor pools as Australia, Vancouver, and Mexico will mean to us one day." He shrugged. "Eventually, however, our need for controlled markets and economic expansion will bring us into direct conflict with America. War with them is inevitable."

And now I've got that *on tape,* Matar thought, triumphant. *What would Washington pay for a copy? No matter. When we need concessions in the future, you will be only too happy to make them. Having your cynicism on record is simply that much extra insurance.*

Matar nodded soberly. "And when that day comes, you would prefer to face an America already weakened by war."

"Of course. We learned rather too well sixty years ago what American industrial might can accomplish." He leaned back in his seat again, fingers laced across his ample stomach. "But as you can imagine, we are concerned about the Islamic Republic's plans. A major war now could reverse America's current trend toward disarmament. If they win, they would end up stronger than they are now, and that would be . . . unfortunate."

"I understand." Matar stood behind his desk, turned, and walked across the luxuriously carpeted room to stand in front of the viewall. Since the bloody revolutions that had swept the fundamentalists into power, no Islamic official had an office with windows, but the wall-sized screen—Sony's latest development in liquid-crystal technology—gave him a dazzling view of the Midan Ahmad Mahir. He could see the faithful thronging the plaza, kneeling in varicolored ranks, facing southeast. As one they bowed, foreheads touching their prayer rugs.

"We cannot hope to destroy the Americans," he said at last.

"It would be a pity if you did. They have much to offer the world economy, but on *our* terms, *neh?*"

"We can hurt them," Matar went on as though he'd not heard. "We can hurt them where we have known them to be vulnerable for these past thirty years. Ultimately, we will dominate them."

"By holding their oil hostage? They no longer rely on the Middle East for oil. Not since they lost the *Abraham Lincoln.*"

Matar frowned. The envoy had found a subtle way of reminding him of the prowess of Japanese military technology.

"True. Now they rely almost entirely on Mexico and South America for their oil. Which is why I dispatched *Sharuq* and her escorts to Cuba. To put additional pressure on the American economy. To put pressure on them politically. Since they must safeguard their oil imports, they will be forced into one of two corners. Either they will surrender to our demands, accepting the UIR as the sole custodian of all of the world's petroleum reserves—"

At his back, Yoshida hissed, a sharp intake of breath. "Even their own?"

"Even their own. The argument will be that petroleum is too precious, too rare a resource to allow it to be dominated by nationalistic interests, that it must be husbanded for the good of all. We would put it under the stewardship of an international agency . . . which in turn would be controlled by us. Their own environmental movement will support us in this, by the way. As the Green Party did in Europe."

"And the alternative? If they do not surrender?"

"They will be forced to intervene militarily in Latin America, again to safeguard their oil. If they cannot ship it safely by sea, they will need to build pipelines through Central America, at enormous cost. Governments that resist will have to be toppled. American troops will be sent to guard pipelines, refineries, and oil fields." He turned from the viewall, shaking his head. "Already, South America grows more restless every day, sinking into poverty while North American business interests grow rich. Mexico already feels dominated by its northern neighbor. We will exploit those feelings. After we have strengthened them. Ultimately, the UIR will control all of Latin America, as today we control North Africa and the Middle East."

"A Catholic population accepting Muslim domination?"

"A poor people accepting succor from friends. It will not appear to be a conquest. At least, they will not perceive it so."

"Ah! The UIR already is everywhere hailed as the new champion of the downtrodden and oppressed," Yoshida said quietly.

"We were oppressed for a long time ourselves."

"And now you are simply taking back your own."

Matar stared at Yoshida for a long moment, measuring him. "You know better than that, my friend. It is more complex than any desire for revenge."

The envoy took another sip of his coffee, draining it, then set the empty cup on the desk. "It always is."

"How much do you know of Islam?"

Yoshida spread his hands. "Some, of course. The job demands it."

"Then you are aware of the differences between Sunni and Shi'a."

"Of course. A division within Islam as profound as the split between Protestant and Catholic."

"A fair enough assessment. But the division stems less from theological considerations than from a simple squabble over who held the authority to rule Islam at Mohammed's death. The Sunnis say that the Prophet's successor was to be chosen from his own tribe, the Quraysh, by the elders of the Islamic community. The Shi'as insisted that Ali, a cousin of Mohammed's on his father's side, was the true successor.

"Actually, the comparison with Protestants and Catholics also applies to the division between the orthodox Sunnis and popular worship. Orthodox Sunni doctrine emphasizes an unmediated relationship between God and man, much as fundamentalist Protestantism does. Popular religion emphasizes the role of mediators, of the Moslem saints and their descendants. They look back to the age of the Four Rightly Guided Caliphs—the last of them was the Shi'as' Ali, by the way—as the golden age of Islam which will be reborn in the final days.

"And then, the Sunnis are further divided by their various sects, each with their own interpretation of the *Sunna,* the customary practices of Mohammed which form the next most important source of Islam after the Quran itself. How much of a woman's body can be legally exposed in public? How far should the community go in enforcing the *Sharia,* Islamic law? With public beheadings and amputations, as called for in the Quran? Or does more enlightened punishment suffice? How far can the Arabic language be permitted to accept new words, words not found in the Quran?"

"A complicated problem in government, Mr. President."

"More complicated than you could possibly know. The *Qaumat,* the great rising that freed Islam from the oppressor, it was supposed to have united us as well. Yet all of these groups hate one another, Tadashi, hate one another with the fervor that only blind and unreasoning faith can bestow. The Sunnis and the Shi'as hate one another, each considering the other to be idolators or worse. Orthodox Sunnis despise the excesses of fundamentalism and fear the people's ignorance, fanaticism, and blind superstition. The fundamentalists hate the orthodox, who, they say, have abandoned the Quran for the comfort of modern ways."

Matar touched his chest. "But in these past few years, Tadashi, I have united the worshipers of Islam. Here, within myself. Without me, there *is* no *Qaumat,* no United Islamic Republic. The Shi'a believe me to be the Mahdi, the hidden, twelfth imam who will be revealed at the last days and lead his people to glory. The Orthodox Sunni accept me as a gifted and charismatic political leader who ended the chaos of the Revolution and made us a great power. The fundamentalists believe me to be the Deliverer who will end the corruption that has plagued Islam since the days of the Four Rightly Guided Caliphs and will usher in the last days.

"There is a proverb, Tadashi, to the effect that you cannot please all of the people at all times. The only way I can hope to keep my people from self-destruction is to give them a diversion."

"A war with America?"

"A war against the Great Satan, against the imperialists who trampled us in the past, who continue to trample the poor and oppressed of the world. A war to give my people an outlet for their God-inspired passions. It will be, truly, *jihad akhil,* the final, the ultimate holy war."

"And you begin this war by attacking their oil tankers in the Caribbean?"

"Perhaps. I have experts of my own, Tadashi, military experts. They predict that America will back down from confrontation this time. With each concession on their part, our position will be stronger. Eventually they will not back down. And then . . ." He shrugged.

"I understand, Mr. President."

Do you? the president wondered. *It is important that you understand enough, for we will depend on Japan for some time to come, for weapons, for advisors, for the intelligence and the protection offered by your satellites . . . just as you depend on us for our oil. But it would be best that you not understand too much. The Islamic Republic cannot depend on outsiders forever. One day, when the Americans are no longer a credible threat, we will need new enemies. . . .*

On the viewall, the worshipers in the square were rising, their second of the day's five obligatory prayers complete.

"Permit me, Tadashi, to pour you another cup of this excellent coffee."

* * *

SSCVN-1 *Leviathan*
Off the Guadiana Banks
Thursday, March 30, 0520 hours

Water hissed and gurgled as it filled three of
Leviathan's missile tubes, spilling through the thin
spaces between the fighter subs and the launch-tube
walls.

"Sierra Foxtrot Flight, your tubes are flooded, your
hatches open," the voice of the Launch Officer said.
"Internal clamps and umbilicals released."

This time, Gray stood on *Leviathan*'s bridge, his
head encased in a SUBVIEW helmet as he watched
three hatches swing silently open on the Typhoon's
long, forward deck. The water was clear and shallow
enough that he could make out an undulating, grassy
bottom several hundred feet below *Leviathan*'s keel.
Charlotte maintained her post off the Typhoon's port
side, while *New Haven* moved unseen through the
deep twenty miles ahead.

It was almost dawn, though the actual level of sunlight at one hundred feet made little difference in
SUBVIEW imaging. At midnight, *Leviathan* and her
escorts had passed forty miles north of Havana, moving swiftly southwest toward Cabo San Antonio at the
island's western tip.

The previous day's patrol, the first full operational
deployment by SFVs at sea, had been a complete success. There'd been teething problems, of course. Not
only had Seegar's computer failed, but there'd been a
control-panel electrical failure on Gray's Barracuda
during the trip back, a failure that could have been
critical if it hadn't been for a backup system, and the
Tube 17 recovery gear had fouled on deployment,

forcing Hanson to recover in one of *Leviathan*'s four empty missile tubes.

Still, the patrol had satisfied Gray that the fighter subs would work as advertised, not only in the sheltered test waters in Long Island Sound, but in the open ocean as well. Aboard *Leviathan* once again, he and his men had had dinner, then retired to the new squadron ready room where they'd gone through a complete debrief of the day's activities. He wanted the impressions, not only of Hanson and Young, but of the men who had readied the fighter subs for the mission, and he wanted to be certain that the faults that had manifested themselves could, and would, be corrected.

Less than twelve hours after his launch the evening before, Gray was witnessing a second launch. The flotilla had slowed as it rounded the western end of Cuba and passed into the Yucatán Channel, and Gray wanted to use the opportunity to further test the fighter subs. Three new boats had been readied. Lieutenants Hernandez and Seegar and Lieutenant j.g. Dominico were aboard them now, readying for launch. Three missile tubes—numbers ten, twelve, and fifteen—were open now, their hatch covers folded outboard to expose the rounded snouts of the fighter subs resting within.

Gray was monitoring the tactical channel over his observer's helmet. "Launch Control, Sierra Foxtrot Leader," Hernandez's voice was saying. "We read green and go for launch."

"Roger that, Sierra Foxtrot Leader," the voice of the Launch Control Officer replied. "Depth is three-zero-zero feet, speed zero-four knots, pressure one-three-three-point-five psi. Stand by." There was a click of a changing channel. "Captain, this is the LCO. Fighter-sub patrol ready for launch. Request permission to proceed."

"Granted," Ramsay's voice said, and Gray could hear him both through the comm circuit and from the man himself, seated unseen at Gray's side. "Launch when ready."

"Sierra Foxtrot, you are go for launch. Counting down from four . . . three . . . two . . . one . . . *launch!*"

This time, Gray watched the explosion of bubbles from the vantage point of *Leviathan*'s sail. The Typhoon was moving slowly enough that the cloud seemed to hang above the deck for long seconds after the roar of the compressed air explosion, and Hernandez's Barracuda rose from the fog, hardening from shadow into dark gray solidity as wings and stabilizer unfolded and locked into place.

Cuban Coastal Defense Force Submarine *San Juan*
The Guadiana Banks
Thursday, March 30, 0521 hours

The black water was just beginning to lighten to deep emerald, illuminated by the glow of the predawn sky above the hiding place of the Cuban *Guarda Coasta* diesel-powered submarine as she crept along at five knots a scant twenty-five feet off the bottom. She was small, displacing 3,000 tons submerged, and she was quiet, much quieter than her larger, nuclear-powered sisters. Even the stealthiest nuclear-powered submarine had cooling and circulating pumps that could be heard across astonishing distances by sensitive hydrophones, but a diesel-electric boat, when running on batteries and moving slowly enough that screw noises and the rush of water across deck fittings and free-flood holes in her hull were kept to a minimum, could be very silent indeed.

Teardrop-shaped, with a flattened ridge along her upper deck and comparatively large sail, she was a Kilo-class attack submarine, manufactured at the United Admiralty Shipyard in St. Petersburg fifteen years earlier, then sold to the People's Republic of Cuba as a replacement for that country's decrepit Whiskey-class boats. For a time her name had been *El Poder de los Obreros,* but then Castro had died, the political pendulum had swung back to the right, and she'd been rechristened with a less ponderous, less ideological name: *San Juan.*

Teniente Raúl Alvarez held the headset against his ear, listening intently as he watched the cascade of sound traces on the sonar screen. "American Los Angeles class," he said. "Definitely."

"She is moving fast, Captain," the chief sonarman said. "Possibly thirty knots. If that is indeed her speed, the traces we have plotted so far give a range of only fifteen kilometers. And . . ." He pointed at the screen, showing additional stacks of Vs, traces of sound ferreted from the depths. "Here . . . and here. At least two additional contacts. I read them as at least two more submarines following the first, perhaps thirty kilometers astern."

"It seems the Americans are rushing an undersea fleet into the Yucatán Passage," Alvarez said thoughtfully. "They act as though they've been stung."

"Contact is closing, Captain. Assuming thirty knots, the range is now fourteen kilometers."

"Continue to monitor them closely, Carlos."

"Sí, Capitán!"

Alvarez backed out of the sonar compartment and into *San Juan*'s control room. With a crew of sixty, the Kilo was crowded, and he had to squeeze past several crewmen to reach the small chart table.

San Juan was lurking at the very edge of Cuba's twelve-mile territorial limit, in the waters off the island's westernmost tip. There, the waters of the Yucatán Passage dropped steadily toward the hundred-fathom line, save in one spot, the Guadiana Banks, where a ten-mile patch of bottom rose steeply from the depths, missing becoming an island in its own right by a scant sixty feet.

The rise provided perfect cover for the sub, which had arrived in these strategic waters hours after the first tanker sinking. Havana was keenly interested in the American response, and the Guadiana Banks provided a well-placed observation post from which a quiet submarine could listen to traffic in the channel beyond while remaining lost in the bottom echoes and clutter of the sea bottom.

"Depth to keel?" he snapped.

"Eight meters, Captain," the Diving Officer replied. "Smooth bottom."

"Very well. All stop. Put us on the bottom. Maintain silence throughout the boat."

Gently, gently, the *San Juan* descended until her keel brushed the bottom, stirring up a cloud of sand and mud like a soundless, underwater explosion. An ominous, rumbling creak echoed through the control room as her hull adjusted to this new combination of stresses.

Then she was silent.

"Conn, Sonar."

"Captain," Alvarez responded, speaking into a hand-held microphone. "Go ahead."

"Sir, we're getting some new noises from one of the trailing targets."

"Noises? What noises?"

"Sir, I know this is strange, but it sounded like a missile sub firing an ICBM."

CHAPTER
11

SSCVN-1 *Leviathan*
Off the Guadiana Banks
Thursday, March 30, 0523 hours

The third Barracuda burst from its tube, the bubble cloud of its launch boiling toward the surface. Through his SUBVIEW helmet, Gray watched the last fighter sub's fins deploy, biting the water as the SFV began picking up speed.

"Damn, those things are noisy when they launch," Ramsay said. "I hope you boys don't plan on sneaking up on anyone this way."

"They do make a racket," Gray agreed. For the former aviators, a fighter-sub launch seemed sedate, almost tranquil compared with the raw violence of a carrier deck cat-shot, but given the way sound traveled under water, he wasn't surprised that the sub skipper thought it was loud. "Still, it's not as loud as a missile launch from one of these things."

"Maybe not. But back in the Cold War, every man aboard a boomer knew that once the missiles started flying, every enemy ASW asset in range was going to be on its way. None of them ever expected to survive a real war. Did you know that?"

"No, sir. At least, I suppose I never thought about it."

"That was the whole point of submarine cat-and-mouse in those days. The goal of the boomers and the guided-missile boats was always to be as quiet as possible, while the attack subs tried to sniff them out. The ideal, of course, was to find the other guys' boomer and plant an attack boat on his tail, close enough that if you heard his missile hatches opening, you could nail him."

Gray was familiar enough with *that* bit of history. It was eerie, standing there in *Leviathan*'s control room, able to see *Charlotte* pacing the big Typhoon a few hundred feet to port, and the trio of fighter subs hovering in close formation just above her forward deck. If his father had had access to technology like this when he'd been tracking that Soviet Echo II . . .

"As for an actual launch," Ramsay continued, "well, that would have been noisy enough to bring down the whole enemy fleet. Nuclear depth charges, SUBROC, torpedoes with nuclear warheads . . . you don't need a direct hit to kill a boomer with that kind of hardware.

"So a boomer's only hope of survival was to stay quiet. Once he gave away his position with a missile launch, well, that was pretty much it. Sound travels too damned well underwater. Five times the speed of sound on land . . . almost a mile a second, depending on temperature and salinity and other factors."

Gray decided to take a small gamble. "Is that why Admiral Delacroix is against SFV technology? Because they're noisy and he used to be a boomer skipper?"

"I suppose that could be part of it," Ramsay said. "But don't make the mistake of assuming the

Admiral's against technology. He knows his stuff, or he wouldn't be here in the first place."

"Yes, sir."

Privately, though, Gray was beginning to think of Admiral Delacroix as a battleship admiral.

Change, especially technological change, always came hard and slow for those charged with making the decisions that guided the military into the next generation of tactics and hardware. Long after Billy Mitchell had proven that even the slow and clumsy aircraft of 1921 could sink battleships, most naval officers had continued to think of the battleship as the centerpiece of all naval tactical doctrine. It had taken Pearl Harbor, twenty years after Mitchell's bombing of a condemned German battleship, to prove that carrier airpower was now the decisive arm of the fleet.

For sixty-five years now, aircraft carriers had occupied the position once held in the fleet by battleships, and it had taken the tragedy of the U.S.S. *Lincoln* to encourage research into new submarine technologies like SUBVIEW.

Gray wasn't sure why the pace of change was as slow as it was. He'd heard, though, that when the Air Force had been holding competitions for its Advanced Tactical Fighter program a few years before, they'd had to decide between two prototypes, the F-22 and the F-23. The F-22 had won, not because it was more powerful or faster or more maneuverable or even less expensive than its sleek, diamond-shaped rival, but because the F-22 *looked* more like the F-15 Eagle it was intended to replace. Truly advanced designs—the Navy's A-12 stealth attack plane, the radical F-29 ATF with its forward-swept wings—had devoured hundreds of millions in research and testing but had ultimately been canceled in favor of more familiar designs.

No doubt steamships had continued to sport masts, sails, and rigging long after there was no mechanical reason to carry them simply because a ship without them didn't look right. There appeared to be a built-in conservatism within the ranks of policymakers that resisted all change, and only rarely—the Air Force's F-117 stealth fighter was an example—did technical considerations outweigh the political demands of what *looked* right.

Not that change, of itself, was good. But it *was* necessary, for the simple fact that technology was changing and evolving and spreading with lightning speed throughout the world, as the sinking of the *Lincoln* by a sliver of ultra-dense metal hurled from space had so spectacularly demonstrated. Those old battleship admirals had been overruled at the beginning of World War II only because America's battleship fleet had been wiped out at Pearl Harbor. If the tactical planners didn't heed the lesson of the *Lincoln,* then a disaster even greater than Pearl Harbor would be necessary to prove that aircraft carriers had just become obsolete as well.

"Home Plate, Home Plate, this is Sierra Foxtrot One," Hernandez said, interrupting Gray's thoughts. "We're clear, all systems green."

"Roger, Sierra Foxtrot. Good luck, and watch out for Cuban submarines."

"Roger that, Home Plate. We'll bring one back as a trophy. Maybe we can hang it up in the wardroom."

The three Barracudas were accelerating now, the SUBVIEW system showing a pale churning astern of each vessel representing the sound and the pressure waves emitted by its drive. In seconds, they were dwindling from view, a trio of faint specks highlighted by computer graphics in Gray's SUBVIEW display.

For Morgan Gray, it was strange to realize that he'd already completely embraced the rugged little fighter subs as the logical next step in the ongoing evolution of naval warfare. Perhaps he, too, felt happier with what was familiar, and had accepted the SFVs not because they represented a new and revolutionary military technology, but because they were so similar to the high-performance aircraft he already knew.

It was an unsettling thought. Maybe he had more in common with Delacroix than he was willing to admit.

Cuban Coastal Defense Force Submarine *San Juan*
The Guadiana Banks
Thursday, March 30, 0532 hours

Alvarez leaned over the sonar operator's shoulder, studying the visual display. The tracks there were ragged and crossed a broad spectrum of sound frequencies, like an explosion, rather than the narrowband traces of a propeller or a power-plant pump. "You could not possibly have heard a missile launch," he said. "Why would the Americans be launching ballistic missiles?"

"I know, Captain," the sonar operator said. "But . . . it is what I heard. Listen. I was able to separate it from the background."

He pressed a button, rewinding the recording

made moments before. Alvarez listened intently. The
sound was faint, at the very limit of the Kilo's sonar
range, a thump, a hiss, and the gurgle of compressed
air rocketing toward the surface. It could be a missile
launch . . . or something more prosaic, like divers
exiting an escape trunk.

An American SEAL team? They operated with
greater stealth than that. Alvarez was beginning to
wonder if the Yankees *were* launching missiles, unlikely
as that was. And there was something else, too . . . a
soft, rhythmic pulsing. It might have been another
sub, except that there was none of the usual chirring
of screws.

"Let me hear everything."

"*Sí, Capitán.*"

There was the thrum of a power plant, the stealthy
swish of a Los Angeles–class attack sub. Behind it was
another. And the big submarine . . . certainly not an
American design. For a moment, he wondered if
Carlos had picked up the Islamic Oscar, but *Sharuq*
was operating south of Cuba, and its missile launches
sounded nothing like this.

The big sub's sounds were quite similar to the
Oscar's, though. Twin screws. Almost certainly one of
the American Typhoons.

"If they maintain course, Captain," Carlos pointed
out, "they will pass within eight kilometers of us.
Close enough to smell them."

Alvarez nodded, then handed the headset back.
He was tempted to go active on his sonar. That would
reveal his own position, of course, but it would give
him precise ranges on the targets and, more important, tell them that they were being observed, perhaps
even warn them off.

But his orders were to remain unobserved and to report on any foreign naval activity close to Cuba's twelve-mile limit.

"Are we going to attack, Captain?" one of the other sonar operators asked.

"We will continue to wait," Alvarez said. "And listen. I want more data on this . . . peculiar sound. We will attack only if Cuban waters are violated."

But he was worried by the presence of a missile boat. Why was it here, so close to Cuban waters?

SSCVN-1 *Leviathan*
South of Cabo San Antonio
Thursday, March 30, 0730 hours

"You look damned silly with your head shaved, Commander. You know that, don't you?"

"I *feel* pretty silly, Admiral." Gray passed a hand over his scalp and grinned. "Still, as a combat tactic, it worked. My boys tell me the submarine officers and crewmen already seem to be more open with them. More accepting. The sub people are working well with ours and—"

"It was a stunt, Commander, and I don't like sophomoric stunts in my command. It makes me look bad, and it decreases the fighting effectiveness of this force."

"I would have to disagree, sir. Anything that helps my people work better together, and with the rest of the crew, is going to increase efficiency and morale."

"Bull shit, Commander."

"Yes, sir."

So that was how it was going to be. Delacroix, for

whatever reason, had taken an active dislike to Gray, with the result that almost anything Gray did would be subject to indifference at best, to criticism or out-right attack at worst.

They were in Admiral Delacroix's office, a cramped little cubbyhole off of his cabin, with barely room for a desk, a single chair, and a bookcase mounted directly to the bulkhead. Gray stood while the admiral sat. Two framed photographs rested on the desk, one of an attractive, older woman, the other of a clean-cut young man in an Air Force uniform. On the bookcase, along with the inevitable copies of *Jane's Fighting Ships,* issues of the Naval Institute *Proceedings,* and technical manuals, was an eighteen-inch-long model, painted dark gray and red, of an Ohio-class submarine.

"I can't very well order you and your men to wear wigs," Delacroix went on, "but I can require that you refrain from demonstrations of a similar nature in the future. Your presence aboard this boat is already a disruption, Commander, and one that cheap theatrics are not likely to ease."

"I thought, sir, that the point was to learn how to work together with the sub people." He gestured at his head. "Sure, this was a cheap trick. But the sub-mariners have accepted us now." He chuckled. "They've been holding competitions for the best name for the Barracuda squadron. The latest favorite, I gather, is 'the Chernobylists,' and some of the guys in engineering have shaved their heads, too. That says something, I think."

"I think it's sick, Commander. This is no place for pranks of this kind. I should report you, you know. Conduct prejudicial to good order and discipline. Conduct unbecoming an officer."

"With respect, Admiral, I didn't do this as a prank and I didn't do it to spite you. I did it to bridge the . . . the *social* gap between my people and yours. We're hardly an effective force if we're fighting each other."

Delacroix gave him a cold look. "You needn't lecture me, Commander. I'll not stand for it." He seemed about to say something, but then reconsidered. "We'll forget the disciplinary problem, for now at least. I called you here because I wanted a report on the patrol you have out now. Specifically, I need to know if there's been any sign of foreign submarine activity."

Gray shook his head. "No, sir, none that they've been able to report over the ULTRA-C net, anyway. Lieutenant Hernandez might be able to tell us more when they get back aboard."

"I'll expect a full briefing."

"Of course, sir."

"What kind of search track are you running?"

"They're not on a search track, Admiral. Their orders are to maneuver independently of *Leviathan,* testing communications and sensor systems. If they pick anything up, they'll report it, of course, but they're not specifically hunting for foreign subs."

Delacroix looked up, his brows coming together like thunderclouds. "What's that? What the hell are they doing out there, then?"

"This is still a shakedown for the Barracudas, Admiral. I want my people proficient with the equipment before they enter the waters south of Cuba. And I want to know what both the men and the machines can do before I send them up against a UIR Oscar."

"I needn't remind you, Commander, that we are

on a *combat* mission. Any 'shakedown,' as you put it, should have been taken care of before your squadron became operational."

"There hasn't been time, Admiral. This whole project has been so rushed—"

"That's as poor an excuse as I've heard. If your minisubs aren't ready for combat, they shouldn't have been declared operational and deployed with a *working* task force."

The way he said it made it sound as though he thought Gray himself had ordered the squadron made operational, though that, of course, had been a decision made by COMSUBLANT. There was no point in trying to correct Delacroix's impression, Gray decided. The man would hear it as excuse making, and that would get them exactly nowhere.

"I should disabuse you of one notion," Delacroix continued. "I certainly don't expect your toy subs to go up against an Oscar."

"There's no reason why we couldn't, Admiral."

"Don't give me that crap. An SFV-4B can mount two Mark 62 torpedoes, right? Eighty-pound warheads, right?"

"Yes, sir."

"Enough to peel open the outer skin of an Oscar, but not nearly enough to punch through the pressure hull. You could hurt him, sure, maybe even slow him down, but you'd never kill him. For that, you need one of the big Mark 48 ADCAPs."

True enough. One reason ex-Soviet monster subs like the Oscar and the Typhoon were as large as they were was the standoff distance—as much as three or four feet—between the inner pressure hull and the streamlined outer hull. In the Oscar, there was separation enough amidships between the hulls for the vertical-launch missile tubes. The tiny Mk 62 Seasparrows—more like underwater missiles than true torpedoes—would never breach an Oscar's pressure hull. The Advanced Capability Mark 48s, on the other hand, each with 660-pound warheads, had been specifically designed back in the eighties to kill large Russian submarines.

"I envision using the minisubs in the reconnaissance role, Commander," Delacroix continued. "With their high speed, they could be employed as scouts at the van and flanks of a formation of attack subs. I suggest you begin working on an operational plan to that end."

There was no point in arguing. Gray had the impression that Delacroix was looking for an excuse to relieve him of command or eliminate the squadron, and it suddenly, and quite unexpectedly, was very important to him that that not happen.

"I'll tell you quite frankly, Commander, that I have my eye on you. I do not believe you can fit in aboard this boat, you or that pack of rugged individualists who call themselves 'aviators.' I intend to get the lot of you off my boat and back ashore where you belong just as quickly as I can get you there. For the moment, however, we are stuck with one another. Whether you like the way I run things or not, I will expect you to obey my orders and stay out of my way. Clear?"

"Very clear, Admiral."

"Report to me as soon as your patrol has returned. I will attend the debriefing in person. Now clear out of here."

"Aye, aye, Admiral."

He left.

Fifteen minutes later, Gray was on *Leviathan*'s bridge, accepting the observer's SUBVIEW helmet from an enlisted rating. Captain Ramsay was in the skipper's chair, his head encased by his own SUBVIEW gear.

"Well, Commander?" Ramsay said. "How'd it go?"

"Not so good, Captain," Gray confessed. He slid the helmet down over his head, blinking as the surrounding sea flooded his brain with a deep and dazzling blue. From his vantage point atop the sail, he could see the three open missile hatches forward, each now sprouting something like a badminton net stretched on end between two slender poles and leaning outboard, across the open hatch covers. The fighter sub retrieval gear was designed to fold into a compact cylinder stored in the missile tube beneath the Barracuda but was extended hydraulically for a recovery.

"Sorry to hear that," Ramsay said. In the background, Gray could hear the chatter of the LCO and his staff as they talked to the approaching Barracudas. The fighter subs were still invisible, save as a trio of computer-generated red circles adrift against the blue-green panorama. *Leviathan* had slowed to less than three knots for the recovery operation.

"If I didn't know better," Gray said conversationally, "I'd say he had something against naval aviators."

Ramsay didn't answer immediately. Gray could see the first Barracuda now, coming bow-on toward *Leviathan*, tiny in all that empty water. It gave a different perspective on the recovery, standing here on the bridge and watching the approach instead of sitting in the SFV's cockpit as the LCO guided the craft home.

The Barracuda drifted in above the Typhoon's immense forward deck, nose high, throttles pulled back until the tiny, one-man sub was on the point of stalling. At the last possible moment, it cut power and drifted belly-down into the embrace of the retrieval net raised from Hatch 15. The net sagged with the fighter sub's weight, and magnetic grapples locked home. With its systems shut down, the Barracuda was then drawn slowly, tail-first, back into the gaping maw of its launch tube. Once the outer hatch was sealed and the water was pumped from the tube, access hatches could be opened from the missile deck, allowing the pilots to clamber from their vessels and the squadron support personnel to fuel and service the machines.

The second SFV-4 was on final approach as the first vanished into its tube. The sequence reminded Gray forcefully of carrier-deck operations, with fighters dropping in above the carrier's round-off, landing gear striking the deck in a clatter of noise and sparks as the tailhook snagged the arrestor cable.

"Unhook, Commander," Ramsay said.

The blue-green vista, the gray shadow of *Leviathan*'s forward deck, the incoming Barracudas all vanished, replaced by the fluorescent lights and low-voiced murmur of *Leviathan*'s control room. On the big TV monitor above the helm and diving planes stations, the second SFV-4 was making its final approach.

"Come with me," the Captain said, handing his helmet to an enlisted rating. "Mr. Parker, you have the conn."

"Aye, aye, Captain," the Exec replied formally, stepping up to the low platform and taking the SUBVIEW helmet himself. "I have the conn."

Ramsay led Gray forward to his office, ushered him in, then closed the door behind them.

"I'm going to tell you something, Commander," he said quietly, turning to face Gray, "though maybe I shouldn't. It's not really any of your business, or mine . . . except that everything that affects the operational efficiency of this vessel is my responsibility. You follow me so far?"

"Uh, yes, sir. It's confidential."

"Damned straight, and if you breathe a word, I'll fire you out a missile tube without putting you in a Barracuda first. I brought you up here because what I'm about to tell you is private, and I wasn't about to shout it to the whole control-room crew. Copy?"

"Yes, sir."

"Okay, here it is. The Admiral had a son. Bright kid. Went Air Force instead of Navy, God knows why."

"'Had'?"

"He was killed in 1992. He was a pilot, and he augured in while driving the F-117."

Gray felt cold. "I see."

America's ultra-secret stealth fighter, the "Black Goblin," had been one of those few radical departures from the tried and true, an aircraft that looked more like something from outer space than a jet. So different was the F-117 stealth aircraft that the thing couldn't even stay airborne without microsecond-to-microsecond adjustments to the flight surfaces by the onboard computer. There'd been several nasty crashes even after it had been declared operational.

"So," Captain Ramsay continued, "if Admiral

Delacroix distrusts the high-tech Buck Rogers stuff, maybe he has his reasons, huh?"

Gray had not considered that possibility, and it gave him something to think about. The revelation could explain a lot about Delacroix's conservative approach to military technology, though it didn't explain what he was doing in command of America's first submarine battle group, itself a unit that depended on advanced technology.

"I appreciate your telling me, Captain."

"Bullshit. I never told you a thing."

"Yes, sir."

He felt the deck shift ever so slightly beneath his feet. The last fighter sub had just been captured.

"You'd best get forward and see to your people," Ramsay said. "Dismissed."

"Thank you, sir."

He left the Captain's office with mixed feelings. Having an explanation for Delacroix's attitudes didn't tell him how to deal with them. He still had to work with the man to carry out his orders.

And that, he knew, was going to be a problem.

**Cuban Coastal Defense Force Submarine *San Juan*
Northeast of the Guadiana Banks
Thursday, March 30, 0930 hours**

The *San Juan* waited in absolute silence until the American subs passed. An hour after their sounds had dwindled into the background susurration of the sea, Alvarez ordered the vessel to head northeast at its top speed of sixteen knots, putting as much distance between the Guadiana Banks and itself as possible.

Then, three hours after the Yankee passage, he raised *San Juan*'s radio mast and risked a single, brief, coded transmission.

Cuba's new allies, he knew, would be most interested in the presence of American submarines in these waters.

CHAPTER
12

Situation Room Support Facility
Washington, D.C.
Thursday, March 30, 1053 hours

"We have something on Cuba," the DCI
said bluntly.

The other National Security Council
members listened intently, leaning forward around
the conference table with an air of hushed expectancy.
The way he'd said the words told the President that
Cabot had bad news. He leaned back in his chair, his
left arm folded across his chest and the fingers of his
right hand propping up his head. "All right, Dick.
Let's have it."

Cabot took his place at the podium, turning partly
to face the big projection screen. "Series one," he
called.

Seconds later, a black-and-white photograph
appeared on the screen, an aerial view of a city built
along a waterfront. To the President's eye, it
appeared to be an oblique shot taken from an aircraft flying past the city at low altitude. Details stood
out in sharp relief . . . warehouses, a line of palm
trees, ships tied up at the docks, a track-mounted

hammerhead crane. The city beyond was one of modern-looking buildings along broad avenues laid out along a rectangular grid. Looking carefully at the docks in the foreground, he could make out individual people in the shot, though details of clothing or activities were lost. Code data stripped across the bottom of the picture indicated that the scene had been shot almost a year earlier from a KH-15 satellite orbiting 150 miles overhead.

"This is Cienfuegos, on the southwestern coast of Cuba," Cabot said. "Population about ninety thousand. It's one of the island's principal ports, one hundred seventy miles southeast of Havana. Next."

The picture changed, now clearly a view from space, with rugged folds of mountains enfolding a rectangular bay. The colors were the harsh pastels of a false-color image. Dark purple-blue for water, mottled reds, grays, and yellows for the land.

"This is an infrared photograph taken this morning from orbit," Cabot continued. He removed a pointer from his pocket, extended it, and lightly outlined the bay. "North is at the top. We're looking down on the Bahia de Cienfuegos, a bay roughly ten miles long by four wide with an extremely narrow entrance here to the south." The pointer touched a ragged gray patch on the northeast side of the bay. "This is Cienfuegos up here. During the Cold War era, there was considerable speculation about Soviet naval activity in the area. Specifically, large areas of construction and extensive dredging observed during the late sixties and early seventies suggested that the Russians might be building a submarine base inside the harbor.

"By the late seventies, we were able to verify that

the Russians were using Cienfuegos as a port of call for some of their submarines, particularly their diesel SSKs and their nuclear attack subs. This suggested special facilities had been built here, including, possibly, hardened bunkers housing underground submarine pens. However, there was no hard proof that the Soviets were permanently basing their subs at Cienfuegos, or that they were using it as a staging area for their SSBNs. During this period, you may remember, there was also speculation that the U.S.S.R. had based as many as several tens of thousands of troops on Cuban soil. The administration at that time, however, was eager to play down the possibility of a renewed Soviet presence in Cuba, and, well, let's just say that, by order of the administration, the Agency didn't look for it all that hard. Next, please."

The next shot was also in false color. It zeroed in on the two narrow triangles of land across the bay from Cienfuegos, where they nearly met to cut the bay off from the sea. The water outside the bay was a dark, dark blue, almost black; the water of the bay itself was lighter, with a distinct greenish tint. Boats—a freighter and several small craft—were clearly visible both in the harbor and moving through the straits, their wakes describing clear-cut Vs on the water.

"These are the Cienfuegos Straits," Cabot continued, moving the pointer again. "The bay to the north, the Caribbean to the south. Here on the western headland, you can make out an octagonal structure north of a small, coastal village. That's Castillo de Jagua, a fort built in the seventeenth century to protect the bay from pirates. Notice how narrow the entrance to the bay is . . . less than a mile wide at the narrowest point, and about four miles long, from sea to bay. During the eighties, we photographed Soviet submarines on numerous different occasions, either within the harbor or transiting these straits.

"In 1991, of course, the Soviet Union ceased to exist. Cuba received some further arms shipments from Russia—among them those Kilo-class SSKs—and then fell off the gravy train. Foreign activity in the harbor ceased. Enhance, please."

The view zoomed in on the western headland, and for one dizzying moment the President felt as though he was falling toward that rugged coast. It stopped with a close-up of rugged, seacoast cliffs seen from above, of waves caught frozen in the act of breaking over rocks. It took a moment for the President to recognize several clumps of shaggy, many-armed masses as palm trees, viewed from overhead.

Cabot's pointer tapped an area where green was bleeding from the land and into the blue of the Caribbean. "Thermal imaging has detected a heat plume in the water," Cabot said, "right here. It indicates that water is flowing into the sea from underground . . . from beneath this headland under the castle. The outflow is several degrees warmer than the surrounding seawater and could come either from the bay—which is also warmer than the ocean—or from underground submarine pens. Either possibility suggests a network of large caverns or tunnels beneath this headland and open to the sea, *underwater*."

"It's also possible the Cubans don't follow our environmental standards," someone joked, and there was a titter of laughter from around the room.

"It *could* be sewage being dumped into the sea,"

Cabot agreed, smiling. "Or industrial waste. But there is absolutely no sign of pumping stations or pipelines in this area. Most waste enters the bay proper or is pumped into the ocean at a more accessible spot, further up the coast.

"More likely, in our estimation, is the possibility that the Soviets built far more extensive submarine facilities here than we thought they did, back twenty years ago. If so—and there are now good reasons for thinking they did—then we have to consider the possibility that those facilities have just been reactivated."

"For the UIR?" the President asked.

Cabot nodded. "Yes, sir. We know there's been a lot of high-level traffic between Havana and Cairo lately. And with Tokyo, too, for that matter. There are hints of some kind of special deal in the works, with the UIR paying Cuba in oil for . . . well, we didn't have any idea what the Islamics wanted. Now it's possible that we do. Next."

Another satellite photo of a submarine appeared on the screen. Again it was a Russian boat, alien and dangerous looking, a lean teardrop shape with the long, low sail smoothly blended into the hull. The size of the sail in comparison to the rest of the sub suggested that this was an attack boat, half the length of the monster Oscar.

"An Alfa," Cabot said. "Former Soviet hunter-killer, a high-speed interceptor originally designed to dash into the Atlantic at forty-five knots to engage our subs, then run before we could hit back. These have been upgraded so they're even faster. They can outrun our best attack boat by fifteen, maybe twenty knots, and they're more maneuverable, too. Titanium hulls, so they can go deeper than anything we have.

They have an advanced liquid-metal-cooled reactor, noisy at full output but very efficient.

"This is one of four Alfas purchased from Russia by the Japanese seven years ago, then resold to the Islamic Republic. We caught her five days ago, leaving Alexandria Harbor. Since she didn't leave with the Oscar, we didn't make the connection right away, but we now think it's possible that she was heading for the Caribbean—"

"My God, Dick!" the President exploded. "What the hell do you mean, you didn't 'make the connection'? We were in here yesterday speculating on whether or not the Caribbean situation could be a trap!"

"Yes, sir. To tell the truth, sir, these photos got held up at NPIC for a week, and we kind of lost track of them. It was sheer, damned luck that an analyst from OIA remembered seeing them when he was in at the NPIC lab."

It was, the President thought, the bane of modern intelligence: too many departments, too much compartmentalization, and soon the right hand didn't know what the left was doing. NPIC, the National Photographic Interpretation Center, was slotted under the CIA's Deputy Director for Science and Technology, but it had its own building, right here in Washington. The OIA, the Office of Image Analysis, answered to the Deputy Director for Intelligence and was located at the Agency's headquarters out at Langley.

"So how many of these Alfas are our people facing?"

"Actually, Mr. President, we don't know that they're facing any. As I said, this one Alfa was picked up leaving Alexandria, and we don't even know for sure that she headed west."

"I doubt very much that she's now blockading the Thames. What else?"

Cabot sagged, almost as though admitting defeat. "We've been taking a close look at Alexandria Harbor. Two more Alfas are gone from their usual berths besides that first one, plus two Akulas."

"Two what?" the Secretary of State demanded.

"Akulas," Admiral Shapley explained. "Word's Russian for 'shark.' It's another attack sub, larger than the Alfa. Fast, quiet, and very dangerous. Japan bought two of them from the Far Eastern Republic three years ago, then transferred them to the UIR."

"So, what you are saying, Dick," the President said, "is that we could have as many as six UIR subs in the Caribbean. And that they might be holed up in a former Russian base in Cuba that we never happened to notice before. Is that it?"

"It is," Cabot said stiffly, "a possibility. On the other hand, the Cairo press has been playing up the UIR's crisis with France lately. It's just as probable, maybe more so, that those attack subs are watching France's SSN fleet at Brest."

"If they *are* in Cuba, Mr. President," McIntyre, the National Security Advisor, pointed out, "they've got a safe haven. We're not at war with Cuba."

"We're not at war with the UIR, either," General Paul Drummond, the Chief of the Joint Chiefs, said. "At least not yet. Mr. President, we're operating in an intelligence vacuum here. I recommend that we get a closer look at that Cienfuegos facility, see what's really going on down there."

"Satellite reconnaissance—" Cabot began.

"Isn't worth shit," the general finished. "Not here. Hell, we know the Japanese spy-sat schedule well enough that we can time our most sensitive operations around their passes. Don't you think the Islamics could do the same? And spy sats can't see *beneath* the water, even with blue-green laser technology. Not yet. We need to have a look at the base of that cliff, find out if it's a sewage pipe or Highway One for Islamic submarines."

"That would mean violating Cuban territorial waters," the Secretary of State pointed out. His sour expression made it clear that he didn't approve.

"God damn it to hell." The President drummed his fingers on the hardwood table before him. *Another Cuban missile crisis,* he thought. *But in '62, Kennedy won because he knew the Soviets weren't ready to go to war with us over Cuba.*

But the UIR acts like they're looking *for a shooting war with us. And we can't afford a war right now . . . any more than we can afford to have our oil imports cut by half.*

In 1962, Kennedy had responded to aerial photos of Soviet missiles in Cuba with increased surveillance flights, a naval blockade, and an eyeball-to-eyeball confrontation with Moscow. How, he wondered, would he have handled this?

"There is another possibility," McIntyre pointed out.

"And that is?"

"That they've deployed those attack subs to sink tankers. That seems to be their game, doesn't it? Sink our tankers, make the price of oil skyrocket. How about it, Admiral?"

"Could be," Shapley admitted. "Three Alfas, two Akulas, and an Oscar. That's a force that could do our surface shipping some serious damage."

"And *Leviathan*'s sailing into the middle of it," the President said.

"Actually," Drummond said, "I doubt very much that our subs are the target."

"They're after our tankers."

"That would be the logical conclusion, Mr. President."

"And how do we respond?"

Drummond clasped his hands together before him on the table, studying them intently. "Mr. President, the very best way to kill a sub is with another sub."

"Admiral?"

"It's true, sir. It takes a sub driver to think like a sub driver, and our submarines are better equipped for tracking and identifying hostile subs than planes or surface ships, especially now that we have ULTRA-C and SUBVIEW."

"Exactly," Drummond continued. "I would suggest that we detach *New Haven* and *Charlotte* from the *Leviathan* battle group. We put them on convoy duty, escorting our tankers up from South America. If the Oscar or anybody else tries to take a shot at our tankers, the attack subs'll nail 'em."

"And *Leviathan*?"

"I want to hold her back," Shapley said. "She's got Orca."

"The submarine fighters."

"Yes, sir."

"I suggest," Drummond said, "that we use her to check out the base at Cienfuegos. If there's anything there, *Leviathan*'s people ought to be able to pick it up. And we would not be risking *Leviathan* herself, especially if the attack sub force is in the area."

"Dividing my fleet in the face of the enemy?"

Admiral Shapley said with a crooked grin. The President noticed the slight stress he put on the word "my." "I seem to remember reading somewhere that that is a tactical no-no. Wouldn't it be better to keep the force together? Our first duty is to kill that Oscar."

"Our first duty," the Secretary of State said, "is to protect our shipping in the area . . . and to avoid an incident that could cause an all-out war. This country is sick of war, Admiral, especially after what happened to the *Lincoln*. They will not sit still for another such disaster, especially when elections roll around again in another couple of years. Mr. President, I support General Drummond's idea of escorting our tankers. As for nosing about that Cuban port, well . . . if we can do it without getting caught ..."

"That's what minisubs are for, Henry," Drummond said. "Mr. President, there's no problem with dividing our force. Perfectly sound military doctrine in a situation like this, where we don't really know how the enemy is deployed or what he is deploying. It'd be dangerous if the Islamics were after our subs, yeah, but I'll bet my pension to yours that the Izzies don't even know we're down there yet. Splitting our force gives us a better chance of covering all possibilities and protecting our own assets in the region. It also gives us a better chance of flushing the bastards out and getting the drop on them."

"I hope you're right," the President said. "I hope to God you're right, because you're betting a damn sight more than your pension on this. Three of my subs and over three hundred of our boys, that's what you're betting on this, this hunch!"

"Should we tell *Leviathan* that those other subs may be in the area?"

"Christ," Sarlucci, the Secretary of Defense said. "What do we tell them, that there *might* be attack subs there? Hell, we don't have a thing to go on, don't even know that those other subs are in the Caribbean. My guess is that they're in the Bay of Biscay. We need confirmation first, so we don't go running off half-cocked."

"Dick?" the President said, looking at the DCI. "Can you get confirmation?"

"We're working on it, sir. We'll pass it on as soon as we get it, of course."

"If those subs are in the Caribbean," Shapley said, "two SSNs and a refitted boomer aren't going to be a match for them. If the UIR gets even a hint that our battle group is in the area, well, we might as well pack it in."

But the President already knew that he was going to have to accept Drummond's plan. If six UIR subs were in the Caribbean—and if they were operating out of Cuba—then the United States was looking down the barrel of an all-out world war.

And with Japan behind the UIR, it was a war that America would almost certainly lose.

SSCVN-1 *Leviathan*
Eighty miles southeast of Cabo San Antonio, Cuba
Thursday, March 30, 1405 hours

A bell chimed as the message came off the printer in *Leviathan*'s radio room, where a seaman tore it off, then handed it to the officer of the watch for decoding. The "Z" prefix gave it FLASH priority; within ten minutes it was in Admiral Delacroix's hands.

Originating at the NSA's ultra-secure satellite communications facility at Fort Meade, Maryland, the message had been transmitted by ground station uplink to an Oscar, not the UIR submarine with that code name, but OSCAR-1, the Optical Submarine Communications by Aerospace Relay, a laser communications satellite in geostationary orbit 22,300 miles above the South American equator. Milliseconds later, the burst transmission had been encoded as a modulation in a five-hundred-nanometer laser beam and fired into the Caribbean off Cuba's southwestern coast.

By this time, OSCAR had nearly replaced the old ELF network that had allowed strategic communication with missile subs during the Cold War. That system, relying on the Extremely Low Frequency range from three kilohertz down to three hundred hertz, was low enough that the radio waves were not attenuated by water. Unfortunately, an unalterable law of physics states that the lower the frequency the slower the data transmission rate; it had taken fifteen minutes to transmit a single, three-letter code group meaning, say, "launch your missiles."

With OSCAR, any submarine equipped with ULTRA-C could receive direct transmissions by blue-green laser at depths of up to several hundred feet. Greater depths would be possible someday—assuming that satellites could carry more powerful lasers . . . and assuming precautions could be taken to protect the eyes of aircraft pilots who happened to be caught in the beam.

Delacroix frowned as he read the decoded orders.

Z081715ZMAR
TOP SECRET: ECHO/GREMLIN

FM: COMSUBLANT
TO: CONSUBFLOT1
NEWORDERS

1. POSSIBLE UIR SSN/SSGN BASE ESTABLISHED CIENFUEGOS, DESIGNATE GREEN ANCHOR. SAFE HAVEN UIR SSN/SSGN FOR SUBOPS, WESTCARIB. REQUIRE CONFIRMATION, URGENT.

2. SUBFLOT1 WILL DIVIDE FORCE.

3. NEW HAVEN/CHARLOTTE HEREBY DETACHED ESCORT DUTY, RNDVZ TANGO.

4. LEVIATHAN TO INVESTIGATE GREEN ANCHOR, USING MSS ASSETS AS DEEMED ADVISABLE COMSUB-FLOT1. RECORD UIR TRAFFIC IN AND NEAR HARBOR.

5. USE ALL DUE DISCRETION TO AVOID ENEMY CON-TACT OR DISCOVERY BY LOCAL NATIONALS. LEVIATHAN NOT REPEAT NOT TO VIOLATE CUBAN TERRITORIAL WATERS. USE MSS ASSETS FOR CLOSE APPROACH AND/OR SHADOWING UIR SSN/SSGN UNITS.

6. DESTRUCTION OF ENEMY SSGN REMAINS HIGHEST REPEAT HIGHEST PRIORITY. TACTICAL OPS SHOULD BE DEVELOPED ACCORDINGLY.

7. LEVIATHAN REMINDED THAT UIR SSN ASSETS IN WESTCARIB ARE A POSSIBILITY.

VADM MCCAULEY SENDS.

Delacroix didn't like losing the *New Haven* and the *Charlotte,* but he understood the reasoning behind it. If that UIR sub tried to take out another tanker, a Los Angeles operating in the area ought to pick him up.

More troubling were the orders requiring him to investigate Cienfuegos. Washington didn't have to tell him not to take *Leviathan* in close to the Cuban coast. Hiding a Typhoon within a few miles of the beach was like putting a whale in a swimming pool.

On the other hand, Delacroix wasn't sure the Barracuda squadron was up to handling such a delicate mission. Clearly, this was the sort of mission minisubs were best at—sneaking in close to an enemy's coastal defenses, penetrating harbors for intelligence or sabotage, and slipping away again unobserved.

But after sounding the man out that morning, he was pretty sure that Gray was still thinking in terms of jet fighters and science fiction. Could the man be trusted with a mission with these parameters?

"Use MSS assets," his orders read. That meant the minisubs, and *that* meant that Gray, as squadron commander, was going to *have* to be trusted. There was no way around it.

But maybe there were ways of ensuring that Gray and his aviators stayed within the limits of their orders.

CHAPTER
13

"No *weapons!"* Gray cried, astonished. "My God, Admiral, that's—"

"The ROEs of this mission are specific," Admiral Delacroix said quietly. "You will be penetrating Cuba's territorial waters. There's a lot of commercial shipping going in and out of those straits and, I needn't add, we are not at war with Cuba. The last thing we need in there is an accidental torpedo launch."

"I think," Gray replied with barely restrained anger, "that my people know how to observe the ROEs."

ROEs—the Rules of Engagement. Naval aviators had to deal with them every time a patrol took them close to a potential enemy's airspace. In most situations short of actual war but still involving the possibility of combat, standard ROEs allowed the participants to fire if fired upon. Some missions put special additional restrictions on the participants, like requiring a "weapons free" order from a higher authority before engaging in combat.

But Delacroix was sending the fighter subs in to probe the Cuban harbor completely unarmed.

Gray and the eleven Barracuda officers had gathered in the compartment designated as the squadron's ready room, seated in wooden folding chairs. Admiral Delacroix had assembled the entire squadron in order to pass on his orders personally.

That in itself was out of the ordinary, Gray thought, since admirals generally made their wishes known through their Chiefs of Staff. But there was very little about *Leviathan* or her complement that was *ordinary*.

"It is absolutely vital that this operation be carried out in complete secrecy," Delacroix said. "Arming the SFV-4s would be superfluous . . . and it could jeopardize the mission."

"I'm not sure you want Barracudas on this one at all," Gray pointed out. "I'd think the Dolphins would be better suited to an op like this."

The SFV-4, though brand new, had already gone through several versions and revisions before it had even reached the Navy. The one-seater fighter subs Gray and the others "flew" were SFV-4Bs, since the original production model—the SFV-4A—did not have folding wings and could not be deployed from a boomer's modified missile tubes. The SFV-4C was an experimental, deep-diving research vessel designed for probing extreme depths. The 4D was a two-man sub-launched version, slower than the fighter subs but specifically designed for submarine reconnaissance. Orca researchers had already taken the B, C, and D designations and given them names that fit the character of the vessels. The 4B had become the Barracuda, a fast, vicious killer; the 4C had become the Cachalot, an older name for the Sperm Whale, a champion deep-diver; and the 4D, the sonar-reconnaissance vessel with its blunt snout and rounded hull, had become the Dolphin.

In her twenty missile tubes, *Leviathan* carried twelve Barracudas, one Cachalot, and three Dolphins, leaving four tubes in reserve in case of recovery problems. It seemed clear to Gray that each minisub had its own particular strength. Dolphins might not be able to make eighty knots, but they were far better equipped than Barracudas to lurk around harbor entrances and record the sonar tracks of hostile submarines.

"An excellent point, Commander," Delacroix said. "We will include one 4D in the force composition. Plus four Barracudas. The Dolphin's electronics suite is considerably more sophisticated than the 4B's and its communication laser has a greater range. Who do you suggest as flight leader?"

"Myself," Gray said icily. He could tell that this was one exchange with the admiral he wasn't going to win, and to fight the no-weapons order would get him thrown in hack or worse.

But poking along at a forty-knot crawl, riding shotgun for a sneak-and-peek recon minisub was emphatically *not* his idea of how to best use the 4B's capabilities tactically.

Seegar was sitting in the folding chair next to Gray. "S'okay, CAG," he whispered, leaning over so only Gray could hear. "You can put this down in your report as what *not* to do!"

"At this point," the admiral went on unperturbedly, "I will turn the briefing over to Mr. DuPlessis."

Lieutenant John Henry DuPlessis was *Leviathan*'s

intelligence officer, a young, black-haired Cajun from
Louisiana. He had already tacked two large nautical
charts to the bulkhead, one of Cienfuegos Harbor
and its approaches, the other a larger-scale map
showing all of Cuba and much of the northwestern
Caribbean Sea. Both showed depth soundings in
fathoms; the large-scale chart showed fathom lines, a
topographical map of the sea bottom.

DuPlessis approached the Cienfuegos chart with a
red felt-tip marker in his hand.

"Thank you, Admiral. This chart shows Cienfuegos,
and the area you'll have to cover. According to
Washington, infrared satellite imagery has picked up
a heat plume in the water about here. . . ." He
marked a red box onto the map two miles west of the
narrow entrance to Cienfuegos Harbor. "Washington
isn't sure whether this might represent an undersea
opening to a sub pen built underneath this headland,
or the mouth to a tunnel leading all the way through
the headland and into the harbor. Since the water
inside the harbor is several degrees warmer than the
sea, and since the holding pools in a sub pen would
also be warmer than outside, there is no way to tell by
satellite which possibility, in fact, is the case. Careful
surveillance from orbit has turned up no sign of submarine support facilities either in the harbor or along
the coast outside. If such facilities exist, they must be
hidden underground."

He turned his attention to the large-scale map.
"Our underwater surveys of the region show a mix of
rock bottom and sea grass rapidly falling away from
the beach. The one-hundred-fathom line is quite
close to the coast here, less than two miles out. As you
can see on the larger chart, right here, an arm of the

Yucatán Basin actually reaches up toward the coast from the south. You have readings of twenty-two, even twenty-five hundred fathoms within fifty miles of shore. That's one reason this area was always suspected as a location for a secret Russian submarine base."

Twenty-five hundred fathoms—15,000 feet. On the chart, the Yucatán Basin was like an enormous trench scooped from the sea bottom between Cuba proper and an undersea rise called the Cayman Ridge. The sides of that underwater valley would be as steep as the walls of a canyon.

"The mission profile calls for the minisub reconnaissance force to be released outside Cuba's twelve-mile territorial limit," DuPlessis continued. "Tactical deployment will be at the flight leader's discretion, of course, but it is recommended that the individual minisubs operate as a single unit for mutual close support, with flank and lead elements. . . ."

As the lieutenant droned on Gray listened with half an ear as he thought about the tactical requirements for the op. The more he thought about it, the less he liked it. Using the Barracudas as guards for the slower 4D was about like using Mach-2 Hornets to escort a big, slow prop plane, a Hawkeye or a C-2A. It was done sometimes, certainly, but the mission was by no means an indicator of the F/A-18 Hornets' real abilities. He would have preferred to use the opportunity to push the SFVs' performance envelope, possibly with extended patrols in a large-scale search for the UIR Oscar. How the hell was he supposed to carry out his orders and work out Barracuda tactical doctrine when Delacroix's prejudice kept getting in the way?

"In conclusion," DuPlessis said, "COMSUBLANT

included a reminder that there could be other UIR sub assets in the region, specifically attack subs. We've had no clarification or other alerts from either COM-SUBLANT or the NCA, so we can assume that the cloak-and-dagger types haven't seen any hard evidence of Islamic hunter-killers. Watch your backs, is all."

Then why bring it up? Gray wondered. It sounded to him like a typical committee job, with lots of input from different factions, and other factions trying to tone down the finished product. He raised his hand.

"Yes, sir?"

"Just wondering, Mr. DuPlessis. Will we have access to TENCAP?"

TENCAP—the Tactical Exploitation of National CAPabilities—had been on-line for several years already. It allowed military units in the field, those equipped with the appropriate ground-station equipment and computers, at any rate, to tap into certain American spy satellites directly without having to wait for imagery and data to be routed down the pipeline from NPIC and the Washington intelligence establishment. It would allow *Leviathan* to watch over the mission through a spy satellite's eyes, in detail that would reveal individual soldiers ashore—or the raising of a UIR attack sub's radio mast as it picked up new orders from its base.

"Negative," Admiral Delacroix said from the corner of the room, where he'd been listening, arms folded, to DuPlessis's presentation. "We have the equipment, of course, but tapping a spy sat's transmissions means coming to periscope depth to raise an antenna. Those waters are heavily patrolled by the Cuban *Guarda Coasta*, and, if the Islamics are there, too, I imagine they've added patrols of their own. Not to mention fishing boats, shrimpers, even pleasure boats."

"Yes, sir." Gray kept his voice level and matter-of-fact. "May I respectfully point out that ULTRA-C and SUBVIEW would give us an advantage there? We could be certain that no surface craft were—"

"Commander, I will not risk this command by approaching the surface at any time during the course of this mission. While I grant you that TENCAP is a useful tool, it has little tactical or strategic application in this case. We would be unable to cover a large enough area of land and sea to make the effort *or* the risk worthwhile. In any case, our reconnaissance is being directed against underwater structures or facilities. Are there any other questions?"

Gray said nothing, and the other aviators remained silent, save for the creak of uncomfortable shiftings in their chairs. *In and out,* Gray thought to himself. *We go in close, take a look, and bug for home. And don't worry about whether or not it makes sense. After all, this is the Navy.*

Someone long ago—probably the very first American seaman back in 1775—had pointed out that there were only three ways of doing anything, the right way, the wrong way, and the Navy way, an aphorism that had remained current and fashionable all the way up to the present day. Gray couldn't help but feel a certain amount of cynicism about orders that so clearly reflected Delacroix's bias.

Well, there would be other opportunities to see what the Barracudas could do, *after* Cienfuegos.

And I'm not so sure about those veiled hints about UIR attack subs, he thought. *If they're in the area, it's entirely possible that we'll have plenty of opportunity to push the envelopes on our SFV-4s.*

Except that we're going in unarmed.

Abruptly, irrationally, Gray's thoughts locked onto Wendy, his wife, and on Heather and John, their kids. There'd been no personal communication allowed between *Leviathan* and the shore since the beginning of the patrol. Where were they now? What were they doing? Had they gotten to Kings Bay yet, or were they still back in Connecticut?

As a naval aviator, Gray—and Wendy, too, of course—had always lived with the day-to-day realization that his career was one of the deadliest professions in the world. And if carrier aviation was the most dangerous, sub duty had to run a close second. Navy men were killed all the time, often in shipboard accidents, sometimes in the international "incidents" that continued to mar an uneasy world peace. The U.S. Navy had a splendid safety record, but there were still accidents, "casualties" in submariner terminology. He thought of the crew of that Soviet Echo II.

There were no certainties in such a life, only the hope that they would see each other again.

The no-weapons order left him feeling cornered. If something unexpected happened, they'd be boxed in, unable to fight back, unable to do anything but run. *Damn!* . . .

UIR Oscar-class SSGN *Sharuq*
Thirty miles east of Isla de la Juventud, Cuba
Friday, March 31, 0844 hours

Sharuq was following the hundred-fathom line, traveling east along the steeply sloping canyon wall that roughly paralleled the south Cuban coastline. Astern

lay the Isle of Youth—once Cuba's Isle of Pines—
while to the north, strung east-to-west like the pearls
of a necklace, were the islands and coral reefs and
sandy-bottomed shallows of the Canarreos Archipelago.
To starboard, south, were the black depths of the
Yucatán Basin, where even a vessel as huge and as
powerful as *Sharuq* would be crushed if she attempted
to penetrate more than the upper twenty percent of
those five-kilometer-deep waters.

Captain Siraj al-Badr stood in *Sharuq*'s control
room, hands braced on the chart table as he studied
the Islamic submarine's course. On Yoshio Katatura's
advice, they were on their way back to Cienfuegos,
but al-Badr was beginning to wonder if that was necessarily the right decision.

Clearly, this part of the Caribbean had become the
focus for a tremendous amount of naval activity. At
least four American Perry-class frigates had arrived
within the past twenty-four hours, and some larger
ships as well. But the Japanese advisor was more concerned about the presence of American submarines,
especially their Los Angeles attack subs.

A Cuban Kilo on patrol off the western tip of Cuba
had reported the passage of at least three American
subs early that morning. His government, al-Badr
knew, was paying the Cubans well to act as lookouts
for the UIR base at Cienfuegos. The Kilo captain had
been positive in his identification of two of the passing sonar contacts as Los Angeles attack subs; a third
contact remained unidentified, though the Cuban
captain thought that whatever it was was *muy grande,
muy immenso*. He'd reported it as a possible SSBN.

Al-Badr doubted that the third contact was an
American boomer, and as for the Kilo captain's claim

that he'd actually *heard* a missile launch, well, that was pure fantasy.

Ballistic-missile subs were no longer the muscle behind international diplomacy they'd once been, not with Tokyo's Sky Shield in place and operational. Besides, ICBMs were good for vaporizing cities 10,000 kilometers away but were useless when it came to skirmishes between individual vessels. What would an American boomer in the Caribbean turn its warheads against . . . the *Sharuq*? Cienfuegos, perhaps, assuming the Americans had even guessed that there was a base there yet? Or Cairo?

No. Dropping a MIRVed megaton warhead on *Sharuq* would be like using torpedoes to hunt goldfish in a pond. Nor were the Americans about to drop nuclear warheads on Cuba, not when world opinion—as orchestrated by Cairo—saw them as warmongering imperialists bent on world domination. Cairo and Tokyo both never wasted an opportunity to remind the rest of the world that it was the Americans who'd first used nuclear weapons in war.

And Cairo was certainly not a target, not only because of world opinion, but because by treaty the Japanese Sky Shield had been extended to protect the UIR. In any case, if the Americans were going to nuke Cairo from an SSBN, they wouldn't send the sub to the Caribbean, not when the ICBMs could reach the UIR from Norfolk as easily as from Cuba.

Al-Badr was pretty sure that the Kilo's "very large" contact had been a Seawolf.

Seawolf was a U.S. attack submarine, originally intended to replace their fleet of aging Los Angeles boats by the late nineties. Budget cuts and an increasingly isolationist American Congress, however, had canceled, then revived the expensive Seawolf program several times, and, in the end, only a handful had been built.

At 106 meters from bow to prop, the Seawolf was actually three meters shorter than a Los Angeles sub, but its submerged displacement of 9,150 tons made it almost thirty percent heavier. The bigger sub's more powerful engine and pumps might well make a sonar operator unfamiliar with the Seawolf's sound signature think he'd tagged a much larger vessel, even though it was supposed to be an extremely silent sub.

In any case, Latinos had a tendency toward exaggeration almost as notorious as that of Arabs; it was easy to imagine how a *large* contact could be reported as a *very* large contact . . . and grow with each telling of the story.

Seawolf had extremely sensitive sonar and was ideally equipped to hunt down a marauding missile sub. In al-Badr's estimation, the Americans must have deployed one of their few Seawolfs plus a pair of Los Angeles SSNs to the Caribbean to find and destroy the *Sharuq*.

Katatura agreed with al-Badr's assessment. In fact, that was why the Japanese advisor had urged him to put about and return to Cienfuegos. The Americans would not be able to find them in the underground pens there even if they suspected the base's existence. There, they could wait out the storm of American protest and saber rattling, emerging to strike again after their ASW aircraft and ships had returned to base.

But al-Badr was not so sure. Traveling at an estimated thirty knots, the American attack subs could be anywhere northwest of the Cayman Islands by now, and that included the waters right off Cienfuegos itself. In his opinion, if the Americans *did* suspect the presence of the base, their best strategy would be to post at least one of their SSNs astride the approaches to Cienfuegos, waiting in silence to ambush *Sharuq* as she returned to port. It might actually be safer for the Oscar to stay at sea, relying on her eight-hundred-miles-per-day range to elude her trackers. *Sharuq* could strike, move a hundred miles in three hours, then strike again. So long as she didn't allow herself to be trapped against the Cuban coast or spotted by American aerial or satellite reconnaissance, he could keep up the game indefinitely. At the very least, he could draw the Yankee hunters off to the west long enough to make a dash for Cienfuegos.

And to do that, he needed to find at least one more good target.

"Conn, Sonar," a voice called over the intercom.

"This is the Captain. Go ahead."

"Sir, we're tracking a very large contact at two-one-zero."

Very large? The words brought a shiver to the back of his neck. "How large?"

"Sir, it sounds like another supertanker. It's hard to tell the range, of course, but we're tracking it through a Convergence Zone. The target might be fifty kilometers away, possibly one hundred."

Al-Badr felt the relief wash over him like a splash of cold water. Another tanker, and not the mysterious contact tracked by the Cubans. The timing could not have been more perfect.

Thank Allah for such a conveniently placed Convergence Zone!

In the dark and murky depths in which they sought one another, submarines depended on sound to find their targets and their enemies. Unfortunately, sound was rarely predictable. In particular, the boundary layers between cold and warm water could sometimes trap and channel sound waves across vast distances, allowing submarines to track a target at ranges far greater than would be possible by listening for them directly. The catch was that the focused sound waves emerged from the deep channel only periodically—typically about every fifty kilometers. A sub had to be in just the right spot to catch the reflected sound; ten kilometers to either side, and the distant target could not be heard.

Al-Badr did not believe in coincidence. This *had* to be the hand of Allah!

"Diving Officer!" he snapped. "New course!"

"Ya sidi!"

Al-Badr glanced around the control room, looking for Katatura's familiar shadow. Then he remembered that the Japanese officer had retired to his bunk hours before, after a long, long night in *Sharuq*'s sonar room, listening for the American SSNs. Well, even advisors needed to sleep some time.

"Bring us to new course, two-one-five." He wanted sufficient lead on the target to position *Sharuq* in its path. "Make revolutions for thirty-five knots."

"New course, two-one-five, thirty-five knots."

He glanced at the clock on the bulkhead, mentally juggling the schedules of the Japanese *Me* satellites. "And come to periscope depth." *Me*-three was almost directly overhead now, in a perfect position to capture the distant target. Better and better!

"Ali," he called to his executive officer. "Sound Battle Stations."

A klaxon sounded. *Sharuq*, readying for war, raced southwest toward her new prey.

CHAPTER
14

U.S.S. *New Haven*
Forty-five miles southeast of Isla de la Juventud, Cuba
Friday, March 31, 0855 hours

Commander Charles T. Logan, captain of the Los Angeles–class attack sub *New Haven*, held the sonar headset against his ear, straining to pierce the murky cloud of sound that surrounded the vessel. *New Haven* was at a depth of 400 feet, traveling northwest at the rather leisurely speed of fourteen knots. Three techs sat at the sonar console, looks of intense concentration on their faces.

"You sure you were listening to a truck on this thing, Lucky?" he said to the sonarman 1st class who ran *New Haven*'s sonar department. "I don't hear squat now."

"Lemme play it back for you, Skipper." Vincent Lucciano—his tough-guy Italian image made him "Lucky Lucciano" to his shipmates—reached up and flicked a switch. Logan closed his eyes as he listened to the recording Lucciano had pulled moments earlier, shutting out the pervasive, background hum of electronics, the clattering, ghostly click of shrimp, the distant rumble of surf. . . .

There. Faint, almost lost in the background, but he could hear it, the faintest of rumbles, overlaid by a faint buzz, almost a whine. Opening his eyes again, he looked at the sonar screen where Lucciano was displaying again the multichannel cascade of sonar traces.

"I make it twin screws, Skipper," Lucciano said. "And a big mother of a pump. Definitely nuclear, definitely a cow. I say it's an SSGN."

"Shoot, Lucky. You tagged *Leviathan*. She's up that way somewhere."

"*No,* sir." The sonarman looked hurt. "I've been listening to the *Levy* for a week now, an' you think I'd make a mistake like that?"

"No offense, Lucky," *New Haven*'s captain said. "Just covering all the bases. What'd the library say?"

All American submarines carried a digitized library of sounds, everything from biologics—whales, fish, and other noisy sea creatures—to every logged sub and skimmer. Often, the library could tell you not only what class of vessel you were listening to, but which individual ship you'd caught.

Of course, a good sonarman could do that too, and often with a hell of a lot less to go on than the computer could work with.

"Well, Lucky?"

"Aw, shit, Skipper—"

"What did the computer say?"

"'Insufficient data.' 'Possible Soviet PLARB.' Hell, I think the poor thing misses the good old days when it was hunting Russian boomers."

"Like *Leviathan*."

"But Skipper, the computer don't know diddly. It's got the *Levy* in its database but not that murderin'

Izzy. Closest thing it can figure given that heavy, twin-screw signature is a big ol' PLARB. But I'm tellin' you this is something else. I think it's a PLARK."

The Russian acronym stood for *Podvodnaya Lodka Atomnaya Raketnaya Krylataya*, the old Soviet designation for their nuclear-powered guided missile boats. Like their Oscars.

Logan lowered the headset but kept studying the visual sonar trace. Lucky Lucciano was good, damned good, though as with any talented professional you had to handle him with gloves some times. The man rated careful handling, though, even more than the several million dollars' worth of sound equipment that was his domain. All the fancy ULTRA-C and SUBVIEW gear in the world couldn't match a good set of ears behind *New Haven*'s state-of-the-art sonar system. If Lucciano claimed he'd heard someone on the other boat *say* they were aboard an Oscar, he'd be willing to believe him.

"Best guess on the range, Lucky."

"Extreme. We're getting a little bit of leakage through a deep sound channel northeast of us. I'd say thirty-five miles, at least. If we're getting some scattering off the thermal layer, maybe forty."

Over an hour at top speed . . . and while *New Haven* was racing along at thirty-three knots she wouldn't be able to hear a thing but the rumble of her own passage. She'd have to play the submariner's usual hunting game—a fast dash, followed by drift and listen, then another dash.

And pray the other guy wasn't as good with his hydrophones as your boys were.

"You done good, Lucky. Designate the contact Oscar One and keep on her."

"Yes, *sir*!" Lucky tilted the blue ship's ball cap back on his head and beamed. Logan glimpsed money changing hands as he turned and walked out of the compartment.

Back in the control room, he fished his reading glasses from the pouch he carried in his pocket, perched them on his nose, and took a hard look at the chart where a seaman had already marked in grease pencil the best guess at Oscar One's position.

The *New Haven,* after receiving her new orders the previous afternoon, had proceeded to Point Tango, a featureless spot on the water south of Grand Cayman, where she'd rendezvoused with two northwest-bound vessels. One, the *Corinthian Challenge,* was a supertanker, as long as an aircraft carrier and carrying 200,000 tons of petroleum. The other was the U.S.S. *Taylor,* a guided-missile frigate of the Oliver Hazard Perry class.

Taylor was the official escort for the tanker and was preceding the lumbering *Challenge* on a fourteen-knot crawl toward the Yucatán Channel. *New Haven* had taken up station twenty-five miles off the tanker's starboard side. Logan had guessed that an attacker lurking somewhere south of Cuba would have to make an approach on the convoy from that direction. Twenty-five miles, he'd thought, would give the *New Haven* plenty of maneuvering room.

Studying the parallel black arrows marking *New Haven*'s course and that of the two skimmers, he decided he'd made a pretty fair initial deployment. It would have been nice to have the bad guy pop up a little closer . . . but he'd not wanted to risk having the Oscar get between him and his lumbering charges.

"Helm, come to zero-two-zero, please. Mr. Hood?" He peered up at his Executive Officer over the tops of his glasses.

"Yes, sir."

"I'll have General Quarters sounded, please."

"Aye, Captain. Are you going to alert the *Taylor* to the contact, sir?"

Logan considered this, balancing a submariner's almost instinctive need for stealth against the need to warn *Taylor* and the supertanker of the threat to the east. "We'll use a delayed message drop," he decided. "Fifteen minutes." It would take at least that long for the enemy to prepare for firing, if he was really there, and if that was what he was planning to do. And in fifteen minutes, *New Haven* would be eight miles away.

"Very well, Captain. Sounding General Quarters."

A moment later, the klaxon sounded three short bursts and *New Haven*'s crew was moving with quick, silent efficiency to their posts.

U.S.S. *Taylor*
Forty-five miles south of Isla de la Juventud, Cuba
Friday, March 31, 0910 hours

The signal buoy, released from a hatch on *New Haven*'s afterdeck, had risen rapidly through the water and broken the surface. Fifteen minutes later, its timer had triggered the digital recording loaded into its compact memory.

Aboard the U.S.S. *Taylor,* her captain, Commander Michael C. Dixon, read the printout handed to him by a radioman, then checked the numbers against the hourly markings on the big chart table behind the bridge.

"*Haven* thinks she's flushed something," he told his Exec, a straw-haired Kansas boy named Gary Wentworth. "Maybe an Oscar. Whatever it is, it's sixty miles to the northeast, maybe more."

"An Oscar?" Wentworth asked. "Damn, those suckers could nail us from four times that far."

"Agreed. Let's sound GQ. And tell the boys in radar to stay sharp."

"Aye, aye, Captain. I'll pass the word."

"Now General Quarters, General Quarters" sounded from the bulkhead speaker a moment later, interspersed with the harsh rasp of the alarm. "All hands, man your battle stations."

Ignoring the racket, Dixon walked over to the starboard side of *Taylor*'s huge, box-shaped bridge, peering aft at the rust-streaked metal mountain that was the *Corinthian Challenge*. That monster was plowing along through gentle seas a mile astern of the *Taylor*, and still she looked as big as an island. She would make a splendid target for a cruise missile's radar.

An aide approached with helmet and life jacket. "Helm!" Dixon snapped as he shrugged into the jacket and let the aide help him with the straps. "Come to zero-four-zero, speed twenty-five knots." He caught Wentworth's puzzled look and grinned. "We're not doing them any good up here. If that Oscar's to the northeast, I want to be in a position to intercept whatever they send our way. Tell the radio shack to inform *Challenge* of my intention."

Heeling sharply to port, *Taylor* cleaved a broad quarter circle into the surface of the sea with her wake.

*   *   *

UIR Oscar-class SSGN *Sharuq*
Twenty-four miles east of Isla de la Juventud, Cuba
Friday, March 31, 0918 hours

"The American frigate is turning toward us, Captain," *Sharuq*'s Weapons Officer reported. "And increasing speed! Could he have seen us?"

"Calm yourself, Hussein," al-Badr said. "He is fifty miles away. We are not exactly within his line of sight, eh?"

The image on the radar screen relayed from the Japanese satellite had caught the frigate in midturn. It was a wide-angle shot that showed both ships, the immense and lumbering tanker astern, the nimble frigate scarcely half the monster's length out in front. The frigate was turning sharply, her wake showing the froth of suddenly increased power. The next scan came through, showing the frigate now much further into her turn and still accelerating.

"I make the tanker to be the *Corinthian Challenge*," Commander Ibrahim reported, his green book open on the chart table before him. "Liberian flag. Three hundred thirty meters, two hundred thousand dry-weight tonnage. Two days out of Paramaribo."

"And the other?"

"The United States Navy has something like fifty FFGs. Since the satellite's radar cannot read hull numbers, it is impossible to tell them apart."

"But it's definitely a Perry-class frigate."

"Yes, sir. Standard antiair or Harpoon antiship missiles, Mark 46 torpedoes for ASW defense, one 76mm rapid-fire cannon, and one Phalanx close-defense Gatling gun. Single screw, thirty-six-knot maximum speed."

"There, Hussein, you see?" al-Badr said with a smile. "Scarcely a threat at this range!"

Sharuq was cruising at periscope depth, her satellite mast extended above the surface to receive the *Me* reconnaissance satellites telemetry. Al-Badr turned from the radar screen in time to see Katatura entering the bridge. "I'm glad you could join us, Commander," he said, grinning. "I decided that it was not quite time to run for home after all."

"What target?" The Japanese advisor's face was impassive, but al-Badr fancied he read nervousness there. For some reason, he thought, Katatura was not wholly committed to this mission. Why was that?

"Another large tanker. And a bonus, an American guided-missile frigate as escort."

"The frigate is definitely positioning itself between us and the target," a radar officer said. "It's coming back to a course parallel to the tanker, about two kilometers to the northeast."

"The frigate's captain could be positioning himself to intercept our missiles," Katatura pointed out.

"If they even know we're here, Yoshio. In any case, it doesn't matter. We will fire four missiles and saturate their defenses. Range!"

"Seventy-seven kilometers." The Weapons Officer's fingers snapped across the switches on the missile panel, lighting the amber lights one after another. "Inertial navigation set. Self-arming initialized. Missiles are on internal power. All green."

"Flood missile tubes five, six, seven, and eight." He could hear the flushing sound, as water flooded into the open tubes.

"Tubes flooded, Captain."

"Open outer hatches."

"Outer hatches three and four are open, sir. Falcons ready to fire."

"*Taiyib!*" al-Badr cried. "Excellent. Fire number five!"

Compressed air blasted into tube four, lifting its deadly contents clear of the Oscar's hull and into the sea. The deck canted beneath al-Badr's feet, then righted itself.

"Number five is fired, sir."

"Fire six!"

Muted thunder shook the water, echoing through the hull.

"Six fired."

"Fire seven!" A pause. "Fire eight!"

One after another, like whales broaching in the sun, the SS-N-19 missiles leaped into the sky in white spray, smoke and thundering flame. Booster rockets dropped away like tiny bombs, as wings unfurled and ramjet motors took hold.

Like winged death, the missiles raced for their target, skimming the sea at Mach-plus speed.

U.S.S. *New Haven*
Forty-five miles southeast of Isla de la Juventud, Cuba
Friday, March 31, 0920 hours

"Shit!" The 2nd class sonar tech's voice broke with the excitement. "Lucky, did you hear that? Like they just flushed all their toilets at once!"

"I heard, Kelly. Conn, Sonar!"

"Conn." It was the Skipper's voice. "Go ahead, Sonar."

"Captain, we have a definite cruise-missile launch, repeat, definite launch, time zero-nine-two-zero and two-one seconds! I think Oscar One just popped four birds at the *Challenge*."

"Acknowledged."

In the control room, Captain Logan exchanged a meaningful glance with his Exec. "We've got a conflict, Number One."

He was not referring to the battle that had just begun, but to the interpretation of *New Haven*'s orders. The latest directive from Washington specified two objectives: find and sink the SSGN stalking American shipping, and escort and protect that shipping. Until this moment, those two goals had been complementary. Now, however, Logan had to make a choice.

"Diving Officer!" he snapped. "Take us up! Periscope depth!"

"Periscope depth, aye, aye, Captain," the Diving Officer replied. "Diving planes, fifteen degrees up bubble."

"Planes, fifteen degrees up bubble, aye, sir." *New Haven*'s deck tilted sharply as her bow came up.

Logan did a fast mental calculation. By the time they rose from 400 feet, it might be too late.

"Blow main ballast," he ordered. "Emergency surface."

"Blow main ballast, aye, sir. Emergency surface."

As an alarm sounded, compressed air blasted into the attack sub's ballast tanks, emptying them of over eight hundred tons of sea water. With a whooshing roar, *New Haven* rose toward the surface.

*   *   *

UIR Oscar-class SSGN *Sharuq*
Twenty-three miles east of Isla de la Juventud, Cuba
Friday, March 31, 0920 hours

"Captain, Sonar!"

"This is the Captain."

"Definite contact, sir. A submarine is blowing its tanks. Bearing one-eight-five!"

"Convergence Zone?"

"Negative, sir. I think this is a direct contact!"

Al-Badr's face clouded. An American Los Angeles, it had to be, and at a range of less than thirty kilometers! He'd underestimated them. They were shadowing the tanker . . . *using* the tanker as bait to catch him!

"Down mast array! What is the depth here?"

"One thousand meters, bottom falling sharply, sir."

They were still above the steep drop-off of the Cayman Trench. Deeper water lay to the south, shallower to the north.

"Helm, left full rudder! Come to course zero-nine-zero. Stand by to dive!" He would swing back to the north, seeking to lose the big Oscar in the sonar shadows of the cliff face.

"If I might offer a suggestion," Katatura said.

Al-Badr glared at him. "What is it?"

"If this is a trap, the situation offers us an opportunity to trap the trappers."

The captain's face cleared. Katatura was right, damn him. He'd reacted hastily, without thinking the situation through. Reacted as the Americans must be expecting him to react.

"Very well. Ali! Raise the radio mast."

Ibrahim blinked at him. "Sir?"

"Raise the mast again!" He touched an intercom switch. "Radio room! This is the Captain! The instant our mast clears the surface, transmit the following message. . . ."

U.S.S. *New Haven*
Forty-five miles southeast of Isla de la Juventud, Cuba
Friday, March 31, 0922 hours

New Haven's radar mast broke the surface, followed seconds later by the upthrust blade of her sail, then the rounded bullet of her bows, streaming water in an explosion of white foam. The Oscar's cruise missiles were fast enough that they would have already passed *New Haven*'s position, but the attack sub was in a good position to illuminate those elusive targets, and possibly make *Taylor*'s job of screening the tanker a bit easier.

Like all radars, the range of the periscope-mounted BPS-15 search radar on a Los Angeles–class SSN depended partly on the target's size. A cruise missile, with its angular wings and boxy air scoops and engine, could be picked up at a range of about twenty miles, though it was easy to lose the low-flying weapons in surface clutter.

"Target!" *New Haven*'s radar operator called. "Multiple targets! I make it four contacts, bearing two-two-three, on course two-one-eight at eleven hundred knots, range one-one miles!"

"Plug it through to the *Taylor*," Logan said. Damn, those babies were traveling! They must have zipped over *New Haven*'s position scant seconds before they'd surfaced. "Priority flash."

A moment later. "Conn, Radio Shack. *Taylor* acknowledges. They say 'Thanks for the assist.'" There was a moment's hesitation. "And sir? ESM's got something screwy from Oscar One. Sounds like they're on the surface and transmitting."

"Transmitting? Transmitting what?"

"No clues, Skipper. It's voice, but it's in Arabic and it's in code. I can tell you that they sound excited."

"Roger. Are you recording?"

"That's affirmative, Skipper."

"A call for help," Lieutenant Commander Hood suggested.

"That's what I think. They heard us blow our tanks and they're calling in the cavalry."

"Conn, Radar. Targets passing out of range."

"Very well. Diving Officer! Get us off the roof. Make depth four hundred feet, course zero-two-zero."

"Four hundred feet, aye, sir. Course zero-two-zero, aye, sir."

"Make revolutions for thirty-three knots."

"Revolutions for three-three knots, aye, aye, sir."

Logan stood impassive, listening to the litany of relayed orders and repeated response. The system, set up half a century before by Hiram Rickover, the founder of the modern nuclear-submarine navy, had the comforting feel of a religious ritual, of something solid and reassuring. *New Haven*, her decks already awash, shuddered slightly as she slipped once again beneath the waves.

"If they are calling for help, sir . . ."

Logan grinned at his Exec. "We've got 'em pinned, Number One. Twenty miles away, with coral reefs, sand spits, and islands just beyond. I think we can nail them before the cavalry arrives."

"That rather depends on just what the cavalry is, doesn't it?"

For response, Logan picked up the intercom mike. "Reactor Room, Conn. Let's see what we can crank out of this old boat. Give me one hundred five percent on the reactor!"

New Haven streaked through the sea toward the northeast.

CHAPTER
15

U.S.S. *Taylor*
Forty miles south of Isla de la Juventud, Cuba
Friday, March 31, 0923 hours

Taylor had not needed *New Haven*'s radar warning. Her SPS-49 air search radar, mounted much higher on her superstructure than a submarine's periscope radar, could track a target as small as an incoming SS-N-19 at three hundred miles, and her SH-60F Oceanhawk helicopters could extend her search range even farther. Thanks to the SSN's buoy-relayed warning, *Taylor*'s entire crew was already on combat alert. They'd begun tracking the four ship-killers almost as soon as they broke the surface.

"Hard left rudder!" Dixon snapped. He glanced at Wentworth. "We'll show 'em our sting."

Taylor had three separate weapons systems that could be brought to bear on the approaching cruise missiles. Her SM1MR Standard missiles, able to track and knock down anything at ranges between three and twenty miles, provided her with her first line of defense. Her Italian-made OTO Melara Mark 75 cannon, mounted on her superstructure amidships, could hurl radar-guided 76mm shells better than two and a

half miles, though accuracy against targets as small
and fast as a cruise missile was questionable.

And finally, there was her Mark 15 Phalanx, an
automated, rapid-fire Gatling cannon mounted aft
above *Taylor*'s helicopter hangar in a fifteen-foot-high,
white-painted silo—a devastating weapon that could
fling streams of 20mm, depleted uranium shells into
the path of approaching missiles at the incredible rate
of fifty rounds per second. The Phalanx—nicknamed
R2D2 by most naval crews for its round-topped, fire-
hydrant resemblance to the character in a popular science-fiction movie—was definitely a weapon of last
resort, however, for its range against aerial targets was
limited to about nine tenths of a mile.

"Bridge, Combat," the Combat Officer's voice
sounded over the bridge speaker. "Range twenty-two
miles and closing."

"Commence fire when they're in range. Countermeasures on automatic!"

The pace of modern naval warfare is terrifying in
its sheer speed and violence. Most weapons must be
aimed by radar and managed by computer, and
human reactions are far too slow to provide more
than minimal guidance. A rapid *thud-thud-thud* sounded
from the deck outside, as *Taylor*'s Rapid-Bloom Off-board
Countermeasures—RBOC for short—began lobbing
chaff shells into the sky from clusters of stubby
launch tubes set into the deck. Like a smoke screen
designed for an enemy that saw by radar instead of
light, the shells burst in midair, flowering into invisible clouds of aluminized plastic designed to provide
the oncoming cruise missiles with multiple false targets . . . and to mask the small island of the *Corinthian
Challenge* a mile beyond.

Forward of the bridge, meanwhile, *Taylor*'s Mark 13 launcher, a Standard missile slung from its single launch arm, spun suddenly, the missile's pointed tip seeking a featureless spot in the sky.

"Firing SM1!" There was a flash from the forward deck, a roar like a magnified *chuff* from a fire extinguisher. Smoke billowed skyward and exploded past the bridge windows as the missile hurtled away at the tip of a rippling white contrail.

In the smoky haze forward, the Mk 13 launcher swiveled, automatically positioning its arm above a hatch that slid open magically in the deck underneath. Another missile from the forward magazine elevated into place and locked home as the hatch slid shut behind it.

With a shrill, hissing roar, the second missile rocketed into the sky, its contrail curving over once it was clear of the ship, following the first as it arrowed toward the northeast. Standard missiles used semiactive homing, following the radar illumination provided by the ship's targeting radar.

A war, meanwhile, was being waged between hostile computers and electronics suites, with the cruise missiles seeking to lock onto the largest target in the area—the *Corinthian Challenge*—and *Taylor* trying to jam their radars. It was a war in which *Taylor* had the advantage in electronic power and range, but in which the approaching missiles had the advantage in sheer speed. Closing at supersonic speeds, those missiles could cover that twenty-mile gap in less than ten seconds, a small eternity for computers, but only a few heartbeats for a human.

What followed, then, happened in the blink of an eye.

The first Standard missile, tracking the lead cruise missile, missed clean. The chances of a kill—given the target's small size and the problem of back-scattering from the waves—were less than fifty percent. The second SM1 locked onto the SS-N-19 a mile behind the first and struck home with a flash and a puff of smoke low in the sky, lashing the water underneath to a froth with hurtling bits of shrapnel.

By the time the third Standard was ready to fire, the lead cruise missile had already passed inside the three-mile minimum range; the Standard shrieked aloft, tracking the last missile of the original four, still five miles out.

Chaff, meanwhile, continued to blossom about the *Taylor,* from close to the surface to a thousand feet overhead. The cruise missiles, guided by rather simple-minded computer brains, were programmed to fly to a certain point fed to them before launch, then switch on their radars, find the largest radar echo within range, and home on that. The lead missile, registering a particularly bright return some ten degrees to port, adjusted its course and began the terminal phase of its flight, climbing high above the sea for a final, high-speed plunge into its target. Seconds later, it arrowed through an expanding cloud of chaff and struck the water, detonating in a thundering explosion half a mile astern of the *Taylor.*

Taylor, meanwhile, was halfway into her turn, a maneuver that gave both her Mk 75 cannon and her stern-mounted Phalanx clear lines of fire on the remaining two missiles. The Mk 75 opened up first, its ringing *crack-crack-crack* echoing across the water as it tried to mark down one of the hurtling targets, slamming shells into the sea in geysering fountains of spray. Both missiles were climbing now, angling higher as they entered the terminal phase of their hunt. One passed within a mile of the *Taylor,* and the frigate's Phalanx joined the fight.

The Phalanx was *Taylor*'s Close-In Weapons System, or CIWS, an acronym usually pronounced "sea-whizz." Computer-guided, radar-directed, the rotating barrels spun, elevated, then fired, the weapon's shrill, buzzsaw shriek deafening at close quarters. The J-band pulse-doppler radar in the silo tower simultaneously tracked the target and the stream of projectiles, automatically correcting the aim.

Half a mile across the water, depleted uranium slivers two and a half times denser than solid steel slammed into the third cruise missile, shredding its metal skin like tissue and sending the wreckage tumbling, a flaming avalanche of debris. At the same instant, the third Standard missed its target. The CIWS spun, acquiring a lock, elevating its rotating barrels—

Too late!

At better than Mach 2, the last cruise missile plunged toward the *Taylor.* The RBOC had broken the missile's lock on the big tanker, but chance and wind had allowed it to lock onto the frigate instead of a decoying cloud of chaff. Though the CIWS Phalanx was swinging to intercept this final threat, this time the advantages of speed and time outweighed those of sophisticated electronics and countermeasures. The cruise missile crashed into *Taylor*'s starboard stern quarter, striking her boxy helicopter hangar just forward of her fantail helicopter flight deck.

And kept on going.

The rugged little Perry-class frigates had been criticized almost since the launching of the first one in 1977. The terrible damage done to the U.S.S. *Stark* by an Iraqi-launched Exocet in 1986 had publicized their weakness. Thin-skinned, single-screwed, and with only a single Phalanx for close-in air defense, they were widely derided as being vulnerable to the point of uselessness in any hard fight. This time, however, a weakness was turned to the ship's advantage.

Had one ton of high explosives detonated inside *Taylor*'s after hull, the explosion would have at least torn her stern off and sent the frigate and 185 men to the bottom in seconds. Taylor's aluminum skin was so thin, however, that the massive cruise missile actually punched clear through the helicopter hangar, smashing in one side and out the other, taking half of an Oceanhawk and part of the deck with it and emerging five feet above the waterline on the port side aft.

The warhead exploded as it hit the water. The blast rocked *Taylor* onto her starboard beam, coming perilously close to rolling her, and it picked up the jagged-edged wreck of the hangar block and peeled it off the afterdeck as easily as a hurricane might flatten a shack of sheet tin and plywood. The Phalanx gun tower was sent whirling into the air; forward, the ship's exhaust stacks in their squat, rounded tower were crumpled and smashed, and forward of *that* the Mk 75 turret was ripped from its mountings and slammed into the frigate's SPG-60 radar tower. On the bridge, Dixon and every man with him were slammed to the deck.

The helicopter's fuel tanks lit off a second later, while the sky was still choked with white mist and smoke and made deadly by scything bits of shrapnel.

Flame exploded across *Taylor*'s fantail, shredding
what was left of the hangar and sending a heavy black
cloud boiling into the morning sky. Below decks,
water was pouring into the engine room, and the ship
began settling by the stern.

The damage was not fatal—yet. But her survival
now depended entirely on the efforts of her damage-
control parties.

And on the determination of her crew.

UIR Oscar-class SSGN *Sharuq*
Twenty-three miles east of Isla de la Juventud, Cuba
Friday, March 31, 0924 hours

"A hit!" the sonarman yelled. Across sixty miles, the
detonation on *Taylor*'s fantail had sounded like a
deep, solid thump in the water. "We got a hit!"

The crew cheered, and joined in chanted shouts,
"Allah akbar! Allah akbar!" Yoshio Katatura watched
and listened. He noticed that al-Badr did not join in
the shouting but stood beside the periscope housing,
a worried look creasing his bearded face.

This is a dangerous time, he thought. *They are so easily
carried away by emotion. They could overreach themselves.*

He walked across the control-room deck, until he
was standing by al-Badr's elbow. "How close is the Los
Angeles?"

"Thirty kilometers. Perhaps less. The technicians
heard him directly, not through a Convergence
Zone."

"If you could hear him, he can hear you. Perhaps
you should restore order with your men."

The eyes al-Badr turned on Katatura were large,

cold, and seemed emptied of feeling. He was a man, the advisor thought, who has come close to losing all, who is still savoring that special dread of risking every-thing and seeing it nearly destroyed. For the first time, Katatura realized how important *Sharuq* was to this man. He looked now as though he were being pursued by the legions of hell.

That Los Angeles scared him, Katatura thought. *Good. He needs to learn caution.*

"Let them cheer," al-Badr said. Clinging to the periscope housing, he paused and looked around the narrow, crowded compartment. "If the enemy is run-ning at full speed, he cannot hear us anyway."

"And when he stops to listen?" The American dash-and-drift tactics were well known.

"Then perhaps—" Al-Badr stopped, then turned a cold grin on Katatura. "Perhaps the cheers will lure him on."

Katatura felt afraid.

Orca Ready Room, SSCVN-1 *Leviathan*
Twenty miles south of Cienfuegos, Cuba
Friday, March 31, 0930 hours

"Stand by to flood tube."

"Ready for flood. Go ahead."

"Flooding Tube Two-zero."

Again, Gray felt the Barracuda shudder as sea-water rushed in to fill the launch tube. His eyes skipped across the control panel one last time. Had he forgotten anything?

"Clamps released," said the voice in his headset. "Deck hatch open. Depth is four hundred feet, speed zero-three knots, pressure one-seven-eight psi."

"Confirm hatch open," Gray said, reading the tell-tale on his console. "Chernobylist Leader is ready for launch."

"Roger, copy that." He heard the laughter in the LCO's voice. The joke about the squadron's members being bald because they were radioactive mutants had taken hold throughout *Leviathan,* a typically skewed piece of gallows humor that appealed to the nuke submariners.

"I read Blue Hunter One, ready for launch," the controller added, using Gray's proper call sign. "Launch in three . . . two . . . one . . . *launch!*"

Acceleration shoved him back in his padded seat, and the SFV-4B fighter sub slid clear of its cradle, rising above *Leviathan*'s forward deck on a billowing cloud of bubbles. He switched on the Barracuda's SUBVIEW, and the ocean surrounded him, emerald and blue and achingly beautiful in a silence that went on and on as his stubby fins deployed behind his cockpit. *Leviathan* filled the sea below and behind him, a gray, man-made mountain hanging in empty blue space. The bottom, reaching toward the light somewhere behind *Leviathan* at the point where tiny, flat Guano Cay pierced the surface, was already a mile beneath the Barracuda's keel. The sea bottom here was lost in the blue darkness below.

Putting the stick over, he dived, gaining speed, letting the pressure in the water intakes build until the hydrojet engine kicked in, filling the cockpit with its soft, pulsing hum. Another Barracuda drifted into view to starboard, pulling close alongside as he angled toward *Leviathan*'s bow. Unlike when he was flying a fighter plane, he could not see the other pilot through a transplex canopy; the bulbous nose was anonymously opaque. But he could see the number picked out in white paint on the other craft's bow: 102. Mimicking the nose number of a naval fighter, it identified the other fighter sub as Seegar's craft.

Seen close up, it was startling how much a Barracuda resembled a dolphin. The swell of the cockpit forward seemed patterned on the marine mammal's bulbous head; the sharply anhedral fins jutting down to either side of the water intakes were like flippers, while the stabilizer rose from the back like a dorsal fin. There were no tail flukes, but the Barracuda's tail extended aft to the trim tabs, lean and flat, like the tale of some sleek undersea beast. It was, Gray realized, a kind of parallel evolution, where environment dictated shape. The same hydrodynamic forces that had shaped the dolphin over millions of years had shaped the SFV-4B during its design and testing.

Gray opened the laser tactical frequency. "Ho, Cigar. I see you made it out of the barn this time."

"That I did, CAG. Where's the bus we're supposed to escort?"

"Coming out last." He checked left and right. The other two fighter subs had emerged from tubes seventeen and eighteen, number 105 piloted by Lieutenant Bob Koch, and number 107, piloted by Lieutenant Hector Vasquez Hernandez.

Choosing the three men out of eleven to accompany him had been difficult, but he'd decided to take the oldest, steadiest, and most experienced men in the squadron. Handling new and experimental equipment was hairy enough; doing it in unknown waters under combat conditions was next to insanity, though by now he and the others had operated the SFV-4s enough that they'd begun to trust their remarkable senses. For so long, submarine operations had been exercises in blind, groping-in-the-dark uncertainty. SUBVIEW had quite literally opened a new window on the world beneath the ocean's surface. The technology was certain to revolutionize man's exploration of the seas.

Just as it was now revolutionizing his wars within them.

From one of the forward hatches, open now to the sea, a cloud of bubbles rose, bearing with it a stubby shape much like Gray's Barracuda, save that the canopy stretched clear back from the rounded nose almost all the way to the stabilizer. The two-man version of the Barracuda, the 4D, was being piloted by Chief Huxley. Gray gathered that he was one of the few men fully checked out on the 4D's systems. His rear seater, operating the sub's sonar and special electronics, was Lieutenant DuPlessis. Gray had been surprised that *Leviathan*'s intelligence officer had insisted on coming. Apparently it was not the Lousianan's style to let others do the dirty work while he sat in the rear and analyzed their reports.

"Okay," he said over the tactical channel. "This is Blue Leader to all Blue Hunters. As we planned it, gentlemen. Maintain depth at devils three. I'll stay tucked in with the Dolphin. Cigar, you've got point. Hernandez and Koch, port and starboard flanks. Don't lose visual with me."

"Roger that, CAG," Seegar said. "Moving to position."

His fighter sub accelerated, Gray's SUBVIEW registering the surge of water emerging from Seegar's jet as a pale blur sharply reminiscent of a Navy Hornet going to full burner. Koch and Hernandez banked left and right. In moments, *Leviathan* was dwindling astern, a gray shadow against the darker shadows of the depths. The water was still deep here, a northward extension of the Cayman Trench that extended clear to Cienfuegos and hooked back to Bahia de Cochinos—the infamous Bay of Pigs—thirty miles west along the Cuban coast.

Gray was beginning to admit that he could learn to love this. Strapped into the cockpit of an SFV-4, he could very nearly recapture the adrenaline-pumping rush of real flying. If there was a problem, it was his driving need to push the outside of the envelope, to cut his machine loose and see what it could *really* do. His test runs during the last few days hadn't even begun to wring the best out of the SFV-4, not by a long shot.

They'd left *Leviathan* twenty miles from the Cuban coast. At forty knots the trip would take them half an hour. He resisted the temptation to race ahead but kept his eyes on his MFD screens.

He wondered what his dad would think if he could see him now.

CHAPTER
16

The bottom was shoaling rapidly now as they approached the Cuban coast. The formation of fighter subs had been forced to climb steadily toward the surface, until now they were cruising at "devils one-point-three," 130 feet. At this depth there was a fairly stiff current moving from right to left, and the formation had to adjust its course several times to maintain the proper heading. The bottom was clearly visible, a rugged, convoluted terrain one hundred feet below the Barracudas' keels.

What interested Gray was the nature of that bottom. From his vantage point, it appeared that an enormous furrow or groove had been cut through the seafloor, with sides as straight and as even as though they'd been laid out by a survey. The water here was deep enough, surely, that no dredging was necessary to keep the approaches to the bay open.

Strange.

"Blue Leader to Blue Hunter Flight," he called over the tac channel. "Flight" still seemed a strange word to associate with submarines, but there was no better pro-word that he could think of. His fighter-pilot background made the association inevitable.

"Blue Leader to Blue Flight," he repeated. "Maintain course and speed. I'm going for a look at the bottom."

"Copy, Blue Leader," Seegar's voice came back. "Don't stop for souvenirs, now."

Gray pushed his stick forward, dropping the Barracuda's nose. At the same time he cut back on the throttle control feeding power to his engine, letting the vehicle's negative buoyancy drag him down into the depths.

Had he been viewing the scene with sunlight and naked eyes, of course, he would have been able to see little. At 280 feet, daylight still filtered down from the surface, but it was a feeble illumination easily obscured by the particles of matter hanging in the water around him.

He was below the current here; the water was nearly motionless. Just above the bottom, he brought the SFV-4's nose up and increased his speed slightly, flying over the bottom at what—in the world of sun and air somewhere above—would have been treetop height.

The landscape was one of eerie desolation, dimly seen, like shadows through a blue-gray fog. Gone were the straight lines he'd thought he'd glimpsed from above. Organic matter suspended in the water was so thick at this depth that his SUBVIEW was losing definition. The Barracuda's ULTRA-C lasers, he decided, were being scattered by the particles, and only sound—the noises of sea life and the hum of his own engine reflected back at him from shadowy rocks and canyon walls—remained to reveal anything at all of his surroundings. It was interesting, he thought, that even SUBVIEW technology had its limitations.

And dangerous. As the murk grew thicker he cut back on his speed to avoid ramming some unseen obstacle, then pushed the throttle forward again when a stall warning lit on his right-hand display screen. Like an aircraft, the SFV-4 needed to maintain a certain speed—about ten knots—just to stay "waterborne." Reducing that speed would quickly put him on the bottom. There was danger, too, that the muck he was cruising through would clog his water intakes and foul his engine, or at least make it overheat. Engine temperature was pushing three hundred already, high enough to be worrisome, at least.

Throttling forward, he rose to some forty feet off the bottom, where he found he was above the worst of the muck. Here, the sense of order, of *design* that had made him want to investigate closer, returned.

Yes! He could see it now, a trench at least two hundred feet wide, running north and south as though laid there by compass. Most of the suspended organic material was filling the trench and obscuring its bottom, which was why he'd not been certain of what he was seeing from closer to the surface. It was like a milky river along the bottom . . . no, a milky *canal*, straight-sided and steep-walled, dug through a jagged ridge of crushed rock and coral.

An eerie, lonely sensation prickled at the back of his neck. He remembered a boyhood interest in lost civilizations and for a moment almost fancied that he was looking at the algae-encrusted walls of sunken roads and temples, the remnants, perhaps, of some vanished outpost of lost Atlantis.

Nonsense! The strangeness of his surroundings, his

isolation, were tugging at his mind. What he was seeing was certainly man-made, but there was no need to
invoke that old fable.

"SUBVIEW," he said, his voice keying the
Barracuda's computer. "Contact display."

Four small blue circles winked on against the dome
of his cockpit, their steady blinking marking the positions of the rest of Blue Hunter Flight above him and
perhaps half a mile ahead. He focused on them for a
moment, took a deep breath, then turned his attention once again to his more immediate surroundings.

Everything he was seeing was being stored in the
SUBVIEW's computer for replay later. "SUBVIEW
voice-over," he said. The feature allowed him to add
his voiced comments to the record.

"I think I'm looking at a ship channel," he said. "A
trench dredged through what looks like a ridge of
old, dead coral, maybe the remains of an ancient
reef. What I can't understand is why anyone would
bother to dredge in water this deep. I'm at two hundred ten feet, now, with the bottom at two-fifty."

The world's biggest supertankers had a draft of
perhaps ninety feet. Monsters like those called at
ports like Tokyo and Galveston, but not Cienfuegos.

Something new attracted his attention ahead. His
SUBVIEW was showing two flashing red beacons on
the bottom, one set to either side of that trench.
Querying his computer, he learned that the visual display represented two radio beacons, broadcasting a
steady, pulsing tone at a frequency that gave it a
range of a few dozen yards underwater. As he passed
over those beacons two more appeared in the distance.
It reminded Gray forcibly of the approach beacons
and runway lights at an airport.

"Those beacons have got to be for submarines," he said aloud. "They wouldn't even register at the surface. My guess is that they mark a safe channel for submarines."

He wanted DuPlessis to see this.

"Blue Hunter Leader to Blue Dolphin," he called. "Blue Hunter Leader to Blue Dolphin."

"Blue Dolphin here." Chief Huxley's voice was faint over the channel, broken by brief, staticky bits of silence. Gray guessed that the murk in the water was interfering with the ULTRA-C communications lasers, shortening their range. In clear water it was possible to talk to another sub across ten miles. Here, contact was breaking up at a range of less than two. "Whatcha got, Commander?"

"I'd like Lieutenant DuPlessis to see what I've got down here. How about bringing him down?"

"Copy that. Shall I come about and meet you where you are?"

"Negative." The channel appeared to continue ahead into the distance, running straight toward the Cuban coast. "Maintain your course but descend to devils two-point-three. I'll rendezvous with you up ahead."

"Rog."

Gray increased his Barracuda's speed.

Harbor Defense Headquarters
Cienfuegos, Cuba
Friday, March 31, 1004 hours

"*Commandante!* I have a contact!"

The Cuban naval officer walked across the room, boot heels clicking on the slick, linoleum floor.

Outside the low, white stucco building, visible through the open windows, palm trees stood silhouetted against the blue morning sky.

"What is it, Escobar?"

"A passive sonar contact," the sonarman said. "Beacon twelve. There is nothing on radar, though. The surface is clear."

"Let me hear."

He pressed the headphones to his ear, listening. Yes . . . he could hear it, too. A faint hum with a curious throbbing quality to it. Definitely mechanical.

But it was unlike anything he'd ever heard before.

"It does not sound like a propeller," he said thoughtfully. "But it *must* be a submarine of some kind."

"Possibly the Yankees?" the sonar operator wondered out loud. Even in Cuba's post-Communist age, the *norteamericanos* were remembered as the villains of the past nearly fifty years, especially by the military, which continued to maintain its uneasy control over a poverty-stricken and volatile population.

"Possibly." The base commandant returned the headset. "Perhaps one of their remote-piloted submarine drones. I don't know what it is, but it is not our responsibility. I will call our friends at Juraguá."

He picked up the red telephone on the console.

Barracuda formation Blue Hunter
Cienfuegos Bay approaches
Friday, March 31, 1016 hours

"What the hell is *that* doing here?" Hernandez wanted to know.

"It looks like it threw a tread," DuPlessis said. "I think they must have abandoned it."

"It" was clearly a bulldozer, painted bright yellow and lying partway on its side close to the edge of the trench. The cab was sealed, and a tangle of long, thick pipes or hoses of some rubbery material stretched away from the watertight engine compartment and dropped over the cliff nearby.

"An underwater bulldozer?" Koch wanted to know.

"The Japanese have had them since the 1980s," Gray said. "Maybe longer, at least on an experimental basis. I remember reading an article about them using them to keep the shipping channels open in Tokyo Bay."

There was so much debris scattered about on the sea bottom that they'd almost missed the sealed vehicle. For as far as SUBVIEW could extend their vision, the bottom was littered with fifty-five-gallon drums, tin cans, plastic garbage bags, even the rusted bodies of old autos, and at first Gray had been willing to think that the bulldozer, too, had been dropped on this undersea garbage dump. The hose and the sealed cabin, however, argued that it was designed for use underwater, while the missing track suggested that it had broken down and been abandoned, at least temporarily. The depth here, outside the trench, at least, was less than one hundred feet. It was possible to imagine someone using a fleet of such vehicles to keep the trench clear of debris and silt, probably in conjunction with more conventional dredging equipment from the surface.

"The channel is probably fairly old," DuPlessis said. The 4D was drifting slowly above the trench, almost obscured by drifting flecks of matter. "Twenty years, at least. But someone's been cleaning it out recently. My guess is that it was abandoned, maybe partly filled with garbage, then cleaned out recently."

"How recently?" Gray asked.

"Within the last few months, certainly."

A Russian sub base, he thought. *Abandoned since the eighties . . . and now its approaches are being cleared out with Japanese dredging equipment. This is what Washington's looking for. I'd bet my captain's bars on it.*

"Blue Leader, Blue Leader, this is Blue Two!" Cigar's voice broke and crackled through the dirty water, but the urgency was unmistakable. He was the lookout, circling in the water a mile closer to shore. "I've got multiple high-speed skimmer contacts at zero-zero-five, heading this way!"

"Heads up," Gray called. Skimmers at zero-zero-five meant surface craft of some kind emerging from the mouth of Cienfuegos Bay. "We've got company."

An instant later, a loud, echoing *ping* sounded in the cockpit, followed by another . . . then another.

"Active sonar," Huxley warned. "Someone up there's looking for trespassers."

Ping!

"Roger that," Gray replied. "And it sounds like they damn well know we're here!"

SSCVN-1 *Leviathan*
Twenty miles south of Cienfuegos, Cuba
Friday, March 31, 1016 hours

"Conn, Sonar!"

Ramsay was under the SUBVIEW helmet, but he reached out and touched the button opening the intercom circuit. "Sonar, Conn. Go ahead."

"Skipper, we're picking up active pinging from up ahead, overlaid with at least four sets of high-speed screws. Sounds like our boys might've stirred up a hornet's nest."

"Acknowledged."

Leviathan was hovering almost motionless, with just enough forward drift to give her maneuvering bite on planes and rudder should she need it. The depth here was over eight hundred fathoms, nearly a mile of water. The bottom was lost in darkness, and only a faint silvery shimmer revealed sunlight dancing on the surface four hundred feet above the top of the Typhoon's sail.

Turning his head until the cross hairs centered on his field of view registered a bearing of zero-zero-zero—due north—Ramsay peered into the darkness. At his command, Crayfish overlaid the scene with red pulses marking the active sonar pings, but their sources were still too far for the computer to image.

"Admiral?" Ramsay said. Delacroix had been in the control room a moment ago. Was he still there?

"Yes, Captain." His voice sounded slightly muffled. Naval protocol demanded that Ramsay remove his helmet so he could look at the man while talking to him, but he didn't want to break the contact, however tenuous, with whatever was going on up ahead.

"Orders, sir?" Everything in Ramsay made him want to go help those men, even though experience and training told him there was little he could do now. If Blue Hunter had been discovered, they were on their own.

"Maintain position, Captain," Delacroix's voice came back.

"I wish we could help."

"We cannot allow *Leviathan* to become involved."

"Of course, sir. You're right."

Ramsay continued to stare into the watery, horizonless depths.

**Barracuda formation Blue Hunter
Cienfuegos Bay approaches
Friday, March 31, 1017 hours**

"Blue Two, Blue Two!" Gray cried out. He could see Seegar's boat now, a tiny dolphin shape racing back toward the rest of the formation. "They can't see us against the junkyard. It's you they're after. Drop to the bottom and see if you can lose them!"

"Copy that, CAG," Seegar replied. "Hard to forget . . . speed is life."

Speed is life. The old fighter's axiom came back to haunt him now. In fighter-to-fighter dogfights it was true, and the faster aircraft usually emerge victorious. Here, though, the former aviators were having to learn the submariner's rule, where stealth and silence meant life.

Gray, Koch, Hernandez, and the two-man 4D were all circling slowly within a few feet of the bottom, where their aquajets were stirring clouds of mud as they banked and turned. There was so much metal—the rusted hulks of cars, the bulldozer, thousands upon thousands of chemical drums—that they might very well be invisible to active sonar.

Seegar, on the other hand. . .

He was descending now as quickly as he could drive his fighter sub toward the bottom, but Gray could see a silvery, turbulent disturbance on the surface now a mile or two away. He queried his Barracuda's sound library for a match.

The ID came back in seconds—

TURYA-CLASS HYDROFOIL TORPEDO BOAT
WEIGHT 215 TONS SPEED 35 KTS

Quickly, he scanned the computer's warbook listing. The Turya was an old Russian design, in service between 1974 and 1979. One hundred twenty-one feet long, with a crew of twenty-four, it had the hull of an Osa II missile boat raised by fixed hydrofoils forward, with stern planes riding the surface aft. Its weapons included antiaircraft cannon forward, a big, turret-mounted 57mm gun aft, and four torpedoes.

Those torpedoes might very well be programmed as sub killers . . . almost certainly were, if someone was using them for ASW patrol.

Who was that someone? It could be the Cuban coast guard, but Gray doubted that very much. The last he'd heard, the Cubans didn't possess hydrofoils, not even ancient, cast-off Russian ones.

Which meant it was an Islamic boat. Here, in Cuban waters.

Using a small joystick on his console, he highlighted the silvery distortion on his cockpit. "SUBVIEW," he called. "Enhance."

A window formed on the cockpit display, showing a magnified view of the approaching hydrofoil. He could see the canted, forward foils leading the churning froth where the Turya's engines were driving the craft forward. It appeared to be slowing. . . .

There was a splash, and a black, pencil-thin shape hit the water alongside the hydrofoil. Gray recognized it immediately.

"Torpedo in the water!" he called. "It's tracking you, Cigar!"

"I see it! I can't make the bottom in time!"

The SUBVIEW image was more detailed than would have been possible had the SFV-4 relied on light alone. Vibrations in the water were picked up by the Barracuda's instruments and processed by its computer. The image showed a slender, black thread trailing astern of the torpedo.

Wire-guided.

Modern homing torpedoes relied on three systems for finding and tracking their prey. A wire-guided torp homed on passive sonar and was steered to the target by a weapons operator who could watch tracking data relayed from the torpedo itself and respond with commands sent back down the wire to the torpedo's guidance system. If the wire was broken, the torpedo could still home by passive sonar, following the sound of its target's engines. And finally, when it had closed the range enough, it could go active, emitting sonar pings and homing on the echoes.

The torpedo, less than a thousand yards from Seegar's Barracuda, was descending faster than he could. Measuring distances and angles with a pilot's eye, Gray rammed his throttle forward, sending his Barracuda into a high-powered climb.

"Blue Leader!" Koch yelled. "What the hell are you doing?"

"Stay put!" he called back. "I'm giving Cigar an assist!"

Seegar was trying to twist away from the approaching torpedo, but it was more maneuverable than his SFV-4, with a tighter radius than his best possible turn. It was on his tail and getting closer, obviously tracking the sound of his engine.

"Cigar!" Gray called. "Cut your engine!"

"Rog!"

An instant later, the sharp *ping* of the torpedo's sonar going active cut through the water. "No good!" Seegar yelled.

"Go ballistic!" Gray yelled. "Outrun the damned thing!"

Seegar's Barracuda began to accelerate, leveling off now and racing toward the south. The torpedo followed, and Gray couldn't tell if Seegar was going to build up enough speed fast enough to escape that deadly warhead or not. It took time to get the Barracudas up to top speed . . . too much time, and time was running out.

Climbing steeply, Gray angled his Barracuda astern of Seegar's, punching the throttle forward until he was hurtling up through the water at forty knots . . . then fifty. He passed Seegar's SFV-4 at a range of twenty yards; ahead, almost comically, the torpedo appeared to hesitate, as though trying to choose between *two* targets now. The weapons operator aboard the Turya was probably trying to sort out a confused blur of returns on his screen.

Though the torpedo was more maneuverable than a Barracuda, Gray had the advantage of already being inside its turn radius as he flashed past it, less than one hundred feet away. The torpedo was starting to turn, trying to follow this new, rapidly moving target. Gray was already behind it, bringing his planes up. . . .

The torpedo's wire hit the Barracuda's bulbous nose, grated aft along the canopy, then fouled across the erect stabilizer fin before parting with a sharp, metallic click. Gray felt the jolt and prayed there was no damage to his control surfaces. Pushing the stick forward again, he dove for the bottom once more, hoping to lose himself amid the junkyard wreckage before the now aimlessly circling torp could acquire either him or Seegar again.

"Thanks, CAG," Seegar said.

"Don't mention it. Where's the torp now? I've lost it."

"Diving for the bottom. It's gone active."

Gray heard the *ping* . . . followed the chirp of a solid echo. The damned thing was ranging on something.

"Heads up, Blue Hunters," he called. "I've cut the torp loose and it's heading for the bottom."

"We're cool," Hernandez replied. "It's locked on something south of here. Ha!"

A savage boom shivered through the water, rocking Gray's Barracuda to the side. In the distance, a white sphere flashed against the bottom, then rose, mushrooming toward the surface.

"Blue Hunter Flight!" Gray called. "Is everyone okay?"

"Copacetic," Hernandez replied. "The Turya just scored on that bulldozer back there!"

Slowing, Gray brought his Barracuda to within a few feet of the bottom. Broken rock thrust up around him, mingled with the eerie, rust-crumbling wreckage of civilization. The Turya was at a dead stop now, floating on the surface a mile away, not moving, not even pinging.

"What the hell happened?" Koch said. "He give up?"

"It's like he's waiting," Hernandez said. "Maybe he's got buddies coming or something."

"'Or something is right," Seegar said. "Take a look at zero-zero-one."

Gray checked his sonar screen, then ordered SUB-VIEW to put it on the cockpit display.

Something was racing toward them at forty knots . . . no, at fifty, something whale large and fast and as black as the shadows it was emerging from. It was deep, too, riding almost on the bottom, following that two-hundred-foot-wide trench through the coral like a locomotive thundering down the tracks.

A submarine. At first, Gray assumed that it was the Oscar they'd come to these waters to find and kill, but one glance at that shadowy form told him that he was wrong. He requested data from the warbook, and got it.

ALFA CLASS ATTACK SUBMARINE

WEIGHT 3,680 TONS (SUBMGRD) SPEED 50 KTS+

Behind the first Alfa came a second, and behind the second, a third. . . .

"My God," Koch said, his voice sounding shaken over the laser circuit. "I'm reading three Alfas."

"At least two more contacts behind those," Hernandez pointed out. "It's the goddamn cavalry!"

"Yeah," Gray said. "*Their* cavalry." He was puzzled. As the cluster of fighter subs watched, the lead Alfa thundered past, still following the trench almost a hundred yards away. The hull was teardrop sleek and rounded, the sail streamlined to the point of looking like a blister growing from its back. The second Alfa passed, trailing the first by nearly three hundred yards. The Islamic attack subs appeared to take no notice whatsoever of the Barracudas but raced off toward the south, vanishing into darkness.

"*Leviathan!*" Seegar said. "They're after *Leviathan!*"

It was the only answer possible, given the information available.

The Islamic attack subs were sortieing from their base to attack the American Typhoon.

CHAPTER
17

"**B**lue Hunter Flight, this is Blue Leader," Gray called. "We've got to warn Home Plate." Those Alfas could be on *Leviathan* before she knew they were coming.

"Roger that, Blue Leader," Seegar replied. "But how? We're way outside of ULTRA-C range, even if the water was clear."

"Eighty knots plus, Blue Two," Hernandez said. "We can outrun the bastards."

Gray had just arrived at the same conclusion. The Alfas could make fifty, maybe fifty-five knots, twenty knots better than the Typhoon's top speed. The Barracudas, however, could make eighty, and maybe a bit more. If they could get within ten miles of the *Leviathan* before the Alfas closed the range . . .

"Right," he said, deciding. "Blue Two, you're with me. Three and Four, you stay with the Dolphin."

"But—"

Gray wasn't sure whether the protest had come from Hernandez or Koch or both. It didn't matter.

He was already throttling forward, feeling the shudder as the Barracuda bucked past forty knots. On his top central display, his computer showed the bottom terrain in 3-D relief, flowing beneath his craft faster and faster. "I want you guys to ride shotgun on Huxley and the Lieutenant. Help them work themselves clear of that hydrofoil."

"Roger that, Blue Leader," Koch said. "But I don't think we're going to have to worry about him. Check your six."

Glancing back over his shoulder, Gray saw what he meant. The hydrofoil, which had been drifting almost stationary while the Alfas passed, was accelerating again.

And it was ignoring Hernandez and Koch, following Gray and Seegar instead.

"Torp in the water," Hernandez warned. Gray could hear the sharp, high-pitched pinging as the torpedo went active almost immediately. The weapons officer must have had a hard fix on the sound of their engines as they pushed to high speed.

Forty-five knots. The torpedo was still gaining.

"Blue Leader, Blue Two. You want me to decoy?"

"Negative, Two. Stick with me." Together, they bucked their way past fifty knots. The torpedo was still closing, but very slowly now, trailing the side-by-side Barracudas by about five hundred yards.

And then they were pulling ahead.

But so slowly! Acceleration in the SFV-4s was painfully low, and at fifty-five knots the pressure cones in the water caused by their passage set up a vicious turbulence that clawed at wings and stabilizer, threatening to wrench the Barracudas apart.

Then, like punching through the sound barrier

and into the silent calm beyond, the shuddering subsided, and the two Barracudas rocketed ahead. The bottom fell away beneath them as they hit seventy knots. By the time they were moving at eighty knots, the torpedo, two miles behind them now, ran out of fuel and dropped away into the depths.

They were in the open sea now, streaking through emerald light for home.

UIR Attack Submarine *Rasul*
Cienfuegos Bay approaches
Friday, March 31, 1018 hours

Commander Kamal Bishara stood in the control room of the lead Alfa. *Rasul* had been on standby alert in the underground sub pens at Jagua when the message had come through from *Sharuq*. According to al-Badr, an American Los Angeles SSN was close behind the Oscar, now less than twenty miles from Cienfuegos.

Alfas had two supreme advantages in submarine combat: they were the fastest full-sized subs in the world, and they were also the deepest divers. Their titanium hulls could withstand sea pressures all the way down to an astonishing 1,300 meters—over 4,000 feet. Driven by reactors using liquid metal instead of water as a coolant, they packed tremendous power into their relatively small, eighty-one-meter-long hulls.

Their single disadvantage was that they made a racket that could be heard a long way off. The pumps needed to handle the molten lead-bismuth coolant were far louder than those on more conventional subs, and at speeds over forty knots, cavitation—the creation of noisy, low-pressure bubbles behind the propeller blades—became a real problem.

But the Alfas' speed and depth made up for that handicap. The Soviets had originally designed the Alfa, during the late seventies, as an "interceptor sub," a fast, hard-hitting attack sub that could dash at high speed from Russian ports or submarine bastions to attack American subs, then make its escape before Western ASW forces could be assembled and brought to bear.

That was precisely the strategy Bishara was employing now. As the Los Angeles SSN drew close to Cienfuegos, the three Alfas had raced out from their hidden base at fifty-five knots, diving deep—deeper than any American sub could go—and rushing toward a point on their charts where mathematics said they should be able to intercept the sub following *Sharuq*. As long as the Los Angeles was moving at top speed, its sonar was unlikely to pick up the high-speed trio, and at 1,000 meters the thermocline far above them acted as a blanket, soaking up their sound and letting them set their ambush undetected.

Bishara glanced at the large clock mounted on the control-room bulkhead. They should be close now to *Sharuq* and the pursuing American. He picked up an intercom mike and depressed the switch. "Engineering!" he snapped. "This is the Captain. All stop!"

"All stop, yes, sir."

And then the throbbing beat of the Alfa's engine died, and the attack sub ghosted ahead through the sea, silent now save for the lesser clatter of sustainer pumps. Sonar was all but useless at speeds of more than twenty knots, necessitating this tactic which the

Americans referred to as "dash-and-drift." The greatest danger now lay not with the American, but in the very real possibility that one of the other two Alfas would ram into the *Rasul* from astern. Their orders were to spread out, abeam of *Rasul* and to her east, and the captains of both *Rais* and *Nabi* were supposed to be listening for such sudden silences as this in order to set their own course changes and speeds, but it was impossible to glean accurate course information from passive sonar alone.

They waited, listening. . . .

Barracuda formation Blue Hunter
Cienfuegos Bay approaches
Friday, March 31, 1020 hours

"Home Plate, Home Plate, this is Blue Hunter Leader. Come in, please!"

The two Barracudas raced through waters as blue as a late twilight sky, pressing eighty-two knots now as they raced toward the waiting *Leviathan*.

"Blue Leader, this is Home Plate." The voice was Ramsay's. "Go ahead."

"Home Plate, we picked up three Alfas and at least two other contacts coming out of Cienfuegos at high speed." In terse, hard phrases, he described the encounter outside of Cienfuegos and explained that two Barracudas and the Dolphin were still on their way in. "We wanted to beat the Alfas here," he said. "They won't be more than four or five minutes behind us."

There was a long pause. "We copy that, Blue Hunter Leader," Ramsay said at last. "You are clear for approach and recovery."

"Ah, roger, Home Plate. But can you spare the time for a pickup? If those Alfas are gunning for you—"

"Blue Leader, the situation has changed. Stand by to recover."

Gray knew better than to argue. *Leviathan*'s undersea senses were better than those of the Barracuda, so Ramsay could see a lot more of the unfolding situation than Gray could. Five minutes later, he was throttling back as the huge shadow of *Leviathan* loomed out of the murk, its sail ULTRA-C laser a brilliant beacon against the gloom. Two missile hatches had already been opened, one to port and one to starboard, and the capture nets, looking like wire-frame Stokes stretchers, had been unfurled. Gray, slightly in the lead, would recover first.

"Blue Hunter One, this is ReCon," a new voice said. Recovery Control was the submarine equivalent of a carrier's Primary Flight Control for landings. "On heading zero-zero-five, speed five knots, depth two-five-zero feet. Pressure one-one-two psi. Call the ball."

The "ball" was a naval aviator's term, referring to the Fresnel lens equipment on a carrier's flight deck that allowed the pilot to acquire visually the proper glide path for a landing. Too high or too low, and the central light appeared red and out of alignment with the lights to either side. When he "called the ball," the aviator was informing the Landing Signal Officer, or LSO, that he had the ball in sight and was on the proper approach.

That bit of carrier lore had been transferred to the recovery gear for the Barracudas. A white light shone on the top of one of the extended mesh baskets, a beacon for Gray to home on. "Blue One ball," he replied. "Ten knots on zero-zero-two, range four-zero yards."

He was approaching *Leviathan* from her starboard side, keeping the white light centered in a red cross hair projected onto his canopy. A second light, a green one, winked on just below the first.

"Blue One, we have you on the LAG. Cut speed to eight knots, adjust right to zero-zero-three."

LAG—the Laser Approach Guide—allowed *Leviathan*'s ReCon to very precisely direct the Barracuda into the net. He adjusted his course and speed as directed, watched *Leviathan*'s forward deck loom huge, her sail a dark gray cliff towering on his left. At exactly the right moment he cut back on his throttle and brought the Barracuda's nose up sharply. The engines stalled an instant before the fighter sub's belly dropped into the wire net with an audible creak and the scrape of metal on metal. A magnetic grapple snapped home.

"Home Plate, Blue One, touchdown," he called.

"We've got you, Blue One. Good trap." With a shuddering grumble of machinery, the net began to draw the Barracuda erect, tail-down, and haul it back into the depths of the open missile tube. Before he cut off his SUBVIEW, Gray saw Cigar's Barracuda coming in from *Leviathan*'s port side, lined up for his recovery approach.

Minutes later, with the echoing clang of heavy metal access hatches and the hiss of released pressure, Gray's canopy swung open, and hands reached in to help him squirm out of his seat and harness. Admiral Delacroix was waiting for him as he got his feet under himself and stood up.

"They're not coming after *Leviathan*," Delacroix said before Gray could say a word. He looked glum, his face long and worried. "They're heading south-southwest and they appear to be deploying for a fight. A few minutes ago they went silent. We think they're setting a trap."

"They didn't see *Leviathan*, sir?"

"Apparently not. We've been at dead slow, silent operation, and they aren't using active sonar."

"Who are they after, then?"

"My guess would be one of our LAs, still out of sonar range to the south, but heading this way. We've picked up some faint CZ traces that might mean a high-speed chase."

"The Oscar."

"A distinct possibility. How long before the rest of your subs can be aboard?"

"Twenty minutes, Admiral."

"Damn! We could lose them in that time!"

"If I could make a suggestion, Admiral?"

Delacroix's eyes narrowed. "What?"

"Sir, Blue Dolphin and the other Barracudas will be in ULTRA-C range any minute now. They also have enough juice for another sixty, maybe seventy miles at forty knots. You could bring *Leviathan* around and follow those Alfas. Use ULTRA-C to tell DuPlessis where to meet you."

"That would work."

"There's more, sir. If those Alfas and other contacts are after one of our attack subs, the odds are five to one . . . six to one if that Oscar is out there. When we show up, odds of six to two won't be that much better."

"Agreed. I suppose you want to deploy the SFVs?"

"Yes, sir." Gray took a deep breath. "Admiral, we can have six Barracudas loaded with Mark 62s inside of fifteen minutes, and we can launch in twenty. That'll narrow those odds a bit!"

Delacroix stared at Gray for a long moment, as though measuring him. Gray was sure the man was about to shake his head and say no.

But Delacroix surprised him. "I don't have much choice," he said at last. "I don't like it, but you're right. Even those play darts of yours would give us something. A distraction, if nothing more."

"Admiral," a rating called from forward. "Blue Two's aboard and in the tube!"

"Very well." He reached for an ICS mike on the bulkhead behind him. "Captain, this is Delacroix. Bring us about to two-seven-zero."

"Aye, aye, sir," Ramsay's voice came back, sharp and curt. Seconds later, Gray felt the sub heeling sharply to port, and he had to grab hold of a pipe on the missile tube at his side to keep from falling. At the same time, the rumble of *Leviathan*'s powerful engines set the deck trembling. The Typhoon was racing at full speed toward the west.

He hoped Hernandez, Koch, Huxley, and DuPlessis would be okay. He didn't like leaving them, forcing them to extend their return trip to a new rendezvous, but every minute *Leviathan* lost could be critical.

A battle was shaping up to the west, a battle unlike any ever fought in the history of naval warfare. Morgan Gray knew that this would be his one chance to prove his theories about fighter-sub combat.

He did not intend to miss that chance.

* * *

UIR Attack Submarine *Rasul*
Cienfuegos Bay approaches
Friday, March 31, 1038 hours

"Captain, Sonar!" an intercom voice called. "We have them! Two high-speed contacts, bearing two-six-six and two-five-one. The contact at two-five-one appears to be chasing the other."

"Sonar, do you have *Rais* and *Nabi*?"

"Yes, Captain. Mixed sounds, close aboard to port."

"Then the contact at two-five-one is our target. Designate it as Target *Alif*." Bishara closed his eyes momentarily, visualizing the unfolding tactical situation. *Sharuq* was already well past *Rasul* and heading north. Given the probable depth, range, and speed of the contacts, the American would be due west of the *Rasul* in another few minutes.

"Helm, come to two-six-zero," he ordered. "Ahead slow, fifteen degrees up-bubble. Come to one hundred meters."

"*Ya sidi!* Course two-six-five." The deck canted beneath Bishara's feet, and the Alfa's engines began their steady, rhythmic throbbing once again. "Ahead slow, fifteen degrees up-bubble. Make depth one hundred meters."

Kamal Bishara was the star of the UIR's crash submarine program, a young Lebanese Palestinian who had started his naval career aboard one of Syria's Kilo-class diesel subs, then—because he was not a native Syrian—managed to survive the political and religious purges of that country's officer corps that had followed the *Qaumat*. Sent to Tokyo to train aboard Japan's recently purchased Sierras and Alfas, he'd become an expert in attack-sub tactics. An Alfa was crowded with its normal complement of forty-five, so there were no Japanese advisors aboard the *Rasul*, but none were needed. Bishara had thoroughly absorbed what his instructors had taught him, and he knew the Alfa's tactical strengths and weaknesses perfectly, and how to best employ them.

"Weapons Officer! Order the torpedo room to stand ready to fire, two shots."

"Torpedo room reports tubes one and two loaded and ready to fire, Captain."

"Depth."

"Passing four hundred meters, Captain."

"Where is the thermal layer?"

"Thermocline at three hundred meters, Captain."

"Sonar, this is the Captain. Where are *Nabi* and *Rais*?"

"They have matched our turn, Captain, and are rising with us. Both are still to the east. We will have a clear shot at the target as it passes."

"Very well." He found himself straining to hear the approaching contact with his own ears.

A little farther, and Target *Alif* would be fully in the trap.

U.S.S. *New Haven*
Twenty-three miles south of Cienfuegos Bay, Cuba
Friday, March 31, 1039 hours

"Captain! New contacts, two . . . no, three new contacts, bearing zero-eight-one to zero-eight nine. Designate Bravo, Charlie, Delta!"

In the control room, Commander Logan turned his head, watching the image swing around him as his

SUBVIEW helmet panned to starboard. There they were, three tiny, dark gray shapes just materializing out of the blue-green gloom, almost dead abeam and low. Red boxes snapped around each, accompanied by the letters "B," "C," and "D," and precise, laser-measured depth and range data.

"I see them, Lucky," Logan replied over the intercom. The contacts were still too far away for *New Haven*'s Crayfish to give a solid ID, but he trusted Lucky Lucciano's ears implicitly. "What's their make?"

"Three Alfas, Skipper. Ain't nothin' else makes that ungodly clanking."

Logan looked back toward *New Haven*'s rounded bow, to the red box marking the UIR Oscar, now some fifteen miles ahead. Damn! The Oscar was just out of range for *New Haven*'s ADCAP torpedoes, but with three Alfas off their flank it was clear that their target had just led them into a trap. His choices were simple. He could keep following the Oscar and nail the trap's door shut on himself; he could turn away and run, and risk losing those high-speed Alfas in his own baffles—the cone of disturbed water astern of a sub that blocked sonar completely and even interfered with the ULTRA-C lasers; or he could turn toward them, keeping them in sight until he knew what their intent was.

He made his decision. "Helm! Come right to course eight-zero. Slow to two-five knots."

"Coming right to course eight-zero," the Diving Officer replied. "Make for two-five knots."

New Haven swung to face the new threat.

*   *   *

UIR Attack Submarine *Rasul*
Cienfuegos Bay approaches
Friday, March 31, 1039 hours

"Captain, Sonar! Target aspect changing! He's turning toward us!"

They'd been spotted. Bishara glanced at the plot table, where the Navigator was recording each new sonar plot. *Sharug* had passed out of sonar range to the north, while *Alif* was almost dead ahead. The other two Alfas were lost in *Rasul*'s baffles, which meant that *Rasul* had the best chance for a shot.

"Depth!"

"Passing one hundred eighty meters, Captain."

"Very well." *Rasul* still needed precise ranging data. "Sonar! Go active for target fix."

"Sonar, yes, sir. Going active."

The chirp of *Rasul*'s sonar rang through the hull as her crew stared up past the overhead and into the blue water beyond. If there'd been any question before, there was no question now. The enemy definitely knew they were here.

"Captain, Sonar. Range to target, seventy-two hundred meters."

A long shot. *Rasul*'s 533mm Type C torpedoes had a range of only about eight kilometers, perhaps a third of the reach of the best American weapons. He would have to fire quickly, or lose this one chance at a kill.

"Flood tubes one and two. Open outer doors. Stand by to fire."

"Tubes one and two flooded, Captain," the Weapons Officer called from his board on the port side of the control room. "Outer doors are open. Torpedoes ready for firing."

"Fire one!"

The Weapons Officer's palm came down on a large button. There was an audible hiss of compressed air, and a lurch transmitted through the deck as the fish slid clear and into the sea.

"One fired."

"Fire two!"

Hiss . . . lurch. "Two fired. Sonar reports both torpedoes running true on passive guidance."

Bishara tried to invoke the calm stressed by his Japanese instructors as necessary to the efficient execution of command, and failed. His heart was pounding in his breast, sweat streaming down his face.

"Ready countermeasures! Engine room! Stand by to come to full speed!"

Rasul's torpedoes streaked through darkness toward her prey.

CHAPTER
18

"**T**orpedo!" Lucciano warned over the ICS. "Torpedo in the water!"

The bastard had fired.

"Snapshot! Two! One!" Logan called. The phrase alerted the torpedo room that *New Haven* had just been fired upon, that they had only seconds to return fire. With the tubes already loaded and flooded in anticipation of a shot against the Oscar, it took only seconds to connect the torps' communications with fire control and open the outer doors.

"Torpedo room reports tubes one and two ready to fire!" the Weapons Officer announced.

"Fire!"

The first sleek, black-and-red Mark 48 ADCAP torp hurtled from *New Haven*'s number-two tube.

* * *

247

UIR Attack Submarine *Rasul*
Cienfuegos Bay approaches
Friday, March 31, 1040 hours

"Captain, Sonar! Enemy torpedo running!"

"Have our torpedoes acquired the target?"

"Affirmative, Captain. Passive lock."

"Cut the wires! Hard right rudder! Go to full speed!"

Rasul heeled hard to starboard, the turn sharp enough to slam some of her crew members against bulkheads and partitions. Her torpedoes, freed from the wires that had connected them to the UIR sub, streaked ahead, homing on the passive acoustical signature of the American submarine, now less than five kilometers ahead. If they missed, they were programmed to go to active sonar, then begin a search pattern that would let them reacquire the target.

"Range to enemy torpedo!" Bishara snapped.

"Thirty-two hundred meters and closing, Captain. Speed twenty-eight meters per second."

Less than two minutes.

The American torpedo had the same speed as the Alfa—about fifty-five knots. Bishara could either run away from the torpedo until it ran out of fuel, or he could try to outdive it.

He decided. "Diving Officer! Take us down!"

"Dive! Dive!"

Still turning sharply to starboard, the *Rasul* plummeted into the depths.

U.S.S. *New Haven*
Twenty-three miles south of Cienfuegos Bay, Cuba
Friday, March 31, 1042 hours

"Release countermeasures!" Logan ordered. "Come hard left!"

Every man aboard the *New Haven* could hear the torpedoes, the noise of their screws sounding like the chugging of steam engines, but sharper and higher-pitched. Every few seconds the chirp of an active sonar pulse would echo through the hull, the chirps coming faster and faster as the torpedoes homed in for the kill.

Logan could *see* them now with enhanced SUBVIEW imagery, a pair of cylindrical missile shapes balanced on white contrails of disturbed water, arrowing toward *New Haven*'s starboard side. *Ping!* One of the torps lit up for an instant, SUBVIEW's device for identifying a sonar pulse. He'd waited until the last moment to execute evasive maneuvering, hoping to give his own snapshot a chance to reach the enemy before he cut the wires guiding them.

A pair of canisters popped from a launch chute on *New Haven*'s afterdeck, drifted a moment, then burst in a cloud of white foam. To SUBVIEW, it looked like a solid blanket spreading out from the burst point, an impenetrable wall shielding the American sub. For a few moments, anyway, the torpedoes' active sonar would be scattered by the bubble wall, while behind that wall, *New Haven* was diving hard and fast as it turned away from the threat. Logan craned his neck, staring back over his right shoulder as the *New Haven* continued to turn to port. This next part had to be timed exactly right. . . .

"Fire decoy!"

There was a hiss and a thump, and a blunt cylinder lurched from one of *New Haven*'s bow tubes. An RSQV-20 decoy, it was essentially a Mark 50 torpedo with a fairly sophisticated computer instead of a warhead, plus a sound system that broadcast the digitally recorded sounds of a Los Angeles–class sub into the surrounding waters as it began maneuvering like a real submarine.

The RSQV was used as a target in combat drills. It could also be used as a lure for enemy torpedoes, if those torpedoes' acoustic lock on the real sub could be broken.

Diving for the thermocline was *New Haven*'s best chance now. If they could survive this attack . . .

There! The first torpedo punched through the bubble wall, which was already thinning and breaking up as he watched. Then the second torp emerged. Both were chirping loudly, both starting to circle in blind attempts to reacquire their targets. One torpedo steadied, centering on the decoy. The other seemed to overlook the decoy . . . or ignore it. It pinged again, then with an infuriating single-mindedness, began to home once more on the *New Haven*.

"Keep her hard left," Logan said aloud. He had to turn almost all the way around now to keep the torpedo in sight. It was coming up on *New Haven*'s baffles now, barely glimpsed from moment to moment through the turbulence of her wake. The range was down to thirty yards . . . twenty. He wasn't going to outrun the thing, so his only chance was to outmaneuver it. Gauging the moment carefully, he waited, watching it close the range to ten yards. . . .

"Helm!" he shouted. "Hard right rudder! Up trim tabs, up planes! Now!"

The aft diving planes mounted in *New Haven*'s cruciform tail were properly known as trim tabs, for their primary function was to maintain the sub's trim when it dove or surfaced. By raising both trim tabs and bow planes at the same time, he brought the sub's nose up and dropped her tail, a maneuver that caused her hull to shudder and buck, and sent men spilling to the deck throughout the boat.

But dropping the stern sharply, coupled with the hard right turn, had the effect of walking *New Haven*'s tail right out from under the speeding torpedo. Plowing through empty water where the aft hull had been a moment before, the torp skimmed past the sail at a range of less than five yards. Its screws were shrill and harsh as it passed . . . and then the sound was dwindling.

Miss!

A deep-throated boom sounded through the water, rocking *New Haven* over to port, then back to starboard as water boiled in the distance. For a moment, Logan thought the torp had detonated on a proximity fuse, but then he realized that the explosion was the first torpedo running down the decoy. The second torpedo, still active, was starting to circle back again . . . but halfway into its turn it seemed to grow tired. The sound of its screw faded away to silence, and the blunt-tipped missile began sinking into the depths.

Logan had been pretty sure that those Alfas were packing short-ranged killers, torpedoes capable of running perhaps five miles before running out of fuel. The Alfas were at that range now; torps launched from that far out wouldn't have juice enough for more than one pass.

Through his helmet controls, he opened an intercom channel and addressed the entire boat. "This is the Captain speaking," Logan said. "They just gave us their best shot, and they blew it. Give me your best effort now, men, and let's see if we can peg us an Alfa!"

The men cheered, a raw, full-voiced sound, instantly silenced. Submariners were not normally a loud or demonstrative lot, but the sheer tension of having an enemy near miss like that, coupled with the battle fever they'd been feeling ever since the Oscar had launched at the *Challenge* and the *Taylor,* exploded now in a brief, warriors' shout. "We'll nail the bastards for you, Captain!" someone yelled, and behind the blank mask of his SUBVIEW helmet, Logan grinned and returned a jaunty thumbs-up.

Still, he wasn't being entirely honest. *New Haven* had survived the first round, but the odds were three to one . . . worse if that Oscar was doubling back. As so often happened in submarine warfare, the hunter had just become the hunted.

Survival for the *New Haven* was now going to depend on skill, speed, superior technology, and a very great deal of luck.

UIR Attack Submarine *Rasul*
South of Cienfuegos Bay
Friday, March 31, 1042 hours

"He's gone active!"

"Fire countermeasures!"

"He has acquired!"

"Depth!"

"Six hundred meters."

A dull, hollow *whump* sounded through the sub, and one of the men whimpered with fright. Another, recognizing the sound for what it was, waved a clenched fist. "We got him! *Allah akbar!*"

In an instant, every man in the control room was screaming and yelling, and Bishara saw with a dreadful clarity that in an instant all traces of discipline were about to vanish.

"*Uskut!*" he yelled. "Silence, or you are all dead men!"

The pandemonium rippled away into silence, and Bishara glared back at pale faces and wide eyes.

"Depth!" he yelled again.

"Passing six hundred thirty meters, Captain! Countermeasures unsuccessful!"

"Torpedo range?"

"One hundred twenty meters, Captain. One hundred . . . eighty . . ."

Less than the length of the boat. Just how good were these American torpedoes? he wondered. The Mark 48 ADCAP, Bishara knew, had been designed specifically to counter the Soviet submarine threat, able to run as fast as an Alfa, powerful enough to break the double-hulled back of a Typhoon. It was said that the things were hellishly smart, that they could distinguish weak spots in a submarine's construction like deck hatches, and home on those with uncanny accuracy.

"Depth!" He could see the depth meter from where he was standing, but he needed to enforce his will on his crew, needed to hold them at their posts, and directing their fear toward the approaching American weapon was the only way he could think of to manage that piece of psychological sleight of hand.

"Passing seven hundred meters, Captain!"

"Torpedo range, now sixty meters."

The Alfa couldn't dive as quickly as it could move in a flat-out run, and the Mark 48 was rapidly gaining. Bishara had brought the boat around, however, and was traveling toward the American sub again, the torpedo gaining from astern.

Seven hundred forty meters. Over half a ton of pressure on each square inch of *Rasul's* aluminum hull. They were still at only half of the Alfa's rated dive depth, but the hull was creaking now, a low, mournful groan peppered by pops and ominous bangs echoing through the control room that sounded like the knock of Death itself.

"Torpedo range forty meters, Captain!" Half a boat length. Bishara could feel his men's fear.

"Fifteen degrees up-angle!" he ordered. "Come right, hard right!" He could hear the oncoming torpedo, a hazy, chirring sound from astern. Sweat dripped from his face; the stink of raw terror was thick in the compartment. The deck was tilting sharply now as *Rasul's* bow came up. . . .

Clang!

The shocked silence that followed was like a physical blow. Bishara and the others in the control room stared at the overhead, not daring to move, not daring to breathe, scarcely daring to think.

The American torpedo had struck *Rasul's* squat, rounded sail—he'd heard it, he'd *felt* it hit—and they were still alive!

It was the pressure. He knew the answer almost before the question formed in his mind. The incredible pressure outside could act in unpredictable ways on merely man-made devices and materials. Below a certain depth there must be a certain percentage of failure, and even the awesome technological know-how of the Americans could not much improve those odds. Another torpedo might have functioned perfectly at this depth, smashing *Rasul* and sending her into a final, fatal dive. In this one, some mechanism—the detonator, perhaps—had failed, and they lived.

His men had their own explanation. "Allah is with our Captain! *Allah akbar!*"

Bishara did not try to restrain his men this time. For the moment, the emotional tide had carried them to new heights of exultation. They were far below the thermocline; the sound would not carry.

And perhaps Allah *was* with them, with him. Bishara was determined to use every advantage in this deadly combat he could win.

**SSCVN-1 *Leviathan*
South of Cienfuegos Bay
Friday, March 31, 1044 hours**

Admiral Delacroix climbed up the ladder from *Leviathan*'s starboard pressure hull and onto the control deck. Enlisted men in dungarees and the chiefs and officers in khaki or blue jumpsuits leaned over their consoles or supervised control-deck operations with a quiet efficiency that nonetheless lent an air of tension and urgency to the scene. Several bulkhead TV monitors showed SUBVIEW scenes outside the hull; one showed sailors forward helping men don aviator helmets and slide feetfirst into the coffin-sized space of Barracuda cockpits.

"Admiral on deck," Chief Delano called.

"Carry on," he replied needlessly. No one in the control room had so much as looked up from what he was doing. Captain Ramsay was in the raised central seat, his head anonymously encased in a SUBVIEW helmet.

Why, Delacroix wondered, had he trusted Gray?

It wasn't, he realized now, so much a matter of mistrusting the man as it was of mistrusting the technology. The SFV-4s were different from anything he'd had to work with in the past, alien, more like experimental aircraft than real submarines. It was difficult to accept them on their own terms.

Basic to modern combat, however, was the doctrine of concentration of mass. The submarine battle group had managed to step into one hell of a concentration of enemy mass here, and the Barracudas offered the only way of balancing the odds Delacroix could see. If *New Haven* was to be saved, he would have to use every trick in the book . . . and perhaps even a few that hadn't been written yet.

Delacroix's thoughts turned to his son, to the last time he'd seen the boy . . . what? Was it fourteen years ago now? Ron had never talked much about the high-tech wonder he'd been given to fly, but it had been clear that he was in love with the technology. That he believed in it, not as an end in itself, but as an extension of the men who used it. A way of balancing the odds in a dangerous world, where the odds were stacked against civilization and reason, and where sometimes the irrationality of war was the only path for reason's survival.

Gently, he pushed the memory aside. He would examine them again . . . later. "Captain Ramsay?"

The blind, alien-looking head turned toward the sound of his voice. "Yes, Admiral. Forgive me for not coming out at the moment. We have a situation developing here."

"No problem. I wonder if I might join you."

"Of course!" The voice alone conveyed a vast surprise. For as long as he'd been aboard *Leviathan*, Admiral Delacroix had never experienced SUBVIEW directly, though he'd watched the displays on the TV monitors. He'd been afraid of stepping too far into this new world.

An enlisted rating handed him the observer's SUBVIEW helmet and helped him lower it over his head. Suddenly, he was swimming in a sea of emerald light. Ahead, red-glowing squares and circles hovered in emptiness, as cryptic alphanumeric displays typed themselves before his eyes. *Leviathan* was flying slowly over a dimly seen landscape nearly lost in the darkening depths. Six of her forward missile hatches were already open as the checklist countdown proceeded for the Barracuda launch.

"You're just in time, Admiral," Ramsay's voice said close beside his ear. "We've slowed to five knots, and we're about to launch."

Through his helmet, he could hear the muted voices of the squadron pilots and the Launch Control Officer in the background. A voice was counting off the seconds.

Then a geyser of compressed air erupted almost in his face, the bubbles unfelt as they streamed past his disembodied point of view. The first Barracuda was rising before him, wings and stabilizer unfolding as its aquajets bit the water and sent the dolphin-shaped machine lancing forward. He glanced up, caught the rippling, silver glint of sunlight on the surface two hundred feet overhead, heard the murmur of voices announcing a good launch. From somewhere, a pair of real dolphins appeared, flashing gray and silver as

they streaked overhead. They escorted the Barracudas
for a moment, until the fighter subs accelerated
beyond even the reach of their powerful flukes and
vanished into the blue haze ahead.

Delacroix's breath caught in his throat as he was
momentarily lost in wonder.

UIR Attack Submarine *Tarhib*
Cienfuegos Bay approaches
Friday, March 31, 1050 hours

Several miles astern of *Leviathan,* another hunter
moved into position. The two Akula-class attack subs,
now the Islamic hunter-killers *Hayal* and *Tarhib,* had
emerged from Cienfuegos behind the Alfas at a more
leisurely speed of thirty-five knots and were only now
approaching the combat area.

Akulas were not as fast as the Alfas, nor could they
dive as deep, but they were very, very quiet. When
they'd appeared with the Soviet fleet in the mid-1980s,
they'd at first been called Walker-class submarines—a
gallows-humor admission by the Americans of the
damage done to the U.S. Navy by the Walker family
spy ring. Until the Walkers had begun passing secrets
to the GRU, the Russians had not been aware of just
how easy their relatively noisy subs were to detect. The
Akula and the other Soviet attack subs that appeared
in the eighties, the Sierra and the ill-fated Mike, were
all as quiet or quieter than anything the Americans
had even yet.

Commanding the *Tarhib* was former Captain
Second-Rank Aleksandr Ilyich Azizov, a remarkable
man . . . an expatriate mercenary in the service of

both Cairo and Tokyo. Son of a Tatar father and a Great Russian mother living in Kazakhstan, he'd joined the Red fleet in 1984, only to find himself without a country seven years later when the Soviet Union came crashing down. For a time, he'd served with the Russian navy, but as the political and economic situation throughout what had been the U.S.S.R. collapsed completely, he'd emigrated to Japan.

His talents had been much in demand there. He'd served as second officer aboard one of the Russian Akulas, and he knew them as well as any man alive. He also spoke passable Arabic, and that made him valuable indeed to his hosts, who often had more difficulty with that alien language than they did with English. The Japanese and the UIR both were paying him handsomely to command the Akula-class *Tarhib*.

The term "mercenary" bore no particular onus for Azizov, who saw the arrangement as a convenient way to make his service training pay. He had no intention of ever going home again, not with religious insanity gripping the entire sweep of southern Asia, from Baku on the Caspian Sea to Afghanistan. His contracted year's service with the Islamics, however, would provide money enough for him to retire to a comfortable dacha and a mistress or two somewhere on the Black Sea coast.

"Captain, Sonar!"

He snatched up the intercom mike. "Azizov here. Tell me." His Arabic was crude and broken, and often peppered with bits and pieces of Russian, but he always managed to make himself understood.

"Sir, we have a new contact, bearing approximately one-seven-five. It sounds large, twin screws."

"Is PLARK *Sharuq, da?*"

"No, sir. We're tracking *Sharuq* now at two-six-five, a solid contact. This is something else." There was a pause. "Captain, it could be one of the American Typhoons. There are strange sounds . . . almost like a missile launch."

"So!" Azizov rubbed his beard, a dark and bristly tangle. The Yankees had two Typhoons . . . at last report, test beds for some type of new underwater communications gear. If one was here, it could only be because the Americans were planning on testing their new gear under field conditions. For his part, Azizov was delighted at the opportunity to give them the very best test of their new equipment he could arrange. "The contact," he said. "Is speed, how much?"

"Difficult to say, Captain. For a time it was moving quite slowly . . . a few knots only. But it sounds as though its speed is increasing once more."

A Typhoon, drifting to listen with its sonar, then rocketing ahead at high speed . . . say, thirty-five knots? It would be deaf to the rest of the world for a time now, its hydrophones useless.

"Your suggestion, Captain Azizov?"

Azizov stared at the Islamic officer. Technically, Abdul Sabah was the real Captain of the *Tarhib,* but that was a diplomatic twisting of words designed to soothe prickly nationalist feelings that might have been offended by a foreigner—and an infidel at that—commanding a UIR vessel. Sabah and Azizov had a working understanding with one another, and both knew who was in command. In any case, Sabah was useful. His Russian was better than Azizov's Arabic.

"*Da!* We approach large *podvodnaya lodka*. Half

speed, quiet. Very quiet, *da?* We move into rear, come from behind. . . ."

"His baffles."

"*Da!* Exactly. Is like game, *da?*"

He remembered the Cold War all too well. Cold War it might have been, a sham of feints and bluff, of shadowing the enemy's vessels and waging pretend war from the Arctic ice pack to the waters off Long Island and Vladivostok . . . but men had *died* in those mock battles, including friends of his, good friends. The Soviet submarine service, largest in the world, had still been a close and intimate family, and the death of one was felt by all.

A few had been more than friends. Azizov's older brother, for instance, had been a *starpom,* the second-in-command aboard the *Komsomolskiy Arkhangelsk,* an older PLARK of the class known to NATO as Echo II. Grigor Azizov had never returned from his last patrol; his death somewhere in the cold Atlantic had been no easier to bear just because the Soviet Union had technically been at peace at the time.

"Is like old game," he continued, though he doubted that Sabah understood a word of what he was saying. "But this time, we move in close, and kill. . . ."

CHAPTER
19

Gray felt the power of the Barracuda's magnetic drive throbbing at his back. As he pushed the throttle forward his speed increased smoothly until he hit the pressure barrier at sixty knots. The fighter sub shuddered and bucked . . . and then he was past the wall, rocketing ahead through a blue-green blur. He checked left and right. The other five fighter subs were holding flanking positions to port and starboard.

He and Seegar both had climbed into new Barracudas rather than wait for their old ones to be refueled. His fighter sub was number 103, while Cigar had drawn 108. The others were piloted by Monk Young, Oz Franklin, Wildman Wilder, and Dom Dominico. Each was loaded with two sleek, delta-finned Mark 62s, rocket-propelled weapons that had far more in common with a Navy fighter's Sidewinder or AAM-RAM missiles than with a submarine's torpedoes.

"Okay, BARCAP Sierra, listen up," Gray called. BARCAP, for BARrier Combat Air Patrol, was another holdover from naval aviation, referring to a flight element placed between the carrier and a possible enemy airstrike. Since they were probing ahead of the undersea carrier, it had seemed logical as a call sign. "We've got two PROBSUB contacts dead ahead, range seven miles at approximately devils three. Those might be our Alfas."

"Where's the third one?" Dominico wanted to know.

"Probably went deep," Oz replied. "We haven't heard a solid hit yet."

"We'll split up," Gray decided. "Sierra Four and Sierra Six." That was Oz and Monk. "You two go deep. Get below the thermal and see if you can find that Alfa."

"Copy, Sierra Leader."

"Roger that. We're outta here."

The two fighter subs to port nosed over, streaking into the depths.

"Sierra Two, Sierra Five." Seegar and Dominico. "See if you can locate the Los Angeles. We still don't know for sure she's out there, but it's the only explanation for all the banging and shooting. See if you can find her and lend her a hand."

"We copy, Sierra Leader. How 'bout we stick with you, though, until we get past those Alfas?"

"Affirmative. Sierra Three, you stick with me, too."

"Uh, roger," Wilder replied. "Are we going after the Alfas?"

"We're going after whatever we can find, kid. And the way my sonar's cluttering up the water ahead, I think we're going to find plenty!"

* * *

UIR Attack Submarine *Rasul*
South of Cienfuegos Bay
Friday, March 31, 1104 hours

Rasul had gone deep, and she'd stayed deep, closing on
the American sub but staying well below it, at six hundred
meters, and keeping her speed to a crawl. Even an Alfa
could move silently when it needed to, and by staying out
of the sound channel at the target's depth, even the noisy
clatter of liquid metal pumps wouldn't give them away.

Now the bottom was rising to meet the Alfa, a steep
jumble of rock and mud connecting the coral-tipped
shallows of the Canarreos Islands with the black gulfs
of the Yucatán Basin a few kilometers to the south.

Bishara had not been fooled by the explosion that
had sounded moments before *Rasul* had been struck
by the dud torpedo. He'd studied the sonar record-
ings and decided that whatever his torpedo had hit
had *not* been a Los Angeles sub. There'd been a solid
bang, but no hull noises or breakup, no sounds of
flooding compartments or crumpling bulkheads as
the wreckage slid into the depths.

They'd hit a decoy with one of their fish and missed
with the other. The Los Angeles must have turned away
after releasing its bubble cloud, away from the torpedoes
and toward the rugged shallows ahead. Perhaps the
American skipper hoped to lose himself among the
sonar shadows of the shallows. No matter. Even resting
on the bottom a nuclear sub made *some* noise; shutting
down the coolant pumps and circulating machinery
meant death. Sooner or later, he would give himself away.

And Bishara was determined to find him.

*   *   *

U.S.S. *New Haven*
South of Cienfuegos Bay, Cuba
Friday, March 31, 1105 hours

"I'm getting two Alfas close aboard, Captain," Lucciano said.

"Got 'em, Lucky," Logan replied. The idea that *New Haven* could still be effectively invisible while the menacing shapes of the two Alfas drifted overhead, clearly visible to SUBVIEW, still seemed like magic to him. When the bad guys started mounting laser detectors on their hulls, this advantage would be lost, he knew. But for now, he intended to press the advantage of seeing without being seen to the limit.

Visibility was pretty bad in any case. The explosion earlier had churned up the water, and there were plenty of other muzzily distorted sounds bouncing off surface and bottom, sounds so garbled that even Lucky couldn't make much of them, to say nothing of *New Haven*'s Crayfish. Lucky was sure he'd heard *Leviathan* approaching from the east, and the Oscar was somewhere to the north, possibly coming back this way. That third Alfa was still out there somewhere—Lucky hadn't heard an explosion or the sounds of a breakup—but it had last been seen heading for the deeps. It might be back, it might not, and there were other sounds that might be other submarines in the area. Logan had decided to concentrate on the targets he was sure of.

The two Alfas were now three hundred yards away and perhaps two hundred apart, in water that was less than four hundred feet deep, only a little deeper in fact than the *New Haven* was long. They'd cruised right past *New Haven*'s position among the rocks and dead coral heads on the bottom, and their tails were to her now. He could see the lazy turning of their five-bladed props, blurred by the disturbance they raised in the water.

"You got a solid lock on 'em, Lucky?"

"Affirmative, Skipper."

"Feed it to fire control. We're going to take a shot."

New Haven was at a sharp disadvantage now. Los Angeles–class subs mounted four twenty-one-inch torpedo tubes amidships. He'd fired one at the Alfas, and another tube had been loaded with the decoy. His remaining two tubes were loaded with Mark 48 ADCAPs, but he wanted to save at least one for the Oscar, which was still his mission target. Reloading took ten minutes, and it was noisy, even with hydraulic loaders to jack the massive fish into their tubes.

With these limitations in mind, then, Logan had decided to fire one of his ADCAPs at one of the Alfas. The explosion close alongside would rattle the remaining Alfa and maybe even knock his sonar gear out of commission. It would certainly roil the water so badly that *New Haven* could put on a burst of speed and clear the area, reloading as she went.

And Logan had already worked out a course that would bring the attack sub into a good position for a firing solution on the Oscar.

He watched the Alfas a moment more as they slowly drew away, ahead of the *New Haven* and well off to port. It griped him, bushwhacking them from behind this way . . . but that was the essential nature of submarine combat. There was no chivalry in this kind of warfare, only the cold and steel-edged efficiency of machine pitted against machine. The Alfas were trying to kill him; he would kill one to make good his escape.

"Ready to fire on tube three," he said.

"Number three, ready to fire," the Weapons Officer announced quietly. "Tube already flooded, outer door open."

"Fire three."

The torpedo hissed from its tube, raced ahead, then began swinging about in a wide loop to port.

The Alfas responded at once, one breaking left, the other right, their props thrashing to white-water blurs as they tried to put on a lifesaving burst of speed.

"Skipper! Contact close astern and to starboard!"

Logan swung his head, looking back over his shoulder. The third Alfa was there, two hundred yards away, rising like some evil, nightmare beast from the black depths beyond the shallows. It had damn near come in from *New Haven*'s baffles, and it was sheer, dumb luck that he'd been far enough to starboard that Lucciano had been able to spot him.

"Engineering, full speed!" he shouted. "Up planes!"

"Our torpedo—"

"Cut it loose! Emergency maneuvering, now!"

"Enemy torpedo running!"

The Alfa had launched. He saw it coming as *New Haven* sluggishly lifted off the bottom and crawled forward. "*Shit!*" Logan spat, an uncharacteristic burst of anger at himself.

"Conn, Sonar! ADCAP has gone active." So had the Alfa's shot. He could see the blunt warhead now, eerily flashing white with each sonar pulse as it homed straight for Logan's vantage point.

"Hard right rudder!"

The ADCAP hit one of the Alfas, the explosion a

shattering, close-range blast of raw sound that hammered the *New Haven* and rang her hull like a gong. Logan's SUBVIEW image blacked out, then returned, the water around him a seething blur of white foam and noise. Then he saw the enemy torpedo, yards away and hurtling directly toward his face. "Hang on!" he yelled. "Collision alert—"

Barracuda formation
BARCAP Sierra One
Friday, March 31, 1106 hours

"Commander! It's going to hit!"

Gray watched helplessly from half a mile away as the huge, lean cigar shape of the Los Angeles moved slowly off the bottom, a single torpedo streaking in from astern. The first explosion had lashed the water into a murky turmoil; it was difficult to see anything except the attack sub and the deadly torpedo. Trailing a white contrail of sound, the torpedo slipped across the big sub's afterdeck, and for one breath-catching instant looked like it was going to miss. . . .

It hit, striking home on the LA sub's sail. There was a flash, a violently expanding storm of black water. . . .

U.S.S. *New Haven*
South of Cienfuegos Bay, Cuba
Friday, March 31, 1106 hours

Logan was slammed to one side in his chair, the explosion engulfing him, a savage shock that tore at his body and left him helplessly blind. Blind! No . . . it was his helmet. SUBVIEW had been knocked off-line.

The first shock was followed by another, a drawn-out, grinding crunch as the *New Haven* struck the bottom. Fumbling with his chin strap, he pulled the dead helmet off and blinked into a smoke-filled, eerie darkness point-lit by the sputter of electrical fires and a cascade of falling sparks.

"Fire!" someone yelled. "Fire in the control room!"

"Close all watertight doors and hatches!"

"Damn it, get that extinguisher over here!"

"We're flooding in number four! Shit! Granger! Hit those circuit breakers!"

"Helm!" Logan yelled. "Do you still have control?"

"Negative, sir! We're on the bottom!"

The overhead lights flickered once, died, then came on once more . . . but subdued. Fire extinguishers *shooshed,* extinguishing the flames. Logan picked up the ICS mike and tried it. Amazingly, it still worked. "Engineering! Conn! Are you there?"

"Affirmative, Captain!"

"Stand by to give me power!" If he could blow all of *New Haven*'s ballast tanks, they should be able to get off the bottom; if Engineering could keep the prop turning, they could maneuver.

If . . . if . . . if . . . Water splattered on him, a steady drizzle from overhead. Looking up, he saw the trickle spilling from the circular hatch at the top of the control room's ladder, the ladder leading up to *New Haven*'s sail and the weather bridge. If that hatch was leaking, it could only mean that the sail had taken a direct hit, worse, that the integrity of the control room's pressure hull was in immediate danger.

"All hands, this is the Captain. We've taken a fish

in our sail, but we're still alive and still in one piece. Everybody grab hold of something now, because this is going to get a little rough." Replacing the mike, he turned to the Diving Control Officer. "Hit it, Steve. Blow all ballast! Surface! Surface!"

A deep-throated flushing sound erupted in the sea around them. *New Haven* stirred, the deck creaking back toward horizontal . . . and then they were rising slowly through the tortured water.

"Conn, Sonar! Contact astern is opening another torpedo tube door!"

God, how could Lucky still hear anything? Logan's own ears were still ringing from the impact. The bastards were about to put another fish into the *New Haven.*

And there wasn't a damned thing he could do about it.

Barracuda formation
BARCAP Sierra One
Friday, March 31, 1108 hours

"The Alfa's firing again!" Gray yelled. He snapped the Barracuda's stick over, putting the fighter sub into a sharp turn, angling down. "I'm on the torpedo!"

"Roger, Sierra Leader! Sierra Two! I'm on the Alfa!"

There was no time to plan, no time to consider options. There was time only for action as Gray's Barracuda streaked in low across the rocky sea floor, aiming now for the slender thread of distortion in the water that marked the torpedo's guide wire.

New Haven was rising in a cloud of bubbles a football field away. Gray was close enough now that his

Barracuda's ULTRA-C could pick out her hull number, still visible on her bow and on her badly mangled sail. Beyond her, the sea was a roiling mass of white, indecipherable by his computer. The water was rough, bucking against the Barracuda like a living thing. Gray pushed everything from his mind except the need to hit that slender, whiplashing wire.

As before, he caught the wire on his canopy, heard it grating inches above his head, then snagging hard against his stabilizer. He put the stick over, giving the wire an extra twist as he snapped it free. Perhaps the shock would knock the torp off course.

Barracuda formation
BARCAP Sierra Two
Friday, March 31, 1108 hours

Michael Seegar held his Barracuda in a tight bank, then pulled the fighter sub into line with the Alfa. From less than a hundred yards away, the Islamic attack sub was enormous, a dark gray shadow backlit by the seething fury of the torpedo detonation in the distance.

"SUBVIEW, targeting!" he said aloud. The Barracuda's computer system switched on a target reticle drifting along the Alfa at the base of its sail. Words and numbers flickered alongside, counting off the range. On his bottom center MFD screen, a line winked at him steadily: WEAPONS ARMED.

"Target lock! Acoustical!"

TARGET LOCK. ACOUSTICAL HOMING. READY.

"Fire one!"

His Barracuda lurched upward as the first Mark 62 slid free of its pylon and arrowed toward the Islamic sub.

UIR Attack Submarine *Rasul*
South of Cienfuegos Bay
Friday, March 31, 1108 hours

Successor to the waterjet-propelled Mark 50 lightweight torpedo was the Mark 62, twelve feet long and a foot thick, powered by a rocket motor burning liquid oxygen and hydrogen and guided by wire, by acoustical homing, or by any of several programmable options. "Flight" time was brief and range was limited to less than a mile; drag on the Mark 62 kept it from reaching a missile's speeds.

But it was considerably faster than the Mark 50, and it carried an eighty-pound, shaped-charge warhead, enough to cripple or destroy any smaller sub, and do serious damage to most larger ones. Its one serious disadvantage was that it was noisy. Tearing along through the water at better than one hundred knots, it sounded exactly like ripping cloth . . . but very, very loud.

"Captain! Sonar!"

Bishara heard the terror in the man's voice. "Steady! What is it?"

"I don't know! Something coming very fast! It sounds like—"

The explosion smashed the *Rasul* hard over, flinging men and loose charts and equipment in a shower against the port bulkhead. The lights went out, plunging them all into a stygian blackness alive with the screams and shrieks of struggling, panic-stricken men as the sub slowly rolled back the other way.

Bishara landed on the deck, his head throbbing from the impact of a logbook. "Be silent!" he yelled, struggling to get out from under another man when he could see nothing in the pitch darkness. "Silence in the boat!"

As the screams and panicked yells died away, only the moans and sobs of the wounded remained. One voice continued to plead and gibber for light, another whimpered, "My arm! My arm!" over and over again.

But above the cries, he heard another sound, a throaty, pulsing noise strangely like the engine of a jet aircraft. And it was coming closer.

Barracuda formation
BARCAP Sierra Two
Friday, March 31, 1109 hours

Seegar held the Barracuda steady as it cruised thirty feet above the Alfa's forward deck. The Islamic sub was still moving ahead, but slowly, and a steady stream of silvery bubbles was rippling from the jagged hole in the side, halfway between the bow and the sail.

His shot had hurt the Alfa bad. Their main sonar was probably shot, and it was possible that the pressure hull had been breached. Those air bubbles were coming from somewhere, and he didn't think it was from a ballast tank or air storage bottle.

Seegar was just trying to decide what to do next when the Alfa's torpedo, running wild after Gray cut its wire, slammed into the bottom. There was a sharp boom, and the pressure surge sent Seegar's Barracuda tumbling. One fin grated against the Alfa's deck with a sound like fingernails on a chalkboard . . . and then he was drifting clear, fighting to regain control of his fighter sub.

His controls weren't responding.

U.S.S. *New Haven*
Friday, March 31, 1110 hours

The second explosion rocked the *New Haven* almost as hard as the first one had. The lights failed again, and this time refused to come on. Logan had time only to hear that three ballast-tank valves were jammed when the ICS, too, failed, but the planesman reported that he still had control. Logan could feel the crippled sub still moving, miraculously moving up, rising through the water.

Someone had a battle lantern out now, the pale glow illuminating faces with a death-white pallor. Most of those faces were turned toward the center of the control room and up to the overhead, where the trickle had become a hissing cylinder of water showering into the control room from the hatch to the sail.

They were rising slowly from a depth of three hundred feet. Logan estimated it would be two or three minutes before they broke the surface.

It was anybody's guess how long that hatch would hold.

*   *   *

BARCAP Sierra One
Friday, March 31, 1110 hours

Gray had also been rocked by the blast of the stray torpedo, but he maintained control of his fighter sub, steering it swiftly clear of the turbulence. One part of his mind wondered at the fact that the Barracuda had survived; all his life he'd heard how deadly the shock waves of underwater explosions were. In World War II, submarines had been crushed by the pressure waves alone of depth charges detonating within a hundred feet or so of their hull, and everybody knew that fish could be killed by dropping explosives into a lake.

In fact, SFV-4s were neither fish nor large and vulnerable submarines. It was the uneven *wrenching* of hulls three hundred feet or more in length that had sprung hull plates and cracked welds more often than not in a depth-charge attack, and fish or divers subjected to underwater blasts were killed by the trauma of having their soft tissues suddenly compressed by the shock wave.

The Barracudas, only twenty-five feet long, were small enough that they bobbed like corks in the passing shock wave, and hulls strong enough to resist tons-per-square-inch pressures protected their soft-bodied contents. Gray was slammed back and forth in his seat, but his helmet and his harness kept him from hitting the side of the cockpit. He was bruised but alive.

He checked his MFD screens, watching for telltales warning of damage. There were none. Still trying to clear the ringing in his ears, he guided the Barracuda northeast. The bottom dropped away into emptiness.

He was over the Yucatán Basin.

Turning in his seat to look behind him, he could see the wreckage of one Alfa, the hull torn into two jagged pieces, lying on its side at the edge of an undersea cliff. The *New Haven* was visible as well, halfway to the surface now, and rising slowly in a cloud of bubbles from her vented tanks and from the shattered ruin of her sail.

Of the two remaining Alfas, or of Seegar, Wilder, or Dominico, there was no sign.

But a red square was flashing on his SUBVIEW display, a winking indicator of a new target. It was coming from the northeast, and the visual sonar reading on his number-four MFD showed a solid contact, something big. He thought at first that it was *Leviathan,* which should be arriving in the area any moment now.

Increasing his speed, he slid forward, trying to see the newcomer. He could see something now, a rounded, blunt-nosed shape, growing clearer as it loomed out of the depths.

He was still half a mile away when the image grew clear enough for a firm ID, so close that he could make out the torpedo tubes opening in the bow.

It was the Oscar, joining the fight at last.

CHAPTER 20

UIR Oscar-class SSGN _Sharuq_
Friday, March 31, 1112 hours

❝I protest, Captain," Yoshio Katatura said. "You are throwing away this vessel, throwing away the lives of your men, all to no purpose!"

"Be silent!" al-Badr snapped. "Or I shall have you placed under arrest!"

Siraj al-Badr turned his back on the Japanese advisor and snatched a microphone from the bulkhead. "Sonar, Conn! Go active now!"

"_Ya sidi!_ Sonar is active!"

Despairing, Katatura watched the man. Despite his training, despite Katatura's patient coaching, he was a barbarian . . . worse, a _child_ entranced by his high-tech toys.

It had been a mistake to give such toys to such children.

"Captain, this is Sonar! We have multiple contacts. The American Los Angeles is directly ahead, at one-eight-five, range three thousand meters, and rising slowly toward the surface. We are picking up clear sounds of damage from her hull, possibly a major leak. The vessel may be in serious trouble.

"We are picking up another large contact to the east, bearing zero-eight-zero, range eight thousand meters. Twin screws. It may be an American Typhoon."

"What else?"

"Nothing definite. We may have one of our Alfas on the screen, damaged but still under way. There are other . . . sounds, unusual sounds that we cannot identify."

"Then identify them! Weapons Officer!"

"Yes, sir!"

"Stand by to fire. We will put two torpedoes into the damaged Los Angeles, then fire two more at the Typhoon."

Katatura wasn't quite sure when he had lost control of the situation, but al-Badr was not listening to him at all now. *Sharuq* had been clear of the battle and on her way to Cienfuegos; there'd been no need to bring the Oscar about and rejoin the fight, no reason save al-Badr's stubborn Arab pride, his refusal to run away from a fight, from the glory of battle.

Yoshio Katatura knew all too well that there was no *meiyo,* no glory in battle. Once, perhaps, it had been different, in the days of the shoguns and fluttering banners and proud *sashimono* of the samurai. Now wars were fought with machines, setting computers against computers with their superhuman reactions, toys for dangerous children.

Where was the glory in that?

SSCVN-1 *Leviathan*
Friday, March 31, 1114 hours

Captain Ramsay saw the Oscar materialize out of the gloom ahead. The range on *Leviathan*'s ULTRA-C gear was limited now to five miles or less, as turbulence in the water from the earlier explosions blurred sonar and distorted laser light enough to degrade the SUBVIEW images.

There was no mistaking the broad, flattened cylinder of an Oscar-class SSGN, though. By enhancing the image, he was able to make out the brickwork pattern of anechoic tiles across her hull and the row of ten rectangular missile hatches down her flanks to either side of that long, low sail.

"Admiral," he said quietly. "I believe we've found our target."

"Right, Leonard. Take the bastard down."

It was hardly a ringing call to battle in the tradition of Dewey's "You may fire when ready, Gridley," or even Farragut's "Damn the torpedoes, full speed ahead," but it was enough for Ramsay. He was still recovering from his surprise at having Delacroix join him in the SUBVIEW.

"Stand by to fire," he announced. "SUBVIEW, target lock."

Cross hairs appeared on the shadowy form of the Oscar. Fire-control data typed itself across his field of view.

TARGET LOCKED. RANGE: 7800 M. DEPTH: 250 M.

WPN SELECT: MK48ADCAP, WIRE-GUIDED, ACOUSTICAL HOMING.

STAND BY.

"Captain! Sonar!"

"Ramsay here. Go ahead."

"Captain, we've got a contact on our tail, just coming out of our baffles! Sounds like an Akula!"

Ramsay swung his head, staring back over his shoulder. The Akula was just emerging from the blur of *Leviathan*'s own wake, an ominous, menacing shape, a squat teardrop with an extremely low sail and a streamlined pod housing a towed sonar array perched atop the stabilizer.

"Engineering!" he called. "I want full speed now! Give me one hundred ten percent on the reactor!"

"One-ten percent on the reactor, aye, aye!"

"Hard right rudder! Come to course three-five-zero!"

The Oscar would have to wait. *Leviathan* was in deadly peril.

**UIR Attack Submarine *Tarhib*
Friday, March 31, 1114 hours**

"We have him," Azizov shouted. "We *have* him!"

"Torpedoes ready, Captain!"

"Fire one!"

The deck shuddered as the torpedo blasted from its tube. "One fired, sir!"

"Fire two!" Thud—*hiss!*

"Two fired, sir!"

Two Soviet-built 533mm torpedoes streaked through the water toward their target.

**BARCAP Sierra Four
Friday, March 31, 1115 hours**

"Sierra Six! Sierra Six! This is Four!" Lieutenant Gary Franklin, "Oz" to his squadron mates, could see the confrontation unfolding three hundred feet above him. "Eleven o'clock high at devils two! The Big Vi's in trouble, man!"

"I see it, Oz," Monk's voice came back. "Let's goose it!"

Oz and Monk had searched fruitlessly for the missing Alfa and were on their way back toward *Leviathan* when both the Oscar and the *Leviathan* had appeared. They'd been vectoring toward the Oscar when a third sub, the sinister whale shape of an Akula attack sub, had crawled out of the gloom a mile astern of *Leviathan*.

And in the next instant, the Akula had fired, two fish running flat out. *Leviathan* had seen the danger, was turning ponderously away from the Oscar, but too slow . . . too slow . . . !

Thinking fast, Oz slapped the weapons-programming select on his console, arming his port torpedo and selecting acoustical homing, feeding into its brain the passive signature he was recording at that moment from the two Islamic torpedoes.

TARGET LOCK.

ACOUSTICAL HOMING: PATTERN SET.

ACOUSTICAL PROXIMITY DETONATION: COMMIT

READY.

"Fox one!" he shouted over the open combat circuit and squeezed the red grip trigger on his control stick. His Barracuda lurched hard as the seagoing missile slid free.

He'd used the old Fox-one code without even thinking about it. In air-to-air combat, "Fox one" was the code phrase meaning a radar-homing missile had just been launched, while "Fox two" meant that a heat-seeking Sidewinder was airborne.

With a sound like tearing cloth, the missile streaked upward at a fifty-degree angle, the angle growing steeper as its tiny brain homed on the sound of the lead Islamic torpedo. At 110 knots, the Mark 62 howled up out of the depths.

Pinpoint accuracy with passive sonar and at such speeds was impossible. The Mark 62's guidance computer, however, could detect when the sound it was tracking began to fade and trigger the detonation at that moment. The rocket-propelled torp narrowly missed the lead Islamic fish, rising several feet above it before detonating with a savage flash and a roiling vortex of violently disturbed water.

The trailing torpedo hurtled into the blast's expanding pressure wave an instant later, slamming into a near-solid wall of water with force enough to trigger the detonator. The warhead, over eight times heavier than the small Mark 62 charge, exploded with a savage fury that blanked out all ULTRA-C imaging for nearly a mile in all directions and smashed at the two Barracudas with hurricane force.

The lead torpedo wavered, the wire connecting it to *Tarhib* severed by the twin blasts, but it had been programmed to go active if it was cut loose, and the closest, largest target within range was the ponderous, submarine mountain that was *Leviathan*.

Prop whining, it swung out of the blast area, locked on to the Typhoon, and closed in for the kill.

SSCVN-1 *Leviathan*
Friday, March 31, 1117 hours

"Release countermeasures!"

Ramsay could see the torpedo, less than one hundred yards astern. Damn, but driving a Typhoon was like trying to jockey a big, eighteen-wheeler trucking rig in the Indy 500. Everybody else was faster . . . and the bitch just didn't have the *oomph* when it came time to put the pedal to the metal.

An explosion of bubbles flowered astern, cutting off his view of the torp. A moment later, it punched through the cloud, still coming, undeterred.

"Torpedo is hunting," the voice of the sonar operator said in his helmet. "Torpedo has reacquired. Range eighty yards and closing."

"Come right three-five degrees." If he could spoil the thing's angle of attack . . .

No such luck. It reacted immediately, turning smoothly with *Leviathan*'s maneuver, bearing in now on the Typhoon's starboard side.

"All hands," he announced over the ICS. "Brace for collision!"

There was nothing else to do.

In the last second, Ramsay heard the torpedo singing as it raced in from astern.

The torpedo struck *Leviathan*'s hull halfway between her sail and her stern and well down on her starboard side. The detonation of over six hundred pounds of high explosives slammed the big sub over to port and sent ragged pieces of hull metal and dozens of anechoic tiles fluttering into the darkness of the depths below.

Air tanks stored between *Leviathan*'s twin hulls ruptured, loosing a cloud of air gleaming like molten silver toward the surface. Trim lost, *Leviathan* heeled back to starboard. Dive controls failed. Her diving planes and trim tab, already set for a dive, locked in place. Her starboard prop, the shaft bent by the shock, froze.

Trailing a stream of bubbling air, *Leviathan* plunged toward the deeps of the Yucatán Basin, some two miles below.

*   *   *

UIR Oscar-class SSGN *Sharuq*
Friday, March 31, 1117 hours

Katatura heard the explosion ringing through
Sharuq's hull. A hit! The Oscar's sonar room confirmed it a moment later.

"Captain, this is Sonar! The American Typhoon
has been hit! We are picking up what sounds like hull
damage!"

"I wish to hear for myself," he told al-Badr.
Quickly, he made his way aft past wildly cheering
men. As he squeezed into the sonar room two of the
operators were hugging each other, a third dancing
before the console.

"Kafi!" he barked. "Enough! Return to your stations!" Snatching up a headset, he raised it to one
ear, trying to hear over the racket from the control
room behind him.

Yes . . . he could hear the fluttering sound of
escaping air and a kind of thready, ripping noise,
water flowing over jagged leaves of metal that vibrat-
ed with its passage. The big American sub was badly
holed . . . and it was sinking.

Al-Badr was at his back. "Well?"

"He is going down."

"Allah akbar!" He turned away, leaning back into
the control room. "Weapons Officer! We will kill the
American Los Angeles. Fire one!"

Through his headset, Katatura heard the torpedo
burst into the sea.

*   *   *

BARCAP Sierra One
Friday, March 31, 1117 hours

Gray was thunderstruck. From his position, *Leviathan* was just barely visible, a dark gray whale shape against the blue-gray murk of the sea, but he'd seen the flash and felt the hard thump as a torpedo struck the Typhoon from behind. He could see her now, turning away from the Islamic Oscar and falling . . . falling into the deep.

The realization that the American squadron was *losing* . . . that both of the large subs on the scene were now out of the fight, that only the six midget fighter subs remained and that *they* were now completely scattered and disorganized, jolted him hard.

With *Leviathan* dead, the fighter subs could hope for nothing better than to surface and await rescue . . . in these waters almost certainly by the Cuban Coast Guard and their Islamic allies.

Those dark thoughts were interrupted by a warning flash on his cockpit display and the appearance of a new contact box. The Oscar had just launched another torpedo, and it was humming through the water toward the crippled *New Haven*.

Damn them!

If it was to be Davids against Goliaths, so be it. Judging the angles between himself, the Oscar, and the torpedo, he decided that his best move would be to go after the torp.

Throttle full forward, he raced toward the Oscar's torpedo.

*   *   *

BARCAP Sierra Four
Friday, March 31, 1117 hours

"Damn, Monk, he got the Big Vi!" Oz watched in horror as *Leviathan* dropped past his level at five hundred feet, nose at a fifteen-degree down-angle, plunging for the bottom.

The Akula was starting to circle away, two hundred feet overhead and half a mile away. "So let's get the bastard!" Monk replied. "Fox one!"

Savagely, Oz programmed his remaining torp, then squeezed the trigger. A second Mark 62 streaked after the first, climbing toward the Akula.

UIR Attack Submarine *Tarhib*
Friday, March 31, 1117 hours

"Hit!" Captain Azizov sang. "We got hit!"

The crew echoed his joy, screaming and yelling *"Allah akbar!"*, their clenched fists shaking in the air.

"Captain! Sonar!"

He couldn't hear. "Eh? Repeat!"

"Captain, this is Sonar! Something approaching at high speed!"

Damn these raghead pigs! He could hardly hear a word. Reaching into the holster he always wore at his hip, Azizov slid a Makarov PM automatic pistol from leather and snicked back the slide to chamber a round. Angrily, he glanced around the control room, looking for a safe place to fire—not easy in a compartment cluttered with pipes, gauges, and electronic displays.

There . . . an ample thickness of fireproof insulation between the overhead fluorescent lights and the bulkhead. He aimed one-handed in classic, Soviet military form and squeezed the trigger.

The shot, painfully loud in the enclosed compartment, rang through the control room and brought instant, stunned silence.

"*Ushkut!*" Azizov bellowed into the sudden quiet. "*Ushkut,* damn you all!"

"Something coming!" the sonar operator's voice called desperately over the intercom. "Something coming in at high speed!"

The first torpedo struck amidships, almost below Azizov's feet, the shock throwing him and the others on the bridge almost to the overhead as the deck buckled beneath them. Though the warhead was small, its shaped charge compressed and funneled the force of the blast, sending a torch of white-hot plasma searing into the inner pressure hull with the intensity of an industrial laser. Sea water, backed by a pressure of over 130 pounds per square inch, surged in behind the flame. *Tarhib*'s battery compartment was holed, then flooded almost immediately.

The second Mark 62 struck several seconds later, slamming into the Akula's after hull. Her highly automated engine room was savaged by the blast, her reactor SCRAMed into shutdown, and water came boiling into her number-two engine room. Sluggish already with the damage amidships, *Tarhib* staggered at this second, killing blow, her stern sinking lower and lower, her bow coming up. In her control room, plunged into darkness absolute by the failure of the electrical system, Azizov clung with one hand to a forward bulkhead stanchion, his broken arm awkwardly pressed against his chest.

His crew had often had difficulty understanding the rough, loudmouthed Russian. The sub's Arabic captain, Abdul Sabah, clung to the chart table a few meters away, listening to the man's frenzied, angry shouts. Sabah spoke fairly good Russian, but he understood little of what he heard.

Something about vengeance, about someone named Grigor, and about the damned Americans . . .

Then the control room's after watertight door gave way with a loud bang, and water came flooding up from the engineering section.

The Akula dropped stern-first into blackness. It would take almost ten minutes to reach its crush depth of 1,400 meters.

BARCAP Sierra One
Friday, March 31, 1118 hours

Gray was too close to try firing a Mark 62 at the Islamic torpedo, and he knew that if he broke the wires, the hellish thing would simply go active, reacquire the *New Haven,* and complete its mission. The crippled American attack sub, now nearing the surface, didn't look like it would survive another shot.

His only option, then, was to try an extremely risky maneuver, risky because he had no way of knowing how the Islamic torpedo was armed. If it was set to detonate on *New Haven*'s acoustic signature or on impact, there was no problem. If, on the other hand, it was set to trigger magnetically, when a large mass of metal disturbed its own magnetic field, then Gray was about to commit a rather spectacular suicide.

His breath was coming in short, hard gulps as he

put the Barracuda into a long, flat dive. His computer gave him the proper bearing and descent slope, but the last few seconds had to be navigated entirely by eye and by the *feel* of his craft as it dropped through the water at fifty knots, his fighter pilot's instincts bringing torpedo and submarine together, first in his mind, then in fact.

It looked as though the Islamic torpedo, fully nineteen feet long and almost two feet thick, was coming straight into his cockpit, but he held the SFV-4 steady, sweeping in above the warhead in an instant, kicking the throttle to full power at the last instant. . . .

Whang!

The Barracuda struck the torpedo's tail empennage with a combined speed of over one hundred knots. It was a glancing blow, about like coming in on a runway for a wheels-up belly-smacker, but it felt like he'd just slammed into a brick wall. His seat harness cut into his shoulders and chest as he was thrown forward by the impact, and suddenly he was tumbling to the side. His engine, deprived of water pressure in the intakes, stalled out with a rumbling cough, and he was sinking. . . .

Glancing back over his shoulder, he glimpsed the torpedo, one stabilizer fin flattened by the collision, its propeller shroud twisted to the side. It was actively pinging now, its wire link to the submarine broken, but its drive had been put out of action.

And it hadn't exploded! The realization brought a hot rush of sheer relief to Gray and left him shaking, but he was able to concentrate now on bringing the falling fighter sub back under control. He read the array of winking alert lights on his console. There was damage . . . but not bad. His engine had stalled when he lost intake pressure. Holding the stick forward, he managed to bring the nose down, feeding water into the intakes, gently coaxing the engine back to life. . . .

UIR Oscar-class SSGN *Sharuq*
Friday, March 31, 1118 hours

"We have lost the torpedo, Captain!"

"What do you mean, 'lost it'?"

The sonar operator sounded uncertain of himself. "It sounded as though the torpedo hit something halfway to the target, but it did not explode. The wire's gone dead . . . I can't hear the torpedo's engine. And there's something . . ."

"What is it?" al-Badr demanded.

"Something unusual, sir. Engine sounds like the pulse jet of an American Mark 50 torpedo, but larger, heavier. It could be a submersible, but quite small . . . less than ten meters. It may have rammed our torpedo."

"A minisub? Was it damaged?"

"Its engine noise changed for a moment, sir . . . but it has resumed. I would say it is still maneuverable."

"A fighter sub," Katatura said at al-Badr's side, his eyes widening.

"A what?"

"A fighter sub. Think of it as a fighter plane that maneuvers underwater. We have been working on them for some time in Japan. I . . . I had no idea that the Americans were so close to having a working prototype."

"They will not have one for long. Weapons Officer! Can you track that target!"

"Yes, sir. We've recorded its sound trace and programmed it into fire control. Also, Sonar could steer a wire-guided torpedo close enough to destroy the craft."

"Prepare to fire, then!" Al-Badr turned excitement-bright eyes on Katatura. "We will teach them the error of sending windup toys against an undersea battleship like *Sharuq!* Eh?"

But Katatura was not entirely sure on which side the lesson's ax would fall.

BARCAP Sierra One
Friday, March 31, 1119 hours

Gray was in trouble. He'd restarted his engine only to find that he couldn't restore full power. Worse, the Barracuda was handling clumsily. Possibly there was damage to his undercarriage; possible a control surface had been bent.

Worse, the Oscar seemed to have forgotten about *New Haven* and was coming after him. The Islamic SSGN's blunt prow was swinging slowly in his direction, as though trying to mark him down with the hard, ringing chirps of its sonar. He could see its torpedo hatches open, like six beady, black eyes set three to either side of the hull.

"If that's the way you want to play it," he murmured. Normally, a Barracuda could outrun any torpedo made except for its own Mark 62s, but the damage to his fighter sub might be too severe for such a simple evasion. The real trick would be staying far enough away to avoid the blast if the thing was set for proximity detonation.

Throttling forward, he began angling up through the water and banking to the left. "SUBVIEW!" he called. "Weapons lock!"

**UIR Oscar-class SSGN *Sharuq*
Friday, March 31, 1119 hours**

"Fire one!"

The torpedo hissed from *Sharuq*'s number-one bow tube, its 660-pound warhead set to detonate on magnetic proximity, its guidance computer programmed to home on the throbbing pulse of an SFV-4 Barracuda. If the sonar operator steering that warhead by wire missed, the torpedo itself would home on the fighter sub nuisance and crush it.

CHAPTER
21

The Islamic torpedo was three quarters the length of a Barracuda. Gray suspected that its warhead would smash the SFV-4 to splinters if it exploded anywhere within fifty yards of him.

And the fighter sub was so slow to respond! It was the damage, partly, but more than that Gray's aviator instincts were screaming now for speed, speed, and more speed . . . and that speed simply was not there. The Barracuda was bucking and shuddering now as it passed fifty-five knots.

Speed is life. The old fighter pilot's slogan had deadly meaning now. If he'd been at the controls of an F/A-18, there would have been no problem, but the slower pace of undersea warfare had boxed him into a trap . . . and the lid was about to slam down with a very loud noise.

"C'mon! C'mon!" The magnetic pulse drive *thuttered* at his back, straining. It is an inviolable law of physics that the higher an object's speed, the wider its turn. Gray had to balance his speed with the Barracuda's turn radius; it would be a mistake to try turning a full one-eighty. In fact, his best hope lay in turning as little as possible, making the torpedo miss him and forcing it to loop back for another try . . . at which point he would be escaping at eighty knots.

The trick was guessing how far the torpedo could correct its course as it homed on him, and avoiding its deadly envelope of destruction when it exploded.

There were no computer simulations to test such tactics, and even his training in evading SAMs was no more than suggestive here. Gauging distances and angles by eye, he held the turn for a critical few seconds more . . . then flattened out the Barracuda's course and rammed the throttle full forward.

The Islamic torpedo was turning to meet him. . . .

The explosion sent him spinning through the water, wing over wing over wing, and for one horrible, nightmare of an instant he was blind as his cockpit display dissolved in white noise.

Then as the turbulence cleared, his view of the surrounding water returned. The Oscar was two hundred yards away and to starboard, moving past him with the ponderous grace of a slow-drifting mountain.

The combat between the Oscar and the midget SFV-4 had suddenly become an intensely personal thing. Clearly, the Islamic SSGN had organized the trap that had killed *Leviathan,* even if it had not fired the killing warhead, and now it had just tried to kill him with a torpedo damned near as big as his fighter sub.

Gray intended to take that monster SSGN down, if he had to climb out on her afterdeck and start dismantling her deck plates by hand to do it. The mental image of himself somehow attacking the giant Oscar with a screwdriver was so incongruous that he laughed out loud. It steadied him, helped him focus his attention on the closing vectors of Oscar and Barracuda.

"SUBVIEW!" he called. "Weapons lock!"

TARGET LOCK.

ACOUSTICAL HOMING: PATTERN SET.

IMPACT DETONATION: COMMIT

READY.

He hesitated before squeezing the trigger, wanting to maneuver the Barracuda just a bit closer to its huge target.

SSCVN-1 *Leviathan*
Friday, March 31, 1120 hours

Leviathan had not been destroyed, not yet, though the situation was serious as the huge carrier sub continued to drop into the depths of the Yucatán Basin. Her double-hull construction had saved her. The Akula's torpedo had blasted a hole in her outer hull and ripped open several compressed-air and diving-trim tanks, but her pressure hull was still intact. She was shuddering as she fell, the effect of turbulence tearing at the jagged edges of the hole in her flank. Ramsay could hear the shriek of wounded metal from somewhere aft.

"After planes are jammed, Captain," Parker announced. His voice was calm, though he looked scared. "We're passing one thousand feet."

Ramsay dropped the SUBVIEW helmet as he rose from the chair. SUBVIEW was useless now, the electronics knocked out by the torpedo hit aft. The Typhoon's control room seemed claustrophobic now, after the unlimited visibility of Crayfish's electronic wizardry. The control-room crew remained at their stations, the emotions playing over their faces ranging from stoic resignation to tension to stark terror, but Ramsay was proud to note that not one man had left his post. He reached out to cling to the back of his chair, bracing himself against the angle of *Leviathan*'s deck.

"Blow all ballast!" There was a flushing, rumbling sound. *Leviathan* shivered, her descent slowing . . . but not enough. The Typhoon's nose was still down, the deck sloping forward a full ten degrees. With her aft trim tabs jammed in the dive position, the Typhoon's speed forward was holding her nose down . . . and she kept going down.

"Negative effect, Captain. Our pressurized air reserves are gone. Passing twelve hundred feet."

They weren't finished yet. "Set bow planes for surface."

"Bow planes to surface, aye, sir." the Diving Officer said, and then he repeated it for the enlisted man at the planes controls.

"Bow planes set to surface, aye, aye," the rating repeated once more. The clockwork precision of orders repeated three or four times, each repetition reinforcing the others, had the steadying effect of routine.

"Passing fifteen hundred feet." There was a ratcheting creak from somewhere overhead, gunshot loud, terrifying in its volume.

"Engine room! Conn!"

"Engine room, aye."

"I need revs for full astern!"

"Revs full astern, aye, aye, sir."

"Hard left rudder."

"Hard left rudder, aye."

"Eighteen hundred feet, Captain."

"Where's our bottom?"

"Depth reads . . . nine thousand eight hundred feet beneath our keel, Captain."

Deep. Achingly deep. *Leviathan* would crush long before she reached the bottom.

"Captain! We're slowing!" And her nose was coming up. The deck's slant was about five degrees now.

"Two thousand feet."

There was a serious problem with a submarine as large as a Typhoon. Once moving in any given direction, including down, it was hard to stop with so much sheer inertia behind its 30,000-ton mass. By setting the forward planes for surfacing, reversing the sub's one remaining screw, and putting the rudder hard over, he'd worked *Leviathan* back against her jammed aft planes, slowing her fall and bringing the nose up.

Another groan sounded from the hull. "Twenty-one hundred feet." There was an anxious pause. "Captain! We're leveling off at twenty-one hundred ninety feet!"

"Engineering! Full power, forward revs for thirty-five knots! Helm, set rudder amidships."

"Full power. Make revs for thirty-five knots."

"Rudder amidships, aye." "Making revs for three-five knots."

The deck was tilting again, this time up. Ramsay suppressed a shudder that ran down his spine. That had been close.

Grinning, he winked at Parker, who was watching him from across the chart table with a fright-pale face. "And our crush depth is twenty-five hundred,"

Ramsay said with a bored drawl. "Shoot, that wasn't even close!"

Slowly, slowly, *Leviathan* began rising once again toward the surface.

BARCAP Sierra One
Friday, March 31, 1122 hours

Gray squeezed the trigger, not knowing what was going to happen next. The telltales on his MFD screen indicated that both Mark 62s were still operational, but his earlier collision with the torpedo meant for the *New Haven* might well have bent or broken something, making it impossible to launch.

There was a heart-stopping hesitation . . . and then the reassuring whoosh of the rocket torpedo arrowing clear of the fighter sub, leaving a trail of bubbles and white sound as it streaked toward the Oscar's flank.

UIR Oscar-class SSGN *Sharuq*
Friday, March 31, 1122 hours

Siraj al-Badr was the product of a long and bloody history. What for much of the rest of the world was a series of CNN news bulletins was for him his daily life in a short and bitter childhood.

He was Palestinian, born in what once had been occupied territory in a land claimed by too many mutually alien cultures. His father had died in an Israeli jail during the "shaking free," the Intifada of the nineties. His son Ali had been killed by the

Syrians during the military crackdown leading up to the *Qaumat*. His grandfather and an uncle had been killed by Americans, both the victims of a sixteen-inch shell fired from the battleship *New Jersey* into Lebanese hills in the early 1980s.

It was no surprise, then, that he disliked foreigners, *all* foreigners. Any not of his cultural background, not of his language, not of his faith, not of his tribe were immediately suspect. For Siraj, the *Qaumat* had been not so much a long-awaited union of Islam as it had been a final, defiant rejection of the myriad aliens who had dominated his people for so long.

He'd been raised hating the Israelis, of course . . . and he'd hated the *Amirikani* for as long as he'd known the word. He hated the French and their dreams of new empires in the Middle East, and he hated the Russians for their political meddlings and petty intrigues.

And for the same reasons and more, he also hated the Japanese.

The Japanese advisor's presence aboard his vessel had become almost intolerable, a continuing affront to al-Badr's own self-image. He knew the Japanese looked down on his people from the self-assured heights of their technological and economic superiority. In that, they were no better than the Americans . . . and possibly worse.

So when Katatura had so strongly urged that the Oscar return to the safety of Cienfuegos, it had become necessary to do just the opposite, if only to demonstrate to Katatura and to himself that Siraj al-Badr and the rest of his crew were *men*.

And he'd done it. They'd done it . . . despite the

terror that all of them felt now in *Sharuq*'s dank, stinking hell. Two of the hated American subs were dead or dying, and there were only the ghostly thrums of a number of minisubs circling beyond the missile sub's moisture-slick walls.

"Captain!" The sonar operator didn't even bother identifying himself. "There is something—"

The explosion came almost immediately, a shuddering thump from somewhere astern that knocked al-Badr to his knees and slammed one man violently against a water pipe, eliciting a shocked yelp of pain.

"What is it?" he demanded. "What hit us?"

"A torpedo of some kind, Captain," Commander Ibrahim replied. He was holding a headset to his head, listening to a report from another part of the sub. "Our outer hull is pierced, but our inner hull is intact. Engineering reports a leak in shaft two. The pressure seal may have broken."

"Have them fix it!"

"We will need to return to port for that, Captain." He listened some more. "Other damage is not serious."

"What is our position?"

"Depth now one hundred seventy meters, descending at one meter per second."

A gentle descent. But for al-Badr, the thought of continuing to drift down into the terrifying blackness below was more than he could bear just now. Until he was certain of the full extent of damage to *Sharuq*, he would rather have as large a safety factor as possible.

"Up planes, fifteen degrees," he snapped. "Bring us to periscope depth." Suddenly, he wanted to see sunlight again. It surprised him that, at the moment, he couldn't even remember whether it was day or night in the world, the other world above the darkness of the sea.

BARCAP Sierra One
Friday, March 31, 1123 hours

Grimly, Gray continued to follow the giant Oscar. Though a wisp of escaping air trickled from the hole in her aft-starboard flank, the monster seemed unhurt by his first torpedo.

Like *Leviathan*, the Oscar had a kind of built-in armor with the enormous separation between her inner and outer hulls. The American ADCAP torpedo with its six-hundred-pounds-plus warhead had been designed to take out such giants as Oscars and Typhoons. As Delacroix had warned him once, he couldn't hope to penetrate that armor with a Mark 62's eighty-pound sting.

Unless . . .

"SUBVIEW, targeting. Laser designation."

TARGET LOCK. LASER DESIGNATION.

PASSIVE/ACTIVE?

"Active."

DESIGNATE TARGET.

Cross hairs appeared on his canopy. Holding the Barracuda's course steady with his right hand, he reached over with his left to grasp a finger-sized joystick set into the arm of his seat. Gently . . . gently . . . he edged the cross hairs onto the gaping hole in the Oscar's side.

"SUBVIEW!" he called. "Laser designation, lock *now!*"

His cockpit view dimmed, growing dark and murky

as his dorsal ULTRA-C laser disengaged from its steady, flickering sweep of his surroundings and became a target designator for the Mark 62. The Oscar was still visible—hazily—imaged by the Barracuda's computer through sonar and the ventral ULTRA-C laser. An intense, blue-green spark of light remained centered in the crater in the Oscar's flank.

TARGET LOCK.

READY.

Gray squeezed the trigger on his control stick again, and his second rocket torp *shooshed* free of the Barracuda's grasp. Laser sensors in its nose picked up the intense point of reflected laser light and fed course-correction data to its brain.

Accelerating to one hundred knots, the Mark 62 hurtled squarely through the gap in the Oscar's outer hull and slammed into the pressure hull aft of the sail with a savage blast of light and sound.

UIR Oscar-class SSGN *Sharuq*
Friday, March 31, 1123 hours

Yoshio Katatura knew that they were dead as soon as the ripping-cloth sound shrilled again through the control-room bulkhead. The Americans were masters of advanced laser technology; their coordination so far in this battle suggested that they'd developed some new tricks in coordinating their undersea forces . . . and such coordination almost certainly depended on blue-green lasers.

The effectiveness of laser-guided bombs had been known since the Vietnam War, though such high-tech weapons had not received widespread public exposure until their successful and highly visible success in the Gulf War of 1991. Anyone who could use laser technology to coordinate their sub squadron operations would be able to apply the same technology to smart submarine weapons . . . weapons that could home, for instance, on a laser-designated target.

The second blast was far rougher than the first. Katatura found himself lying on the deck, struggling to free himself from beneath the body of a wildly thrashing Islamic sailor who screamed incomprehensibly in the advisor's face all the while. The deck was angling steeply down by the bow and listing hard to starboard as well. Papers, people, charts, the massive, green-covered target book, all were sliding across the canting deck to the starboard side of the control room. Men were screaming, praying, gibbering in panic. Many were trying to claw their way through the watertight doors at either end of the compartment.

Al-Badr was clinging to the periscope mount, his eyes staring, sweat drenching his face and uniform. "Katatura!" he screamed, staring at the advisor but not seeming to see him. "Katatura!"

"I am here." He was surprised at how calm his words sounded, emerging by the chaos around them.

"Katatura! What should we do? How do we stop?"

"Order the engine room to go full speed astern. Bring your bow planes up, your rudder over. Perhaps—"

"Damn you! The engine rooms are flooding! The battery compartment is flooding! We cannot blow ballast! *What do we do?*"

The obvious rejoinder was to tell al-Badr "we die," but so blunt an answer would have been rude . . . and so very un-Japanese.

The samurai of old had been ready each day to die for their lord, likening themselves to cherry blossoms—the embodiment of perfection as they fell. With a sudden rush of mingled sympathy and disappointment, Katatura realized that al-Badr would never understand that concept. Technology could be shared, even learning, but the cultural gulf between them was too great to bridge.

Briefly, Katatura wondered if his own leaders, the politicians who'd placed him here, understood, but that, too, was an un-Japanese thought. "It is our karma to tread the path of heroes," he said simply.

Then the lights failed, and al-Badr screamed. *Sharuq* rolled further onto her starboard side . . . and kept rolling. Katatura landed on the overhead, then gasped as something heavy slammed into his legs, breaking them both.

He thought of cherry blossoms as he heard *Sharuq*'s hull buckling around him. . . .

BARCAP Sierra One
Friday, March 31, 1124 hours

One after another, the Barracuda's systems were failing. His SUBVIEW was still working, giving him a crystal-clear view of the lonely emptiness around him, the dark, flattened cigar shape of the Oscar now rolling to a full inverted position as she continued her death plunge.

But his controls were no longer responding. Something had torn free when he'd fired the second missile, and his MFD damage readouts weren't showing a damned thing. His control stick flopped loosely in his hand; there was no response at all . . . and while his throttle could still speed or slow the engine, he was powerless to change the fighter sub's direction.

He was following the Oscar into the depths.

"Time to punch out," he said aloud. On the deck, set against his seat and between his knees, was a black-and-yellow-striped D-ring. Grasping it firmly, he yanked it back. There was a stuttering crackle of explosive charges going off, charges designed to blow his cockpit pressure capsule free of the Barracuda and send him bobbing back toward the surface.

Nothing happened. The Barracuda continued its descent.

For the first time, real panic clawed at Gray, memories dredged from stories told by Dee-Dee and the other submariners, memories of stories told by his father about the deaths of a hundred Russian sailors. . . .

It was growing blacker now, as though the depths were swallowing even his ULTRA-C laser so completely that there was no return for the Barracuda's computer to image at all. He was approaching 2,000 feet now and dropping at a rate of nearly ten feet per second.

What was the crush depth for a Barracuda? Even the experts weren't sure, though they'd rated the SFV-4Bs safe to 4,000, and the tough little 4D might make it clear to 10,000 or more.

Damn the eject mechanism, anyway! He suspected that the explosive charges designed to kick the escape capsule clear had detonated, but that under the intense pressure outside they'd not been able to effect a release. Or possibly his impact with the torpedo had warped the fighter sub's frame. Whatever the cause, his last test evaluation on the Barracuda would be to learn its actual crush depth . . . the hard way.

His eyes tracked the Oscar, now two hundred feet ahead of him and still falling, upside down. No! He wasn't going to give up, not now. Thoughts of Wendy and the kids were too strong in his mind now . . . thoughts of family mingled with memories of sun and fresh air.

He didn't want to die down here. Not here, in the dark.

With steering out, all he could do was throttle forward. His rate of descent increased as the heavier-than-water sub drove forward, chasing the Oscar's broken hulk. By varying his thrust, he was able to gently adjust his vector, then ram full speed ahead, slamming into the Oscar's hull.

The shock smashed him to one side, and his harness painfully bit at his ribs. He was still falling, damn! He'd been hoping to bring the Barracuda back into a nose-high attitude . . . or shake loose a jammed control surface, or—

The Oscar imploded. With almost half a ton pressing in on every square inch of its surface, the hull gave way at last, folding in around the skeletal frame bracing it, then vanishing in a burst of air and whirling debris.

The cloud of air, tightly compressed by the pressure but rising quickly, struck the Barracuda from below, a savage blow that slammed Gray forward against his harness, ripped one wing free, and bent the stabilizer almost ninety degrees out of the vertical.

His SUBVIEW failed in that instant . . . as did all power and electrical connections. But he felt the shuddering clatter as bolts incompletely severed by the eject detonations tore free.

He was rising . . . rising!

Tears streamed down his cheeks, unseen in the pitch blackness of his capsule, as Morgan Gray rocketed toward the light.

EPILOGUE

"**C**aptain? Request permission to come on the bridge."

Actually, Captain Ramsay had told Gray to report to him up here, but Navy protocol and long-standing tradition required that he ask permission to join *Leviathan*'s Captain on the weather bridge, an open cockpit perched high atop the Typhoon's massive sail.

"Permission granted, son. Come on up."

Gray clattered up the last few rungs of the ladder, an incongruous spiral staircase with wooden rungs left over from her days as a Soviet boomer. The air, salt-laden, wet, and smelling of oil, rotting vegetation, and muddy beaches, assaulted him in a heady wave, like a blanket thrown over his head, but mingled with the harsh glare of full sunlight.

The dank air tasted *wonderful* . . . and the subtropical sun was a lover's caress on his skin.

Leviathan's weather bridge was big enough for several people, and it was protected behind a salt-stained, Plexiglas windscreen. It gave a marvelous view fore and aft of the Typhoon, which was still, after five days, listing ominously to starboard and down slightly by the stern. The damage to her outer hull had been crudely patched by divers working from the surface, but her starboard screw was still out and it had been a long and dangerous limp back around the western tip of Cuba, up the Florida Channel, and back toward home, the sub base at Kings Bay, Georgia. Her surface escorts for that voyage, the frigates *Samuel B. Roberts* and *Davis* and the guided-missile destroyer *John Paul Jones* continued to flank the huge sub, lean, gray shark shapes to port, starboard, and astern.

As he leaned on the edge of the cockpit and looked out over the water, he saw the sub had already navigated the straits of St. Mary's Entrance and was now well into Cumberland Sound. That would be Drum Point Island off to starboard . . . and he could already see the wharfs and jetties and storage buildings of the base, just beyond the final turn into Kings Bay proper.

"Thought you might like to see our homecoming, CAG," Ramsay said with a grin. "I think maybe you earned it."

"I appreciate it, sir. But I didn't earn anything. Not any more than anybody else in the squadron."

"Maybe. And maybe I figure you earned the right when you won those dolphins."

Gray glanced down at the breast of his khakis, still unsure of his own emotions as he saw the glint of the silver device pinned above his left breast pocket. Normally, submariners served aboard a sub for a full year before winning the coveted dolphins, but Ramsay had explained that exceptions were made from time to time, especially when a man had the chance to prove himself to his shipmates in combat. There'd been a special celebration in honor of Gray and the other members of the Barracuda squadron who'd gone out to face the Islamic attack subs, Davids against Goliaths.

He was proud. He was also ashamed. He knew now what his father had felt when that Soviet Echo had gone down, so many years ago.

Gray had been fished from the water by a boat off *Leviathan* an hour after the battle, as Cuban *Guarda Coasta* vessels circled less than two miles away. The Typhoon's sheer size had proven to be an advantage in that instance, for the Cubans had not interfered with the Americans' rescue efforts. They'd picked up Seegar as well, bobbing in his ejected SFV-4 cockpit pod three miles from Gray's surface point. Like Gray, he'd managed to eject after his damaged Barracuda's controls went dead. The party aboard *Leviathan* had started as a welcome-back bash for the rescued men. It had ended as a kind of rite of passage for aviators turned submariners.

The experts would be debating the outcome of the battle for some time to come. On the international scene, the UIR was already both condemning U.S. provocations in the Caribbean and denying that any of its submarines had been there. That morning, the U.S. Ambassador to the UN had charged the UIR with piracy and destruction of American vessels and aircraft on the high seas. Where it would end—with more diplomatic saber rattling or in outright war— was still anyone's guess. The men aboard *Leviathan* knew only that they'd been challenged by a numerically superior enemy, and that they'd won.

Tactically, the battle was an American victory, though it had been a close-run thing. All of the SFV pilots had been recovered, though two Barracudas had been lost. *New Haven* had managed to surface long enough to put her crew off, then sank in 350 feet of water off the Canarreos. Salvage efforts were already under way, though the diplomatic repercussions of an American nuclear sub lost in Cuban waters were going to keep things interesting on the international front for some time to come.

And *Leviathan* had made it home despite the damage to her hull and screw, as had the frigate *Taylor*. The U.S.S. *Charlotte*, racing north after hearing of the battle, had surfaced alongside the damaged frigate, helped fight the fires, and then escorted her at a snail's pace to the U.S. base at Guantanamo Bay. Forty-one out of *Taylor*'s crew of 185 had been killed by the Oscar's attack, and another fifty-six badly wounded, but they'd saved the ship.

As for the UIR forces, the full extent of their losses might never be known. They'd lost one Akula and one Alfa, definitely, with another Alfa badly damaged and presumed lost in the black depths of the Yucatán Basin. Another sub, a presumed second Akula, had never shown up in the confusion of the battle, and the third Alfa had vanished shortly after *New Haven* torpedoed her consort. The last part of the fight had been so chaotic that the American forces had lost track of them . . . and if it had been chaotic for the Americans, equipped with ULTRA-C and SUBVIEW, it must have been impossible for the Islamics to coordinate their forces, relying on sonar alone. Their attempt to concentrate their undersea forces and overwhelm the American sub flotilla had failed completely.

Most important, the Islamics had lost their Oscar the pirate sub that had been targeting American tankers in the Caribbean, beginning this incident in the first place. At least 130 men had died aboard her when she imploded. How many more had been lost aboard the Alfas and the Akula?

Gray didn't like to think about it.

He'd not talked to his dad in a long time, but now he thought maybe it was time he did so. For a long time Gray had felt like he'd had little in common with his father. The dolphins on his chest, the battle in the depths, they'd changed that.

They'd changed *him*.

Leviathan was drawing closer to the docks now, and Gray could see a small crowd of people in brightly colored civilian dress, waiting behind the wire fence that kept the public away from the sub piers. A small thrill of anticipation rippled up his spine. Those would be the wives and sweethearts and kids of *Leviathan*'s crew. Gray knew how information circulated among the families of submariners; it was a fact, long known and accepted, that Navy wives always knew when their men were coming home, even when no official announcement was made. That near-psychic grapevine was even more evident for submariners, for the Navy *never* announced when its subs were coming back, which made such assemblies as this doubly mysterious.

"You might like to use these," Ramsay said, handing Gray the pair of big, 7×50 binoculars from around his neck.

He accepted them eagerly. "Thank you, sir." Through the binoculars, he could scan the faces in the crowd. It was an irrational hope, he knew. Wendy and the kids weren't supposed to come down from

New London for another couple of days, yet. Still …

He saw her, standing just behind the fence, her face turned toward him as she watched *Leviathan* slowly rounding the final point into the turning basin. The sea breeze tugged at her hair. John and Heather were with her, standing to either side; there were tears on her cheeks, and he realized that his eyes were no longer dry either.

"How's it feel, submariner?" Ramsay asked at his side.

Gray smiled and returned the binoculars. "It feels like home."

BILL KEITH, a former U.S. Navy Hospital Corpsman, laboratory technician, and illustrator, lives with his wife and daughter in the hills of western Pennsylvania. For the past seven years he has been a full-time writer, specializing in science fiction and in military techno-thrillers. *Sharuq* is his twenty-seventh novel.